The Light a Candle Society

Also by Ruth Hogan

The Keeper of Lost Things
The Wisdom of Sally Red Shoes
Queenie Malone's Paradise Hotel
Madame Burova
The Phoenix Ballroom

The Light a Candle Society

Ruth Hogan

Published in hardback in Great Britain in 2025 by Corvus,
an imprint of Atlantic Books Ltd

Copyright © Ruth Hogan, 2025

The moral right of Ruth Hogan to be identified as the author of this work has been asserted by her in accordance with the Copyright, Designs and Patents Act of 1988.

All rights reserved. No part of this publication may be reproduced, stored in a retrieval system, or transmitted in any form or by any means, electronic, mechanical, photocopying, recording, or otherwise, without the prior permission of both the copyright owner and the above publisher of this book.

No part of this book may be used in any manner in the learning, training or development of generative artificial intelligence technologies (including but not limited to machine learning models and large language models (LLMs)), whether by data scraping, data mining or use in any way to create or form a part of data sets or in any other way.

This novel is entirely a work of fiction. The names, characters and incidents portrayed in it are the work of the author's imagination. Any resemblance to actual persons, living or dead, events or localities, is entirely coincidental.

10 9 8 7 6 5 4 3 2

A CIP catalogue record for this book is available from the British Library.

Hardback ISBN: 978 1 80546 074 9
Trade paperback ISBN: 978 1 80546 075 6
E-book ISBN: 978 1 80546 076 3

Printed and bound by CPI (UK) Ltd, Croydon CR0 4YY

Corvus
An imprint of Atlantic Books Ltd
Ormond House
26–27 Boswell Street
London
WC1N 3JZ

www.atlantic-books.co.uk

Product safety EU representative: Authorised Rep Compliance Ltd., Ground Floor, 71 Lower Baggot Street, Dublin, D02 P593, Ireland. www.arccompliance.com

This book is dedicated to Kylie Dillon and Jim Gaffey and written in memory of those who die alone.

'All the darkness in the world cannot extinguish the light of a single candle'
St Francis of Assisi

It begins with an ending …

The young man with dark hair styled into an Elvis quiff lifted the gun and nestled the butt into his shoulder. The wood felt hard and cold through the thin cotton of his blue shirt as it pressed into his taut muscle. He took a slow, deep breath and fixed his gaze down the barrel before he fired a single shot. A young woman beside him clapped her hands with delight. Bullseye! All around them coloured lights flashed and spun to the sound of organ music, over the hiss of hydraulics and the rattle and clatter of the rides. A pungent tang of fried onions mixed with the scent of candyfloss and hot doughnuts trailed in wafts through the evening air. It was Saturday night and Dreamland was packed with people looking for excitement and a little bit of magic.

The man running the rifle range took back the gun and grinned at the young woman. One of his front teeth was missing. 'Take your pick, love. Any prize you like.'

The poodle stood on the mantelpiece above the gas fire, its glass eyes glinting in the lamplight. They were still as bright as rubies after all these years, Kathleen thought as she gazed fondly at the cheap little ornament from the comfortable cocoon of her armchair. These days she might not always remember to take her pills or the name of that nice woman behind the counter at the corner shop – but she could recall every detail of that first date with Frank at Dreamland, even though it was a lifetime ago now. Back then he had styled his hair just like Elvis and that night his blue shirt had matched the colour of his eyes. She had thought him so handsome. Kathleen had worn a yellow dress with a daisy print, a spritz of her favourite Avon perfume and a dash of Persian Melon lipstick that she had bought especially for the occasion. Frank had won the poodle for her on the rifle range. She could have chosen anything as her prize. There were some great big stuffed toys and a few lonely goldfishes swimming listlessly in glass bowls, but it was the poodle that had taken her fancy. She had christened her Penelope and she had been with them ever since – through sixty-one years of marriage and several moves.

'But you could do with a clean,' Kathleen said to Penelope a little sadly.

The dog stared back at her impassively. If its sparkling eyes had been able to see, the poodle would have witnessed her mistress's grief at the death of her beloved husband, Frank, two years ago, but also her determination to carry on and make what she could of the life she had left. Kathleen had never been a quitter.

But then, as physical frailty took its toll, the dog would have also witnessed the gradual and inevitable decline of both woman and home into gentle dilapidation. Kathleen had always kept their cosy flat spotless, but now the colours and contours of the sitting room were blurred beneath a fuzz of dust. And whilst her once trim figure may have softened and spread over the years and her complexion puckered into wrinkles like the skin on a rice pudding, she had always dressed well and had her hair washed and blow dried at Sally's Salon once a week. But recently Kathleen had found it increasingly difficult to summon the energy to do anything other than what was essential to keep herself clean and tidy, and fed and watered. Simple tasks had become daily challenges, and every movement that she made required a conscious effort.

Kathleen hated the thought that she had let her standards slip, but at least she still had her independence and was living in her own home and sleeping in her own bed. Well, mostly. There had been the odd occasion when she had woken up to find herself still in her chair, her bones stiff with cold and the TV showing the morning news. But she definitely wasn't going to let that happen tonight. She was going to make herself a cup of tea and take it to bed with a couple of biscuits to dunk. She might even listen to the radio for a bit. Yes, she was lucky, she thought to herself. She had so far dodged the care home ending that she had always dreaded. Of course, it would have been better if Frank had still been by her side, or perhaps a son or daughter – and grandchildren, even great grandchildren by now – to visit her and keep her company. But that hadn't happened and couldn't be helped. Besides, they had always had each other. Kathleen believed in counting her blessings rather than raking over her disappointments, and having Frank as her husband had been the greatest blessing of all. And they had had some lovely friends and neighbours over the years, but at eighty-nine Kathleen was the last woman standing. Or at least she would be if she could manage it, she thought as she gripped the arms of her chair and planted her feet down squarely, ready to haul herself up. She leaned forward and pushed, but the pain in her hips made her gasp and she slumped back for a moment's respite before making a second attempt. She looked up and smiled wryly at the poodle. 'Old age is a bugger, you know.'

She took a deep breath and steeled herself to try again to stand.

'But I can't complain,' she muttered as she finally got to her feet. She steadied herself for a moment. 'It's been a good life.'

An hour later, Kathleen was tucked up in bed listening to the soothing sounds of *Book at Bedtime* on the radio. A cup of tea with two ginger biscuits in its saucer sat cooling on the bedside table beside a framed photograph of Kathleen and Frank on their wedding day.

Yes – it's been a very good life, she thought to herself as she sank back into her pillow and closed her eyes.

The next morning the sun rose as usual. But Kathleen did not.

Chapter 1

'What do you think of my new shirt, then?' George McGlory asked his wife as he puffed out his chest and grinned a little self-consciously. George had a penchant for colourful shirts, and he was particularly pleased with this one, which featured a bright orange parrot print on a navy background.

'It was in the sale,' he told her. 'I've had my eye on it for ages and it was such a bargain that I couldn't resist it.'

George's wife, Audrey, said nothing. Which was hardly surprising given that she'd been dead for almost two years. George put down the canvas bag that he had brought with him and from it he removed a pair of shears. He trimmed the long grass around Audrey's headstone, which the groundsmen on their ride-on mowers weren't able to reach.

'We have to keep you nice and tidy,' he said, remembering Audrey's favourite mantra of 'A place for everything, and everything in its place'. It was mid-September, and although the early mornings now had the nip of autumn, the afternoon sun was pleasantly warm on George's back as he worked.

'I got a nice piece of haddock for my tea from Tesco,' he said as he took the wilted dahlias from the metal vase on Audrey's grave and tipped the putrid water onto the grass. 'I thought I'd have it with some new potatoes and a few green beans from the garden.'

Since Audrey's death, George had tried to fill the void left by her absence with activities, keeping himself busy rather than allowing himself to brood. He still worked at the library three mornings a week, and his fledgling efforts at growing his own fruit and vegetables had proved surprisingly satisfying – digging for distraction rather than victory, as the old Second World War slogan had advocated. George gathered the grass clippings and stood up, slowly unfolding his stiff back, which creaked in protest. Perhaps he should add yoga or Pilates to his schedule, he thought, rolling his shoulders and rubbing at the nape of his neck. He took a cloth from his bag and wiped the dust and dirt from the marble headstone. As he rubbed at a particularly stubborn spot of bird muck, he heard the soft purr of an engine and looked up to see a gleaming hearse arriving at the entrance to the crematorium. It contained a plain coffin unadorned by even a single flower. The undertakers slid the coffin from the car and hoisted it onto their shoulders. Waiting for them was a sturdy-looking woman in her fifties, dressed in a charcoal suit and sensible shoes. She checked her watch as she followed them inside, as though she had somewhere else to be. George stood and watched as the door swung slowly shut behind them. He assumed that the other mourners must already be inside the chapel, although he hadn't noticed anyone going in. Odd, he thought, that no one else was waiting outside to follow the coffin.

He took the metal flower container over to the standing tap, gave it a good rinse out and then filled it with fresh water. Back at Audrey's grave, he removed the yellow roses that he had bought from their brown paper and arranged them carefully in the container.

'There you go, my love. I got you roses this week for a change,' he told Audrey affectionately.

He caught a movement in his peripheral vision, and when he turned to look, he was surprised to see the pallbearers coming out of the side entrance that was used as an exit for funeral parties. Perhaps they were going to wait outside and then go back to usher the mourners out when the service was over. But they were immediately followed by the woman in the charcoal suit, who spoke briefly with one of them before striding off in the direction of the car park, fishing her car keys from her bag as she went. No one else came out of the building. In fact, small groups of people speaking in hushed voices were already making their way towards the chapel entrance to pay their final respects to the next dearly departed on today's list. George strolled across to the rubbish bins with the grass cuttings and dead dahlias. He couldn't help but wonder who on earth had been the unfortunate guest of honour at such a desperately lonely funeral.

The bins were positioned out of sight, at the side of a brick-built storage shed where the groundsmen kept their tools and other paraphernalia. Leaning against the wall of the shed with his eyes shut and his faced turned up towards the sun, one of the undertakers was enjoying a cigarette. George cleared his throat to alert the other man to his presence.

The undertaker opened his eyes and grinned broadly at George. 'Caught me!'

George returned his smile. He had given up smoking years ago, but he still missed it. He pulled a crumpled paper bag from his pocket and from it took a mint humbug and popped it in his mouth. 'I started on these when I gave them up,' he said, gesturing towards the cigarette. 'Much better for my lungs, but not so great for my teeth. Want one?'

The man shook his head.

'I don't blame you. They're no substitute. Don't worry – I won't dob you in to your boss.'

The undertaker laughed. 'It's my wife finding out that I'm more worried about. She's always on at me to give it up. And anyway – I *am* the boss! Edwin Bury at your service. And, yes, it is my real name.'

George grinned. 'How very fortunate. I'm George.'

'Pleased to meet you, George.' Edwin took a final drag on his cigarette, ground it out under his foot and then dropped the butt into one of the bins.

'Not much of a turnout for that last funeral,' George commented as the two men began walking together towards the chapel.

'No. Just us and Big Brenda.'

'Big Brenda?'

'Yes – she's from the council. It was a public health funeral.'

'What's one of those when it's at home?'

'When someone dies alone and no friends or family can be traced, the council are obliged to give the deceased a decent send-off. It's a quick no-frills affair but Brenda usually puts in an appearance – although, I sometimes wonder if she only comes to keep an eye on us,' Edwin added with a wink.

'But that's such a shame – that anyone can end up dying completely by themselves.' George shook his head in disbelief.

'It happens more than you'd think. But at least Mrs Hooley had a good innings.'

'Mrs Hooley?'

'Yes. Today's funeral was for Mrs Kathleen Hooley, aged eighty-nine, who died in her sleep, safe and warm in her own bed. I can think of worse ways to go.'

'It still seems really sad to me. Will she be buried here?'

'Cremated first and then her ashes will be buried in the council plot.' Edwin checked his watch. 'Anyway, it's been nice chatting, but I'd better get a shift on or else the lads will go without me! We've got another funeral 3.30 pm.' He hurried off round the back of the chapel to where his colleagues were waiting with the hearse.

George returned to his wife's grave and collected his bag. He blew a kiss at Audrey's headstone. 'Bye love – God bless. I'll see you next week.'

As he walked back to the car park, he couldn't get the sight of that lonely coffin out of his head. He knew that it was just a wooden box that held only the empty packaging of what had once been a person, but it had looked so forlorn.

'Rest in peace, Kathleen Hooley,' he whispered as he climbed into his car. 'I hope to God that wherever you are now, you're not alone.'

George carried his tray back into the kitchen and loaded his plate into the dishwasher. The haddock had been very tasty and the beans from the garden nice and tender – just how he liked them. He had even treated himself to a can of beer with his dinner to cheer himself up. George McGlory was a good man and kindness was in his DNA. Kathleen Hooley's lonely funeral had touched his heart and left a bruise. He returned to his comfortable chair in the sitting room and settled down to watch an old episode of *The Detectorists*. The familiar programme's gentle humour soothed him, and soon he was completely absorbed by the exploits of The Danebury Metal Detecting Club. At 10 pm he switched off the TV and went upstairs to bed feeling tired and content. But he dreamt of Kathleen Hooley's funeral.

Chapter 2

'It's got a blue cover with a castle on the front. Or a big house.'

George smiled patiently at the woman facing him across the counter, hoping for something more specific to help him identify the book she wanted to borrow.

'It's about a woman who murders her husband and then pretends to be her identical twin sister in order to frame her sister for the murder so that she can be with her sister's husband.'

'I'm afraid it's not ringing any bells. Do you have any idea of the title – or perhaps the name of the author?'

The woman sighed. 'It's got the name of the woman in the title and the author is someone Richardson, or Dickinson – or maybe Parkinson.' The irritation in her tone implied that George was being deliberately unhelpful.

'Nothing springs to mind immediately, but why don't you leave it with me, and I'll see what I can come up with while you're choosing your other books?'

The woman tutted. '*That* was the book that I came in for specifically.'

She waited, as though her presence might encourage George

to conjure the book out of thin air. He smiled at her again but said nothing, and eventually the woman turned away and went off to browse the fiction shelves. One of the things George loved most about his job as a librarian was talking to people, helping them find what they were looking for and recommending books that they might like. Most of the people he dealt with were friendly and polite, but there was always the odd exception.

'Miserable old bat!' hissed George's colleague Roxy as she sat down next to him with two mugs of coffee. 'I don't know how you put up with some of them!'

George nodded his thanks for the coffee and took a sip. 'Maybe she's having a bad day.'

'Well, she doesn't have to turn it into a group activity!'

Roxy opened a new tab on the screen in front of her and began searching for likely candidates for the book that the woman had described. Her intellect and temperament were as fierce as her facial piercings and her purple-streaked hair, but she was a loyal colleague and George was very fond of her.

'As long as I have you to brighten my day, I'll never let the likes of her bother me!' he declared with a wink.

Roxy widened her eyes in mock outrage. 'George McGlory! You'd better not be flirting with me. I'll have to report you to HR!'

George laughed. 'I forgot to ask – how was your date last night?'

Roxy was an enthusiastic user of an online dating app called DateMate, and the previous evening she had been going out for a drink with a tree surgeon called Ezekiel.

Roxy groaned. 'Bloody awful, thanks. I assumed that with his job and a name like Ezekiel he'd be pretty cool with a sort of hipster lumberjack vibe.'

George nodded, even though he was unsure exactly what that kind of 'vibe' might entail.

'I was wrong. He was a proper posho who kept going on about his family's holiday home in Burnham Market, his mummy's home-made gooseberry gin and how brilliant he was at windsurfing. Honestly, what man in his thirties still calls his mum "Mummy"?!'

George could certainly think of one who had – and he was definitely a proper posho with a sort of king vibe. 'So, it didn't go well, then?'

'One drink and I was off! I think maybe I need to change my profile picture for one that looks a bit more like me. The poor bloke nearly choked on his beer when he saw the piercings.'

Roxy continued her online search while George went to retrieve some material from their archive room that had been requested by a lecturer from a local college. When he returned some half an hour later, Roxy was grinning from ear to ear.

'I found madam's book!' she announced triumphantly. 'It had a green cover with a photograph of an abandoned church, and it's called *Sister or Sinner?* by Richard Jones.'

'Well done you! At least she got part of the author's name right.'

Roxy rolled her eyes. 'It was the only bloody thing she got right.'

'And I'm sure she was very grateful.'

'Well if she was, she did a good job of hiding it! She spat out a thank you like a maggot she'd found when she'd bit into an apple.'

George laughed. 'You really should write a book yourself, you know. You have a very colourful way with language.'

'Yeah – I should write a book about working here and some of the oddballs we have to contend with! I could call it *The Secret Trials of a Town Librarian*. I could include some of our Habituals, like Mrs Biscuit.'

The garrulous Mrs Biscuit was a bustling, bosomy woman in her late sixties who came in every Friday to satisfy her seemingly insatiable appetite for crime fiction – the bloodier the better. If ever she was prevented from coming, she would always provide a detailed explanation for her absence to whomever was behind the counter on the day of her next visit.

'I'm terribly sorry I couldn't come last Friday,' she would say. 'But I had a doctor's appointment, and they could only fit me in on the Friday on account of my normal doctor being off sick with kidney stones, which isn't a good advertisement for a doctor if you ask me, so I had to see someone else on the Friday.'

Her soubriquet (her surname was actually Kettle) was the result of her pioneering approach to biscuit baking. Mrs Biscuit was in the habit of bringing them a batch of her latest creations each time she came in. Her choice of ingredients was imaginative but not always very palatable. Their favourites so far had been the lavender and lemon shortbreads, but they hadn't been able to stomach the peppermint and orange creams, which Roxy had fed to some pigeons on the way home from work. Even the pigeons hadn't been that keen.

Mrs Biscuit was one of several regulars – whom Roxy referred to as The Habituals – who used the library more as a home-from-home than simply a place to borrow books.

'I could also feature a list of the things people use as bookmarks and leave in library books for us to find,' Roxy said, warming to her theme.

George laughed. 'What's the strangest thing you've found?'

Roxy answered without hesitation. 'A red lace thong.'

'Good grief! What was the book.'

'Not what you'd expect at all. *A Brief History of Time* by Stephen Hawking. What about you? What's the weirdest thing you've found?'

George considered. 'It's a toss-up between a rasher of bacon in *Harry Potter and the Half-Blood Prince* and a DVD of *Alien* in a Jamie Oliver cookbook.'

'Bacon wins. Was it cooked?'

George grimaced at the memory. 'Unfortunately not. And it was going a bit green around the edges.'

'Is *Alien* the one where that snake thing explodes out of John Hurt's stomach?'

'That's the one.'

Roxy grinned. 'Maybe it was a comment on Jamie's recipes!' Then she grew serious. 'You never know, I might have to give the writing thing a crack if this latest round of staffing cuts goes through. The library will be run by robots if the council has their way.'

George summoned an optimism that he didn't entirely believe. 'They can't get rid of everyone. Who would find Mrs Misery-Guts her books then? Her search data is so inaccurate that any automated system would short circuit! And besides which, they'd get rid of me first because I'm only part-time.'

Roxy shook her head. 'Which is exactly why they'd keep you instead of me – because you're cheaper. No offence.'

'None taken.' George offered her a wry smile in place of any further hollow reassurances. 'Speaking of the council,' he continued, deliberately moving the subject away from things they could do nothing about, 'I saw something really sad yesterday.'

'If this is your attempt to cheer me up it doesn't sound promising,' Roxy joked, but then registered the pensive expression on George's face and allowed him to go on.

'I was visiting Audrey's grave and I saw a funeral with no flowers and no mourners, just the undertakers and a woman from the council. The service barely lasted fifteen minutes. When I think about Audrey's funeral, with all the flowers and music, and all the friends and family that came to remember her and say goodbye – it was heartbreaking, yes, but it was also heart-lifting. It was a tribute to an amazing woman who left her mark on so many people and they came together to remember her with love. It was a validation of her life. And when I saw that funeral yesterday, it made me think – surely everyone deserves that, don't they? Some sort of recognition that they existed?'

Roxy was silent for a moment, considering her response. 'Well, I'm not sure about *everyone*. What about murderers and sex-offenders and people who leave bacon in library books?'

George's brief smile acknowledged the joke, but he was deadly serious. 'But nobody's born bad, are they? And how can a life become a death with so little acknowledgement? The funeral I saw was a practicality and no more. A box ticked off – literally.'

'It does sound a bit grim when you put it like that. But what's it got to do with the council?'

'It's called a public health funeral. When some poor soul dies alone, without any family or friends, the council are obliged to give them a decent funeral.'

'No wonder there weren't any flowers,' Roxy scoffed. 'I'm surprised the coffin wasn't made of cardboard.'

'Actually, you *can* get coffins made out of cardboard.' A man who looked to be roughly the same age as George, neatly dressed and peering out from beneath eyebrows that badly needed pruning, stood at the counter in front of them. 'They're much cheaper than conventional coffins and one hundred per cent biodegradable,' he continued. 'I've requested in my will that I'm to be buried in one myself.'

Roxy pursed her lips and raised her eyebrows to counteract an inappropriate smile. 'That's nice,' she managed to reply. 'How can we help you?'

'I'm looking for a book about the history of fountain pens. I can't remember the title but I'm pretty sure it has a red cover …'

———

It was another warm and sunny afternoon, and George planned to spend the rest of the day tending to his vegetable patch. His walk home took him past Sid's Bargain Emporium on Castle Road, a second-hand shop that sold such a wondrous and peculiar salmagundi of items that George often went in just to look around. The shop's clientele was as varied as its merchandise. Students came to Sid's to kit out the kitchens in their rented accommodation as cheaply as possible. Avid recyclers brought things to recycle, and amateur interior designers bought hidden gems to upcycle. It was the kind of place where people dropped in when they were passing whether they needed anything or not. Sid was a principal part of the attraction. He was a big bear of a man with broad shoulders, a barrel chest and bulging arms that were comprehensively inked with intricate tattoos. His thatch of ginger hair had thinned over the years – sixty-seven on his last birthday – but his irrepressible vigour was that of a much younger man. Sid loved to talk – and people loved to listen to him. His voice was as rich and resonant as a double bass, but more importantly, Sid always knew all the gossip. And he was happy to share it.

When George arrived outside Sid's shop, the man himself was unloading his van. As he stopped to greet George, he tripped up the kerb and the contents of the overfilled cardboard box that he was carrying toppled out onto the pavement.

'Bugger!' Sid exclaimed, but still with a grin on his face.

George stooped to help pick up the items scattered in front of him. There were a couple of small saucepans and a frying pan, some tea towels and cutlery, a crystal vase, a glass jar full of buttons, a Huntley and Palmers shortbread tin and various china ornaments.

'No harm done,' George said as he replaced the lid on the tin, which was full of black and white photographs. But then he noticed that one of the ornaments, a little poodle, had sustained a broken leg. 'I spoke too soon,' he said to Sid, holding up the casualty.

'Never mind – just chuck it in the bin. At least the vase survived.'

'Where's it all from?' George asked, gesturing towards the stuff they had now returned to the box.

'A house clearance. I do a lot of those,' Sid replied. 'I've got a contract with the council to clear out their places when the resident dies and there's no one else to do it.'

George saw once again that lonely coffin. *How can a whole life be reduced to a few boxes?* he thought. Whilst Sid was serving a customer, George noticed that one of the photographs was still lying on the pavement. He picked it up and studied it. It was a picture of a young woman at the seaside. Her hair was tousled by the wind, and she was holding an ice cream and laughing. The camera had captured for eternity a single moment of pure joy.

When Sid returned for the box, George held up the tin. 'How much for the photos?'

Sid grinned. 'Get away with you! You can have them. They're not worth anything – just someone else's memories and no one left to care. They'd probably just end up in the bin with that poodle.'

Chapter 3

The poodle lay on the kitchen table next to the tin of photographs whilst George rummaged in a drawer for a tube of superglue. It was the type of drawer to be found in most kitchens – the one that contained a muddle of useful things along with those that fell into the 'just in case' category. Keys kept just in case you remembered what they unlocked. A couple of small glass jars which might come in handy for storing something. A fridge magnet that had come apart, kept in case you got round to sticking it back together. A packet of birthday candles, an ancient bottle of Olbas Oil, a plastic syringe, a variety of corks and an inordinate number of elastic bands. And a tube of superglue.

When George had returned home that afternoon, he had dug up a few leeks and potatoes, picked some green beans and tomatoes, and watered and weeded where it was needed. He had worked steadily, enjoying the warmth of the sun and the smell of freshly dug soil and newly harvested vegetables. A robin kept him company, chirruping his excitement as he hopped expectantly on toothpick legs and darted down to snatch any worms exposed by the gardener's spade. George had made leek and potato soup for his dinner, with Radio 4 playing in the background for company, and having eaten, he put the remainder of the soup in the freezer. Audrey would be proud of him, he thought. He hadn't done much cooking when she had been alive, but now his repertoire had expanded well beyond the ready meals and cheese on toast that he had survived on for the first year after she had died.

George hadn't had the heart to throw the poodle in the bin. He didn't know why. It was just a cheap ornament – and a broken one at that. But someone had loved it once. Someone had chosen it, kept it, dusted it. Someone had looked into its sparkly red eyes and smiled because it had brought them a little pleasure. And perhaps that was what had stopped George from throwing it away. Because it wasn't just an object. The poodle was a reliquary of someone else's memories and emotions. It was a treasure. George shook his head as he squeezed a blob of glue onto the poodle's leg. Perhaps he was going soft in his old age. But Sid's words had pressed on the bruise that yesterday's funeral had left on him: 'someone else's memories and no one left to care'.

He positioned the leg back onto the poodle, and as he held it there waiting for the glue to take effect, tears pricked his eyes. Grief had shadowed George when Audrey died, a monkey on his back that he couldn't shake off. But gradually it had loosened its grip, supplanted by happy memories of the life they had lived together. He could allow himself to be consoled by the fact that he had been with Audrey until the very end – 'till death us do part' – and that her final hours had been pain-free and peaceful. Her diagnosis of pancreatic cancer at the age of just fifty-nine had been a complete shock and her decline swift, but there had been enough time for Audrey to make her wishes clear and to prepare George as best she could for life without her.

'It's me that's dying, not you, love,' she had told him. 'And if you don't get on with your life when I'm gone, then I'll come back and haunt you – and not in a good way!'

George had held her hand and nodded, but at the time, the idea of a world without Audrey in it seemed almost inconceivable and his survival in such a world impossible. These days his grief was a more comfortable companion – an acknowledgement of the love they had shared. His tears now were for something else. He could fix the poodle, but he couldn't fix the other things. He couldn't prevent people from dying alone. He couldn't stop them being buried or burned in plain coffins with no one to bear witness aside from undertakers and council workers. He couldn't stop their lives being packed into boxes and picked over by people like Sid, who would decide which of their possessions were resaleable and which were rubbish. Until yesterday, George had been blissfully unaware of such things, but now the knowledge – and the sadness that it had brought with it – was like a dull ache that he was finding hard to ignore. He gently wiggled the poodle's leg to test whether the glue had set. It held firm and he stood it on the table in front of him. He noticed that the little dog was a bit grubby and thought that he might give it a wash tomorrow, once he was sure the leg was secure.

George checked the clock on the kitchen wall. There was a programme that he wanted to watch on at 8 pm. It was twenty minutes to. He opened the shortbread tin. The photograph of the young woman with the ice cream was on top.

'I suppose this was the lady that bought you?' he said to the dog.

The photos were versions of the same images taken and kept by so many people before mobile phones became virtual photo albums. He spread them out on the table in front of him – a panorama of the lives of strangers, but the landmarks universal and familiar. Christmases and birthdays, friends and family, homes and holidays. There were numerous images of the same couple recording their journey together through the years. One of them had clearly been taken on the day of the ice cream photograph. The young woman was standing at the entrance to Dreamland in Margate alongside the man with whom she was to grow old. He was tall and handsome, with a shock of black hair and a confident smile, and he had his arm around her shoulders. George wondered if they knew already on that day that they would spend the rest of their lives together. It struck him that there were no baby pictures in the tin. No children riding bikes, building sandcastles or posing on first days at school in uniforms bought to grow into. Perhaps that was why a wholesale house clearance had been necessary – because the couple had been childless. George wondered who had been the one left behind, widow or widower.

He checked the clock. It was five to eight. As he began to gather up the photographs his phone rang. He cursed at the knowledge that he would miss the start of his programme, but his irritation was short-lived when he answered the call.

'Hi, Dad, it's me.'

His daughter, Elizabeth, lived in Edinburgh with her husband, Nick, and teenage children, Angus, known as Gus, and Amelie, known as Lil. George couldn't understand all this messing about with names. Everyone called his daughter Lizzie, but to him she was always Elizabeth. She usually rang him a couple of times a week for a chat. George knew that she was also checking up on him. When Audrey died, Elizabeth had toyed with the idea of them moving back south to be closer to him, but George wouldn't hear of it. The family had moved to Scotland when Nick had got a job as a senior operations manager at the airport. It had been a big promotion for him, and the relocation had worked out very well. The children had still been quite young and had quickly readjusted to their new lives. Once they had started school, Elizabeth returned to the career that she loved: teaching modern languages. When Audrey was alive, the two of them would take a trip up to Edinburgh several times a year, and in the summer, Elizabeth would always come to stay with the kids for a couple of weeks during the holidays and Nick would join them for a few days when he could.

'You've got your own life where you are,' he had told her when she had mentioned moving. 'You and Nick have both got great jobs that you enjoy, and the kids love it in Edinburgh. You've got absolutely no need to worry about me. I'll be fine.'

And he had been fine. Bedford was his hometown, and the familiarity of its landscape and people had been an anchor when Audrey's death had cut him adrift. It had taken a while, and he still missed his wife every day, but he had made a different life without her, and he had grown to like it perfectly well.

Elizabeth told him all about the family's summer holiday in Portugal, her suspicions that Lil might have a boyfriend and Gus's hope of making it into the school's rugby first fifteen in the new term. He had been training hard at the gym and had grown another two inches in height, making him almost as tall as his father. George told Elizabeth about his vegetable patch and his new shirt and regaled her with a few anecdotes from the library. By the time they said their goodbyes, George's programme was almost over, but he wasn't in the least bit disappointed. The photograph of the childless couple still lay on the table in front of him and George knew how lucky he was.

Chapter 4

Case no. 63542-7577

On the day of the move, it rained relentlessly. The sky was dark and disapproving, and water was smashing down on the flowers in the garden, shattering the blooms and battering their torn petals onto the sodden grass. As portents go, it wasn't encouraging. But Derek didn't believe in portents. When the removal man – Dan with a Van – had turned up at his flat in Hackney that morning and announced that they might do better with an ark than his aging Transit, Derek had smiled serenely and offered him a cup of tea – and a chocolate digestive. And now they had arrived in the picturesque, though currently rain-lashed, village where Derek was to make his new home with the love of his life. Jack was at the door to greet them as soon as they pulled onto the drive. A broad smile lit up his attractive face, and he ran his hand through his ever mussed-up mop of silver hair as he stood waiting for Derek to get out of the van. He had remembered to put on the navy check shirt that Derek liked so much, and his usually rumpled chinos were neatly pressed for the occasion.

'Welcome home, my darling!' he murmured, as he pulled Derek into a brief hug and then released him with a quick glance in Dan's direction.

'Don't mind me,' said Dan, pulling the first of the boxes from his van. 'I'm Elton John's biggest fan.'

Between them, they unloaded Derek's belongings – getting drenched in the process – and Jack insisted on making Dan a sandwich and a mug of tea before he set off back to London. They sat in the kitchen, eating and drinking and drying off in the heat of the Aga, which looked strangely incongruous in the 1960s-built bungalow. It had been Jack's retirement gift to himself. He had always dreamt of living in a large country house with a boot room and an Aga – he never missed an episode of *Downton Abbey* – but on a college lecturer's salary, the bungalow had been the best he could afford. He had, however, furnished it as though it were a country cottage, its colourful vintage interiors completely and rather splendidly at odds with the building's plain, boxy exterior. Continuing the theme outside was the epitome of a cottage garden, a feast for both body and soul. The regimented beds of runner beans, carrots, potatoes and onions, the fruit trees and raspberry canes and the riot of delphiniums, roses and honeysuckle made the bungalow they surrounded look like an imposter.

A haughty marmalade cat with tufted fur stalked the kitchen, inspecting them with his baleful yellow eyes before approaching Derek and rubbing his head against his calf. Derek leaned down to stroke him. 'I'm honoured, Kathmandu. You never normally come near me.'

Jack laughed. 'He's trying to get round you now that he knows you're moving in. He's hoping for extra titbits.'

Once Dan had gone, they began to organise Derek's things.

'I've cleared some space on the bookshelves in the study, and your records can go with mine in the sitting room,' Jack told him as he carried Derek's suitcase into his new bedroom. It was cosily furnished with a single bed, a carved mahogany wardrobe and a comfortable looking armchair positioned next to a side table on which stood a handsome brass reading lamp.

'Of course, I hope you won't be *sleeping* in here,' Jack said, with that slow smile that always made Derek's stomach flip. 'I'll leave you to unpack.'

Jack kissed him lightly on the cheek and then left the room, closing the door behind him.

Derek sat down hard on the bed, allowing himself to bounce a couple of times with sheer happiness. He could hardly believe that he'd actually done it. After years of living alone and having no *real* friends – only work colleagues and people he knew from the pub – he had retired, sold his flat and moved to the country to live with his boyfriend. Derek smiled to himself. Boyfriend! They were middle-aged men and both of them drawing a pension. But Derek had never felt so young – and so full of hope for the future. His actual boyhood had been spent in a series of children's homes, or 'in care' as it was so often called. But care wasn't a concept that Derek had been familiar with back then. He had felt lonely, bullied, angry, afraid and sometimes completely invisible. But he couldn't remember ever feeling cared for. Until now. Until Jack.

He got up and lifted the suitcase onto the bed. He opened it and began decanting his clothes. He didn't have that many, having spent most of his adult life wearing the uniform of a police officer – specifically that of a custody sergeant for the past fifteen years. He was sure Jack would soon remedy that. Jack loved shopping for clothes, an activity that for Derek was on a par with filling out a tax return. But with Jack it would be more bearable. He might even learn to enjoy it. Perhaps he could use the John Lewis vouchers he had been given as a retirement gift by his colleagues. His departure from the force had been marked by a few drinks at a local pub. It had been well attended but had only lasted an hour or so before people began to drift away. Derek had never been that close to anyone at work. He had participated sufficiently in the day-to-day banter, pulled his weight and been a reliable member of whichever team he had been assigned to, but he had never socialised with any of them. His childhood had made him stubbornly self-reliant and reluctant to trust anyone, and being gay was an added complication. Yes, attitudes within the force had gradually changed over the years, and some of the younger officers were now officially 'out', but it hadn't been something that Derek had ever felt comfortable sharing with his colleagues. Opening up to a friendship with any of them would have made him feel exposed and vulnerable, and Derek preferred the protective carapace that social solitude afforded him. Until Jack.

As he hung his shirts on the hangers in the wardrobe, he recalled their first meeting a little over a year ago. It had been on a Saturday in The National Gallery. Derek had been standing in front of *Bathers at Asnières* by Georges Seurat. He didn't know much about art, but he knew what he liked, and he enjoyed visiting galleries and museums in his spare time and absorbing rather than analysing what he saw. The painting was one of his favourites. He loved the muted colours and the languid poses of the bathers. The picture conveyed an otherworldly serenity that Derek found mesmerising.

After a while he had become aware of someone standing next to him and had glanced across to see Jack staring at the painting. They had stood in silence for several minutes before Jack said, without looking at him, 'It's wondrous, isn't it?' Jack always chose his words so carefully, and his description had been perfect. They had both been standing there lost in wonderment at the picture before them.

They had exchanged a few pleasantries, Derek reluctant at first – his natural reticence reinforced by the assumption that Jack was an academic and his own ignorance of art would make him look foolish. But Jack's warmth and humour had won him over and they had ended up going for a drink. From that first day, Derek had felt safe with Jack. And over the months that feeling had expanded and elaborated into trust and finally love, and now here he was.

There was a knock on the door. 'Are you done yet?'

Jack came in and glanced at the wardrobe, which now contained the contents of the suitcase but was still half-empty. 'I can see that we need to take you shopping. But perhaps we could start with a few online purchases' he added, seeing the expression of mock horror on Derek's face. 'Now, come and have a glass of wine and talk to me while I cook dinner.'

Derek followed Jack through into the kitchen where the table had been laid with a white tablecloth, silver candlesticks and flowers rescued from the garden. Sade was playing in the background and something that smelled delicious was simmering on the Aga.

Jack handed him a glass of wine and raised his own in a toast. 'To us!'

Derek was horribly cold when he woke up on the floor. He tried to move but a bolt of pain shot through his head. His left side was numb, and his limbs lay immobile – uncooperative and useless. When he attempted to call out, the only sound he could manage was a guttural moan. He tried to remember what had caused him to fall. The headache had arrived without warning – intense and agonising. He had been on his way to the kitchen to get some painkillers when he had suddenly collapsed, as though the headache had blown the main fuse to the rest of his body. How long had he been on the floor? He couldn't move his arm to see his watch, but it had been lunchtime and now it was dark outside. It was dark inside too. Derek wondered if he was going to die. He couldn't raise the alarm. His phone was charging in the kitchen, and he couldn't even speak let alone shout for help. How long would it take for him to be found? Days? Weeks? Months? No one came to the bungalow except to deliver post and parcels. Would anyone in the village notice his absence? He doubted it. They might just assume that he'd gone away for a bit. He wasn't afraid. In fact, it would be a relief.

Since Jack had died, Derek had disengaged from the world, merely going through the motions of a life rather than living one. It had become a mechanical but meaningless process to survive, and after six years he'd had enough. Six years – twice the amount of time that he and Jack had had together. If only he had known that they would have only three years to do everything they had planned, to say everything that needed to be said, to love each other enough for a lifetime. Just three years to squeeze out every last drop of happiness. Jack had died two days before his seventy-first birthday.

Derek tried to lift his head again, but nothing happened. He closed his eyes. He didn't feel so cold any more. In fact, he couldn't feel anything.

Jack, he whispered in his head. And as the blackness closed in, he heard a voice reply,

'*Welcome home, my darling.*'

Chapter 5

'"Heart of Glass",' George said triumphantly to Roxy, who wrote down the answer on their entry sheet.

'Are you sure?' said Gary, frowning. 'I could have sworn it was "Sunday Girl".'

The pub quiz at The Duck and Donkey was a serious business, and George's team rarely finished below the top three of the teams that regularly took part.

'No, "Heart of Glass" was definitely Blondie's first UK number one – "Sunday Girl" was the second,' George replied with complete conviction.

Gary didn't look convinced, but as the official scribe, Roxy decided in favour of George. The team had originally consisted of George and Audrey, and Gary and his wife, Sally. The pub had a decent restaurant where George and Audrey used to have dinner every so often. It was there they had met Gary and Sally, and the four of them had become friends. When the pub had started running quiz nights, they had formed a team.

'Question thirteen – unlucky for some!' joked the landlord, Lachie, who relished the role of quiz master. 'What's the largest lake in England?'

'It's between Windermere and Ullswater,' said Roxy, who had fortuitously holidayed in Cumbria the previous year.

'What about Loch Lomond?' Gary suggested.

'That's in Scotland,' Roxy replied a little impatiently. 'I'm pretty sure it's Windermere.'

After Audrey had died, George hadn't the heart to go to the pub for several months, but Gary and Sally had kept in touch, never intruding but letting him know they were there if he needed anything. One evening, on the spur of the moment, George had decided to go for a drink. He had forgotten that Thursdays were quiz nights, and there at their usual table sat Gary and Sally.

'So,' Gary had said, getting up to buy George a drink, 'are we putting the band back together?'

They were hardly the Blues Brothers – a film they both loved – but George was happy to return to the quiz team. He had subsequently invited Roxy to become their fourth member but now they were a woman down again, as Sally had taken up pottery classes which were also on Thursday evenings.

'I'm happy to go with Windermere,' George agreed.

The pub was even busier than usual on account of a darts match taking place in the adjoining games room, and once the quiz was over there was a rush to the bar to get drinks. While George was standing waiting to be served, he felt a nudge on his elbow.

'Fancy seeing you here!'

George turned to see the undertaker whom he had met at the cemetery standing next to him. 'It's my local,' George replied with a smile, 'but I've not seen you in here before. It's Edwin, isn't it?'

'That's right. I'm here for the darts match.'

'Are you on the team?'

Edwin laughed. 'No, they're not that desperate. I'm just here to cheer them on. Can I get you a drink?'

'Thanks, but I'm getting a round in for my teammates. Pub quiz, not darts,' George clarified.

'That's much more up my street. But two of the lads from work are darts mad, so I tag along every now and again just to keep them sweet!'

For a moment, George was tempted to ask him if he'd be interested in joining their team. But George hardly knew him, and it wouldn't have been right to ask without talking to the others first. Instead, he said, 'Did your lot win?'

'We're only halfway through, but we're just in the lead at the moment. What about you?'

'Lachie's just totting up the scores.' George nodded to where the landlord was sitting, poring over the answer sheets with a pen in his hand.

'Well, good luck,' said Edwin, gathering up his drinks.

'You too,' George replied.

Back at the table, Gary and Roxy were waiting eagerly – both for the drinks and the results.

'I reckon we stand a good chance of winning this week,' said Roxy, taking a swig from her glass of cider.

'My lucky shirt usually does the trick.' George was wearing a black shirt patterned with coloured dice and playing cards.

Roxy laughed. 'You say that about every shirt you wear on quiz nights.'

'That's because they all make me feel lucky!'

'Who was that bloke you were chatting to at the bar?' asked Gary. 'I've not seen him in here before.'

'His name's Edwin. He's here with one of the darts teams. I met him at the cemetery when I was visiting Audrey.'

'Don't tell me he's a gravedigger!' Gary joked.

'You're not far off the mark. He's an undertaker. I got chatting to him while he was having a sneaky fag by the bins. I was asking him about that funeral I told you about, Roxy.'

George explained briefly to Gary about Mrs Hooley's funeral and how lonely it had looked.

'I grant you, it's not a nice thought – dying alone,' Gary agreed. 'But then, your Mrs H wouldn't have known anything about her funeral so does it really matter?'

'She might have done,' said Roxy pensively, tracing her fingertip down the condensation on the outside of her glass. 'She knew she had no friends or family left, so if she'd thought about it, she might have realised that no one would go to her funeral. And that's pretty sad.'

'But is it, though? If it were you, would you really care about what happens after you're dead?' Gary persisted.

George wished that Gary hadn't asked that question of Roxy. He knew that her father was dead, her mother was elderly and frail, and that she had no siblings or significant other. A sparsely attended funeral was a far more possible scenario for Roxy than it was for Gary, who had two sons and a bevy of grandchildren.

Before Roxy could answer, George spoke. 'I just feel that Mrs Hooley and others like her should be remembered as real people and not just names and case numbers. Isn't the whole point of a funeral to show respect and –' George paused while he searched for the right word '– and recognition of a life that must have touched others along the way?'

'But if she didn't have any friends or family, you can't just magic some mourners out of nowhere.'

Before George could reply to Gary's perfectly reasonable but deeply unsatisfying argument, there was the sound of a bell being rung at the bar and Lachie waited for silence before announcing, 'Ladies and gentlemen, the scores have been counted and the results are in!'

Chapter 6

'We are the champions!'

Roxy greeted George with a fist bump and a huge grin when he turned up for work the next morning. They had won the pub quiz by a clear ten points, their greatest victory to date, and their prize was a voucher for a local Indian takeaway. They had agreed that George would host a curry night at his house and that Roxy and Gary would bring the drinks.

'I was thinking about asking that chap I was talking to at the bar if he was interested in joining our team,' said George, shrugging off his coat. 'He said he preferred quizzes to darts.'

'You mean the undertaker?'

'Yes – Edwin. What do you think? We could do with a fourth member and we haven't come up with anyone else so far.'

'Cobweb Dave was angling to join us last night after the result was announced. He asked if we'd found anyone yet to replace Sally.'

Cobweb Dave was a member of a rival team who were rarely placed above the bottom three. Roxy had christened him 'Cobweb' on account of the tragically sparse comb-over carefully arranged across his shiny bald pate – and the fact that, like spiders, he gave her the creeps.

George raised an eyebrow. 'So he's after a transfer? I wonder if his teammates know.'

'He's just looking to worm his way into a better team and bask in our reflected glory. Well, he can bugger off. Anyway, I told him that we'd already got someone, so I'm more than happy if you want to ask the undertaker. I'm sure Gary won't mind.'

'I'm not sure when I'll see him again, but if I do, I'll ask him.'

'Great! Now if we get any questions on cremation or embalming or any other death stuff, we'll have it covered!' Roxy replied with a wry smile.

They walked through from the staff room to the library itself, and while Roxy switched on the lights, George unlocked the main doors. Several people were waiting to come inside, and at the head of the queue was another of the library's Habituals – a stocky man with a white beard and deep-set, flinty blue eyes. George estimated that the man was in his late seventies, and a labyrinth of deep lines crazed his face as though a hard life had etched them there with a heavy hand. In his navy blue felt cap with its silver skull and crossbones badge, he was a familiar figure, not just in the library, but also around the area where George lived. George often saw him in the local shops and in the park, where he was always accompanied by a large white and grey dog with the most astonishingly blue eyes. He would always offer a perfunctory reply to George's greeting in his gravelly voice, which had a faint Welsh inflection, but he never engaged in conversation. He didn't borrow books to take home, so they didn't know his real name, but he was generally known as Captain, something George had learned from Sid who counted Captain as one of his regular customers. He nodded to George and made his way into the library, where he began browsing the non-fiction shelves.

George spent the morning dealing with requests for books that needed to be ordered in from other libraries, and he was surprised when Roxy brought him a mug of coffee. 'Is it that time already?' he said, checking his watch.

'Don't pretend you didn't know,' Roxy replied. 'You just keep your head down and wait for me to make it so you don't have to.'

George laughed. 'It's only five-to by my watch so technically you're five minutes early.'

Roxy went to take his mug back, but he held on to it firmly.

'Enough of your cheek, George McGlory, or that's the last coffee I'll make for you,' she scolded with mock severity.

She placed her own mug on the desk and then took the other one across to where Captain had been sitting for the past two hours in his usual seat, tucked away in a quiet corner of the room, reading a book entitled *More Haunted Houses of London*.

'Don't tell anyone,' she murmured as she handed it to him, 'else they'll all want one.'

He looked up and thanked her with a fleeting smile. The mug of coffee was one of the small kindnesses Roxy sometimes bestowed upon members of The Habituals.

'He's a grumpy old bugger,' Roxy said to George when she returned to the desk. 'But I actually got a smile out of him this morning.'

George looked across to where Captain was once again engrossed in his book – taking small sips from his mug as he read. 'He certainly never has much to say for himself. I sometimes wonder what his story is.'

'Maybe he doesn't have one,' Roxy replied. 'Maybe he's just an ordinary bloke who's retired and lives alone with his dog and comes to the library to save on his heating bills.'

'Ordinary people have stories too,' George said with a frown. 'Every life is a story of some sort.'

'I suppose,' Roxy conceded. 'But you wouldn't want to hear all of them. Some of them would send you to sleep.' She nodded pointedly towards the door where Mrs Biscuit was just coming in carrying a cake tin.

She came straight to the desk and set down the tin in front of Roxy. 'Well, you'll never believe what a morning I've had!' She huffed and rolled her eyes for emphasis before continuing. 'At one point I didn't think I'd get here at all! First, my Norman couldn't find the shirt he wears for bowls, and he's got a match this afternoon. I told him to look in the airing cupboard and he said he already had, but when I looked, I found it straightaway. He'd done what I call a "man's look" – open the cupboard door, and if it doesn't jump into his hand, it can't be in there! Then the phone rang, and it was Norman's friend Bill who wanted to know if Norman could give him a lift to the bowls match because his wife, Sandra, needed their car because she was taking her sister to the hospital for her colonoscopy.'

Mrs Biscuit paused for breath and George tried hard not to picture Sandra's sister having a colonoscopy.

'Then as soon as George put the phone down there was someone at the front door, and when I opened it, it was two very smartly dressed young men who belonged to the same religion as that pop group who were brothers and sang about crazy horses and loving puppies. They wanted to have a chat about their god and what he could do for me, but I told them that I was quite happy with Father Michael's god at St Francis Xavier's and besides which I really didn't have the time to be standing around discussing holy matters at nearly eleven o'clock on a Friday morning when I should be at the library. And you'd think that would be enough, wouldn't you?'

Roxy and George both nodded earnestly.

'But then just as I was leaving the house,' Mrs Biscuit continued, fixing them with her gaze as she approached the scintillating climax of her anecdote, 'the cat sicked up a dead mouse on the hall carpet. A whole one.'

Roxy gasped in sympathy, covering her mouth with her hand to disguise her smile.

Mrs Biscuit leaned in towards Roxy and George conspiratorially. 'I pretended I hadn't seen it,' she whispered. 'I left it there for Norman to deal with. I only hope he doesn't tread in it.'

She straightened up and tapped on the lid of the tin with her fingers. 'I made you some biscuits to have with your coffee – and I'm just in time, I see,' she said, nodding at their mugs.

'That's very kind of you,' George said. 'What sort are they today?'

'You're very welcome, my dears. They're a new recipe I'm trying out so let me know what you think. Peanut and rhubarb.

Norman had rather a surplus at his allotment so I'm using it up. The rhubarb, that is, not peanuts. Now, I can't stand here chatting all day. There's a new Martina Cole book I want to borrow.'

As she turned and walked away, Roxy looked at the tin warily. 'Maybe she should borrow a cookery book every now and again too.' She lifted the lid of the biscuit tin with exaggerated caution as though she expected something from inside to escape. She sniffed the contents tentatively and then offered the tin to George. 'You go first.'

Chapter 7

George stood outside the little flower shop just along from Sid's emporium trying to decide what Audrey might like on her grave this week. There were some beautiful dahlias – oversized pompoms of petals in shades of glowing orange through copper and chestnut to rich chocolate. He gathered a selection and took them inside to pay.

The woman behind the counter smiled at him in recognition. 'For your wife?' she asked in a voice still heavily accented with her native Croatian, despite having lived in the UK for the past ten years.

George nodded.

The first time she had asked him that question and he had explained that his wife was dead and the flowers were for her grave, the woman had reached over and briefly touched his arm. 'I'm sorry,' she had said, looking him straight in the eyes before taking the flowers from George and wrapping them in paper. She had not flinched in embarrassment or confusion like so many people did when unexpectedly faced with the bereaved. Her words had been direct and sincere, and George had appreciated them.

He handed over the dahlias and the woman held them out admiringly. 'You make an excellent choice,' she said. 'Audrey, she will be very happy.'

'I'm glad you think so, Elena. The colours are stunning – and very seasonal.'

September had slipped into October, and George noticed there was a tray of Royal British Legion poppies on the counter. He paid for his flowers and then picked out a poppy. He fished a five-pound note from his wallet and pushed it into the collection box.

Elena smiled at him. 'Thank you, George. You are a good man.'

George drove to the cemetery with the dahlias beside him on the passenger seat. The blooms themselves had no scent, but their stems and leaves had an earthy, slightly bitter tang which always put him in mind of his Grandad Joe. As a small boy, George had idolised his mother's father and had spent many happy hours with him on his allotment. His memories of Grandad Joe could be distilled into a potent cocktail of tastes and smells, each one having the capacity to transport him back to his childhood as effectively as any time machine. The man himself had smelled of camphor, Wright's coal tar soap and tobacco. George's grandma had been an ardent advocate of moth balls and coal tar soap, and Grandad Joe was never without his pouch of baccy and packet of rolling papers. His trouser pocket always contained a paper bag of mint humbugs, which he would offer to young George whenever he lit up a cigarette. On his allotment, Grandad Joe had grown as many fruits and vegetables as he could cram onto his allocated plot. Summers had tasted of the strawberries, gooseberries, blackcurrants and plums that George had pilfered while Grandad Joe had planted and pruned, weeded and watered. The only flowers that had been permitted precious space on the allotment were a few rows of dinnerplate dahlias that had towered above George like a chorus of dazzling showgirls. When he had walked amongst them, their leaves had brushed his clothes and skin, leaving their peculiar scent behind.

George parked the car, and before he got out, he pinned the paper poppy he had bought onto the lapel of his jacket. Grandad Joe had been a soldier in the trenches at the Somme during World War I and he had returned with a long jagged scar on his right forearm that had defaced the tattoo of an eagle that had been there first. A single bullet had mutilated man and bird. Both had survived but both had been changed irrevocably. When George had asked him about it, Grandad Joe had replied only that it was his war wound. He never spoke about his time in France, and it wasn't until many years later that George had understood that the worst scars the war had left were the ones you couldn't see.

As George made his way to Audrey's grave, he spotted a familiar figure over by the bins. This was his chance to ask Edwin if he wanted to join the quiz team.

Edwin greeted him with a smile. 'We'll have to stop meeting like this – people will talk!'

George noticed that Edwin wasn't smoking, but appeared to be skulking – that is, he got the impression that Edwin didn't want to be seen. 'Are you hiding from someone?' he asked.

'Not exactly. One of my lads is running the next funeral. It's his first time in charge and I want to keep an eye on things to make sure it goes smoothly and that he does his job properly. But I don't want him to know I'm checking up on him in case it puts him off, so I'm incognito. I'll slip into one of the chapel side rooms once they're inside.'

'I'd better be off then,' George said. 'I don't want to give you away.'

'No – you're fine for a bit. They won't be here for another five minutes or so – although I see the man from the council's already in position.' Edwin nodded towards the entrance to the chapel, where a man in a grey suit was pacing back and forth nervously and checking his watch.

'It's his first time too,' Edwin explained. 'Big Brenda's been promoted and he's her underling now – poor sod. It seems like she's chucked him in at the deep end. She could at least have held his hand for this one. I'd offer to be his wingman myself, but it would rather blow my cover.'

'You mean it's another one of those lonely funerals.'

Edwin looked at George, puzzled for a moment, and then he nodded, understanding his meaning. 'Yes – it's a public health funeral for a Derek Isherwood. And I suppose it will be pretty lonely because no friends or family were traced for this one either. So it will just be my lads, the appointed celebrant and Nervous Niall from the council.'

They both turned at the sound of a purring engine and the crunch of tyres on gravel as a hearse made its stately progress up the drive.

'I'll leave you to it,' said George and Edwin withdrew into the shadow of the bins.

As he walked, George watched the bare coffin being unloaded from the hearse and his stomach lurched. Or was it his heart? The specific organ responsible for his feeling of disquiet was irrelevant. All he knew was that someone else was embarking on their final journey unacknowledged by any fond farewells or precious memories. It would be another death perfunctorily marked, with scant consequence given to the life that had preceded it, and to George it felt profoundly sad. The poppy he wore was for all those who had died fighting for their country, and far too many of them had been left behind in the mud without even the briefest ceremony or the shallowest of unmarked graves. Many of Grandad Joe's comrades were still there, waiting to be found and given a decent burial. Their fate had been unavoidable, given the circumstances, but what about Derek who had just been carried into the chapel?

'Sorry, Audrey, love – I'll get you some more tomorrow.' George clutched the dahlias to his chest as he set off towards the chapel. Inside, the funeral of Derek Simon Isherwood, widower of Jack Percival Isherwood, was almost over when George strode up to the coffin and laid the dahlias on its lid.

He turned to face the pews, which were empty save for Nervous Niall, and with his hand still on the coffin, George took a deep breath. 'The Lord's my shepherd, I'll not want ...'

Chapter 8

The twenty-third psalm was the first – and only – thing that had come to mind when George had suddenly decided to gatecrash Derek's funeral. Thankfully, years of singing it at school assemblies and then later at weddings and funerals had embedded the words into his brain so that he didn't actively have to remember them, but simply retrieve them from his subconscious. Once he began to sing, the words flowed effortlessly. He wasn't Michael Ball, but he could hold a tune and, anyway, it was better than nothing – better than silence save for the final swish of the curtain. When he had finished singing, the celebrant, who appeared completely unmoved by George's impromptu interruption, committed Derek's body to the hereafter and headed off towards the door as soon as the coffin was out of sight. It was clear, however, from the troubled expression on Niall's face that he was not feeling so equanimous.

'Are you a relative or friend of the deceased?' he asked suspiciously.

'Derek,' George replied, unable to hide his irritation. 'He was called Derek – not "the deceased".'

Niall flushed, and George felt a twinge of conscience, remembering what Edwin had told him about Niall being new to all this.

'No, I'm not a relative,' George replied in a gentler voice. 'And I never met Derek in his lifetime. But I decided to be a friend at his funeral.'

Niall frowned. 'I'm not sure I understand. How did you know about his funeral if you didn't know him?'

'Edwin told me – Edwin Bury, the undertaker. I ran into him earlier when I was visiting my wife's grave. I saw one of these funerals a few weeks ago and it's haunted me ever since. It was more like a package being posted off to its final destination than a ceremony to mark the end of someone's life. I didn't want Derek's departure to be the same. Whoever he was, I'm sure he deserved something better than that.'

'And he got it, thanks to you. Great vocals, George! You'll be doing weddings and bar mitzvahs next.' Edwin was standing in the doorway to the exit of the chapel, and George remembered that he still hadn't asked him about the pub quiz team.

'That's all very well,' Niall replied, sounding decidedly rattled, 'but you really can't go … butting in like that. The deceased – I'm sorry, Derek – may not have been religious. Or he may have believed in something other than Christianity, in which case "The Lord's My Shepherd" is hardly appropriate.'

George was beginning to get irritated with Niall – partly because he might have had a point, but mainly because he was being such a jobsworth. George had tried to do something kind and all Niall could do was pick holes in it.

'I shouldn't worry too much about all that,' Edwin intervened as they joined him and headed outside. 'In the absence of any information either way, surely it's the intention that counts? I think George was just trying to make it a bit more personal.'

Niall's flush had deepened in proportion to his agitation and had seeped down his cheeks across his neck. 'But that's my point! If the deceased – Derek – wasn't religious, then singing a hymn at his funeral wouldn't make it more personal. He may even have been offended.'

George had had enough. 'Well, at least I tried! All you did was stand there while that woman read out his name and check-in and check-out dates. You should be thankful that Derek can't leave a review on Tripadvisor. I don't think you'd be getting many stars for customer service!'

Before Niall could reply, George left them to it and returned to Audrey's grave, where he stood for a moment, his hands clutching the top of her headstone. The black marble was cold and smooth against his skin, soothing his anger and calming his frustration.

'I know, I know – I shouldn't have had a go at him like that,' he sighed. 'But he shouldn't have been so snotty with me. I was just trying to do something nice for Derek, but he had to ruin it with all his bloody rules and regulations!'

'Does she ever answer you back?'

Edwin had appeared at his side holding the dahlias that George had placed on Derek's coffin. He leaned in closer to read the inscription on the headstone. 'Your Audrey. Does she ever reply?'

George conceded a smile. 'She doesn't need to. We were together for so long I know exactly what she'd say.'

Edwin raised his eyebrows. 'And?'

'She'd say, "Give the poor man a break. He's new and probably nervous. He's just trying to get things right and not get the sack. And, besides, whatever he said, you did a good thing."'

'She sounds like a very smart lady to me. And for what it's worth, I'd agree with her.' Edwin handed George the dahlias. 'You might as well have these back now. Derek's being cremated.'

'Where will his ashes go?'

'In the council plot.'

'Where's that? Will you show me?'

Edwin took George to a garden behind the chapel which comprised four small square lawns laid out in a larger square, surrounded by flower beds stocked with rose bushes. The roses were little more than threadbare clusters of tattered petals fringed with sepia now, but still clung precariously to their stems. In contrast, the dahlias that George was holding were vibrant botanical jewels. At the very centre of the garden stood a stone sundial. George removed the paper in which the dahlias were wrapped and set them down at its base. 'In memory of Derek – may he rest in peace.'

They stood in silence for a moment and George felt his shoulders relax and his tension dissipate. And he remembered what he had been meaning to ask Edwin.

'How do you fancy joining our pub quiz team?'

Chapter 9

Briony Harris rang the doorbell at 27 Honeysuckle Close and wondered at the wisdom of whomever at the council had chosen such an inappropriate street name. Perhaps they had envisaged front gardens full of flowers and neatly kept lawns. The reality was a row of ugly driveways whose cracked concrete and weed-infested gravel had subsumed any resemblance to gardens. There was the token potted plant and a few bedraggled privet bushes, but cars and wheelie bins predominated. Briony rang the bell again. Life as a junior reporter for *The Times and Herald* hadn't turned out to be anything like she had imagined when she had joined the local newspaper fresh and keen from her degree in journalism twelve months previously. She had envisaged herself writing investigative pieces about unsolved crimes or corrupt politicians, but Gordon Bullock, her editor at *The T and H*, as it was commonly known, had insisted that she cut her teeth on local human-interest stories, or 'extraordinary stories about ordinary folk' as he was fond of calling her assigned subject matter. And so Briony spent her days writing about sponsored knitting marathons, peculiarly shaped fruit and vegetables, mildly interesting achievements, lost and found pets, children, wedding rings and, in one case, a piano accordion, and an interminable variety of complaints and grievances.

This morning's assignments were typical. The door was finally opened by an overweight man in his thirties wearing a T-shirt bearing the words 'Babe Magnet' that didn't quite cover his hirsute belly. From his dishevelled appearance, Briony wouldn't have been surprised if she had got him out of bed. He hitched up his tracksuit bottoms and scratched his crotch. 'Yeah?'

Briony forced a smile and showed him her ID. 'Briony Harris from *The Times and Herald*. I'm here about the sandwich.'

Realisation dawned on the man's face and he perked up immediately. 'Oh yeah, great – come in.'

He opened the door wide and stood to one side to let her past. Somewhat unexpectedly, he smelled of strawberries. He led her through to a sitting room where a woman of similar age and size to him, dressed in a leopard print onesie, was sitting on a cream leatherette sofa. She held a French bulldog wearing a matching outfit on her lap.

'She's come from the paper,' the man said to the woman, nodding towards Briony. 'About the sandwich.'

Briony stood awkwardly, wondering if anyone was going to offer her a seat. Apparently not.

'Do you mind if I sit down?' she asked, perching herself on the edge of one of the armchairs that matched the sofa. The little dog growled.

'That's enough of that, Paris,' the woman said to the dog, giggling. 'She's a terror, she is. Thinks she's a rottweiler.'

Briony smiled through gritted teeth. 'She's lovely,' she lied. 'And what a pretty name. Have you been to Paris?'

The woman looked puzzled for a moment and then she laughed. 'No – she's not named after the place! She's named after that boxer's wife – the one with all those kids. Paris Fury.'

To be fair, the dog did look pretty furious, but perhaps it was on account of the outfit, Briony thought. She took out her notebook, keen to get on with the interview.

'So,' she said, 'you are Tyler and Paige De Quincey, is that right?'

'That's us,' Tyler replied, vaping hard on an e-cigarette, which explained the smell of strawberries.

'Great. Now tell me about the sandwich.'

The couple looked at one another encouragingly, and then Paige began. 'I was doing my big shop at the supermarket, when I saw that some of the sandwiches were on offer, so I got one for Tyler because he loves a sausage sandwich, don't you?'

'They're my favourite,' Tyler agreed.

'Well, they used to be. But after what happened, he may never be able to eat one again.' Paige spoke slowly and deliberately to emphasise her point.

From the expression on Tyler's face, this was news to him, but one look from his wife and he was nodding earnestly.

'I understand you found something in the sandwich other than sausages?' Briony couldn't believe that she actually had to write about this stuff.

'It was terrible,' Paige replied. 'And they're not getting away with it.'

'When I bit into it,' Tyler chipped in, keen to have his moment of glory, 'I felt something hard, so I spat it out. And it was a little piece of blue plastic.'

'It wasn't that little! You could have choked and then I would have had to do that Hendricks manoeuvre on you!' Paige wasn't going to have the gravity of the situation underestimated.

'Have you still got the piece of plastic?' Briony asked, desperate to wrap things up and move on to her next assignment.

'Of course we have – it's evidence! We're sending it to their head office with our demand for compensation. Tyler could have choked,' Paige repeated. 'He could have died in front of me. He could have been allergic to plastic and gone into that shock thing that makes you swell up so you can't breathe. He could have died of that as well!'

It appeared Tyler was very lucky still to be alive after his encounter with the discounted sandwich. He fetched the piece of blue plastic from the kitchen to show Briony. It was in a sealed bag and Tyler held it up for her to inspect. It was no bigger than a ladybird.

'We haven't got the sandwich,' he explained, 'because I ate it. But I took some photos first on my phone.'

Briony asked him to email them to her and then took a photo of them sitting on the sofa, with Tyler holding the plastic bag aloft and grinning (somewhat inappropriately for someone who had so narrowly and recently escaped death) and Paige appearing suitably upset. Paris still looked furious.

'So when will it be in the paper?' Paige asked as they followed Briony to the door.

'I'm not sure,' Briony prevaricated. 'But I'll let you know.'

Back in her car, she checked her phone for the address of her next assignment. It was only a short drive away, and as she parked the car, she hoped that Mrs Lindsay Lavender, music teacher and keen gardener, would have something of greater substance to share with her than a substandard sandwich. The house was a 1930s semi with a proper front garden and not a wheelie bin in sight. The green front door with stained-glass inserts was opened by Mrs Lavender herself.

'Briony Harris – from *The Times and Herald*.'

Mrs Lavender inspected her ID and then smiled. 'It's lovely to meet you. Do come in. I take it you're here about my homegrown pumpkin that looks exactly like Donald Trump?'

Chapter 10

On the passenger seat beside her sat Briony's compensation for what had turned out to be a thoroughly rubbish day. The interior of her car was filled with the delicious aroma of king prawn and pineapple, curry sauce and chips. It was fitting that after a day investigating vapid nonsense about food and then struggling to write something remotely interesting about it she should console herself with her favourite takeaway. As she pulled into the driveway of the house where she rented a first floor flat it began to rain – and not just a passing shower, but a proper soak-you-to-the-skin-in-seconds downpour. Briony switched off the engine, and as the rain hammered onto the car roof, she debated whether or not to wait for it to pass over. But she didn't want her food to get cold, so she grabbed her things and dashed for the door.

She made it safely inside, but water ran in rivulets from her coat onto the tiles in the hallway, and after a couple of steps she slipped on the rain-slick floor. As she fell, she twisted awkwardly in an attempt to save her supper but succeeded only in landing on it. The flimsy bag split and the foil containers inside burst open, spilling their contents over Briony and the floor. She yowled in pain and frustration and let rip a stream of expletives. And as she lay there in an inelegant sprawl, splattered in Chinese takeaway, the door to the ground floor garden flat opened and Ms Allegra Monteverdi stepped into the hallway and surveyed the scene.

Ms Monteverdi had the poise and posture of a dancer and could have been any age between sixty-five and seventy-five. She was what could only be described as startlingly beautiful and always immaculately turned out. Briony had barely seen or spoken to her in the twelve months that she had lived there, but mail for all the residents in the building was left on a table by the front door which was how Briony knew her neighbour's name. And of course, it would have to be this perfect woman who discovered her in such a humiliating predicament.

'Goodness!' she exclaimed in a low, slightly husky voice without a trace of any accent. 'What a mess. Are you hurt?'

'Just my pride,' Briony replied through gritted teeth as she tried to get up, but slipped back down into the gloopy orange puddle that was spreading across the tiles.

Ms Monteverdi smiled, but Briony couldn't read the emotion behind the expression. She didn't know if the woman was amused or sympathetic. Her green eyes gave nothing away. But then she offered Briony her hand to help her up, and Briony wiped her own on her jeans before taking it. Once she was on her feet, she scooped back into the split bag what she could of the carnage that had been her intended supper.

'I'll just go upstairs and get something to clean this up,' she said to Ms Monteverdi, who nodded and smiled that inscrutable smile once more before turning back towards her flat.

By the time Briony returned with a bin bag, a roll of kitchen towel and some cleaning spray, the mess was almost cleared. Ms Monteverdi, wearing a crisp pinny and rubber gloves, was just wiping the final smears from the floor. She stood up and handed Briony a carrier bag containing the food, its damaged containers and a bundle of soiled paper towels. 'You might want to put this in the bin outside. I'm sure you won't want the smell of it in your flat. Particularly as you haven't even had the pleasure of eating first.' Her assured tone indicated an instruction rather than a suggestion but there was just a hint of mischief in her eyes.

Briony took the bag from her. 'Thank you so much. You really didn't need to – it's very kind.'

She hesitated at the front door, reluctant to go back out into the driving rain, but a glance over her shoulder confirmed what she had somehow suspected – that her neighbour was still in the hallway watching her. The bins were only a few yards away to the side of the house, but by the time Briony had dumped the bag and sprinted back inside she was very wet – again.

The hallway was empty but the door to Ms Monteverdi's flat was still open and, hearing Briony's footsteps, the woman reappeared. 'Would you like to join me for a drink? It appears that your plans for the evening have been rather spoiled and perhaps a vodka martini might lift your spirits?'

All Briony wanted to do was get out of her wet things and have a nice hot bath and some beans on toast – which admittedly would be a very poor substitute for chips and curry sauce but would be quick and easy and satisfy her grumbling stomach. But she didn't want to appear rude and – ever the journalist – she was curious about her enigmatic neighbour and keen to see inside her flat.

'That would be lovely, thank you. Do you mind if I pop upstairs and change first?'

Ms Monteverdi looked appraisingly at her wet shoes and dripping hair. 'I'd prefer it if you did,' she replied in a wry tone.

Back in her own flat, Briony stripped off her wet things and blasted her sodden locks with a hairdryer. She pulled on a pair of clean jeans and a sweater and checked in the mirror to see if she looked presentable. She would have to do. She imagined Ms Monteverdi tapping her beautifully manicured fingernails impatiently on her martini glass if she were to be kept waiting too long. Downstairs, she rang the bell and Ms Monteverdi welcomed her inside saying, 'Please do call me Allegra – and you're Briony, yes?'

Briony nodded, and Allegra motioned her to sit in one of two emerald-green velvet-covered armchairs. There was a small table between the chairs on which stood two full martini glasses, each garnished with two olives and a twist of lemon. There were also three small bowls, containing nuts and crisps and crudités, and a pot of houmous.

Allegra lifted one of the glasses. 'Help yourself,' she instructed Briony. 'It will hardly replace your supper, but it's never wise to drink on an empty stomach.'

Briony took a sip from her glass and the liquid burned her throat as she swallowed. This was a serious martini – delicious, but dangerously strong. She put down her glass and reached for the crisps.

'You have a lovely home,' she said, taking in her surroundings. It was a trite compliment, but in this instance completely justified and therefore sincere.

The flat was considerably larger than Briony's, which was little more than a studio. The walls of the sitting room were painted the colour of ripe Victoria plums – a hue so rich that it almost glowed in the lamplight. They were the perfect canvas for what appeared to be a carefully curated collection of pictures and objets d'art. There were watercolours of Paris, Amsterdam, London and Venice, a selection of film posters fully framed in Perspex and a huge black and white photograph of New York. A trio of Venetian carnival masks were mounted beside a row of fancy gold hooks on which were hung a top hat, a bowler hat, an exquisitely embroidered silk kimono and a large black umbrella with a silver horse-head handle. On another wall a collection of ornate mirrors cast back disparate views of the room and its treasures. A large mahogany bookcase was home to one shelf of coffee table books about travel, one shelf of classic literature and poetry, one shelf of Edwardian postcard albums and another to a selection of vinyl records.

'You have so many wonderful things. Have you been to all these places?' Briony gestured to the pictures on the walls.

Allegra smiled. 'I've been lucky enough to have travelled widely and what you see are just a few reminders and mementoes. Of course, when I moved here, I wasn't able to bring everything with me. This flat is somewhat smaller than where I used to live in London, but it suits me perfectly well now.'

Briony's journalistic antennae twitched. She felt sure this woman's life story would be anything but ordinary. 'Whereabouts in London did you live?'

'Mayfair.'

Briony nearly choked on her olive. How on earth had Allegra been able to afford a flat in Mayfair? There were so many questions she wanted to ask. But she wasn't on an assignment, she reminded herself. Allegra was hardly likely to have a celeriac shaped like Boris Johnson. This was a purely social encounter.

'What made you leave London?'

Allegra took a sip from her glass. 'It was time to move on – to another place, another stage in my life. I thought I'd like somewhere quieter.'

'And do you?' Briony asked, registering that Allegra had given only a politician's non-answer to her first question.

Allegra gazed at her coolly for a moment and then said simply, 'Yes. I do. And what about you? You've been here, what – about a year? What brought you here?'

'My job. I work for *The Times and Herald* as a junior reporter.'

Allegra raised an eyebrow in mock approbation. 'My God – the paparazzi! I hope you're not recording our conversation.'

Briony grinned. She was beginning to relax as the martini took effect. 'Don't worry – your secrets are safe with me. Not that you've told me any. Besides, the only stuff they trust me to cover at the moment is insultingly trivial and incredibly boring – neither of which epithets apply to you.'

'You're most kind,' Allegra replied with a gracious inclination of her head. 'So, what have you been up to today?'

Briony described her encounters with Tyler and Paige De Quincey and Mrs Lavender's pumpkin. 'That's why I'd bought a Chinese takeaway,' she explained. 'To cheer myself up.'

'In that case,' Allegra said, picking up Briony's empty glass, 'you'd better have another martini.'

Chapter 11

'Back again so soon?' Elena asked when George came into the shop with another bunch of dahlias. 'What happened to the other flowers?'

George handed the dahlias over for her to wrap. 'It's a long story.'

Elena shrugged. 'I have time. I'm not so busy today.' She was always happy to chat to George.

'Have you ever heard of a public health funeral?'

Elena looked slightly horrified and shook her head.

'It's what happens when someone dies and has no friends or family to sort out their affairs and organise their funeral and so the council ends up doing it. I saw one a few weeks ago for a lady called Mrs Hooley and it was horrible. There were no flowers, no hymns, no music and no mourners – just a woman from the council and the undertakers. The coffin looked so … forlorn. I couldn't stop thinking about it afterwards.' George sighed before continuing. 'A life that lasted for almost ninety years reduced to a fifteen-minute funeral. That can't be right, can it?'

'So many people live lonely lives these days. Live alone, die alone – none of it is right but it is a big problem to fix.'

'But is that a good enough reason not to try?' George's anger and frustration were so powerful that they were almost physically painful. Ever since Derek's funeral his emotions had been all over the place, and he was beginning to wonder if his reaction was disproportionate and triggered by his grief for Audrey.

Elena gave his arm a gentle squeeze. 'Of course not. My mother always used to say that even the smallest candle can still shine a light. But tell me, what did you do with Audrey's flowers?'

'When I was at the cemetery yesterday, there was another public health funeral. I watched the bare coffin arrive in the hearse, and once I realised that there were no mourners, I went inside the chapel for the service. It was shamefully brief and purely perfunctory. There was no music, no speeches, just a few despatch notices – name: Derek, address, date of birth, date of death – and that would have been it.'

Elena raised her eyebrows 'But …?'

'I couldn't stand it, Elena. I couldn't just stand there and do nothing. So, I put Audrey's flowers on Derek's coffin and I sang "The Lord's My Shepherd".'

Elena clasped her hands together in delight before wrapping her arms around George and hugging him tightly. 'See!' she said, releasing him. 'You did it. You lit a candle and shone a light on Derek. Audrey would be very proud.'

George could feel tears welling in his eyes and he scrubbed them away with the back of his hand. It was such a small thing that he had done, but it felt important. It had mattered. Somehow, even in the great scheme of things, it had made a difference. A bunch of flowers and a hymn had brought a precious touch of humanity to the dispassionate protocol that had marked Derek's lonely death. George took out his wallet to pay, but Elena waved his debit card away.

'Derek's flowers were free – so I owe you these. You did a good thing, and I'd like to be part of it if you let me.'

'That's very kind, Elena, but you really don't have to.'

'I know I don't. But I want to.' She smiled. 'It makes me feel happy.'

George put his wallet back into his trouser pocket and picked up the dahlias. 'Thanks, Elena. You know – in a strange way, although it made me sad, it made me happy too. Such a small thing –'

The bell above the door rang and a young man came in holding a bunch of pink roses.

'Well, I better let you get on,' said George, turning to leave.

As he opened the door, Elena called after him. 'If you go to any more of those funerals, let me know. There will always be free flowers from me.'

'I've been swotting up,' Edwin said as he took a seat with Roxy in The Duck and Donkey. It was Edwin's first quiz night as part of the team.

'Well, you're our designated expert on anything death related,' Roxy told him with a wink. 'And also anything to do with football.'

Edwin laughed. 'Not me! I don't know anything about football. I'm strictly Formula 1 and tennis.'

'Damn!' Roxy shook her head. 'We really need to get someone who knows about football. The only sport George is interested in is cricket.'

'What about you?' Edwin asked. 'What's your sport?'

'Scrabble. I used to play hockey at school, but I was useless. I was always getting sent off for hitting other people's ankles instead of the ball.'

'Accidentally or deliberately?'

Roxy grinned. 'A bit of both.'

George arrived at the table carrying a tray of drinks.

'It's good to have you here,' he told Edwin as he handed him a pint of bitter. 'Especially as Gary's abandoned us. Sally's persuaded him to join her pottery class. I think he's seen the film *Ghost* too many times!'

Edwin laughed and took a sip from his glass. 'Cheers, George, but you might not think that when I tell you who I've invited to come along and support us.'

'Accidentally or deliberately?' Roxy asked, raising an eyebrow.

'Completely deliberately, I'm afraid. But I couldn't help myself.'

'Well, come on then – put us out of our misery,' said George, taking a seat.

'Niall. Nervous Niall from the council.'

'Oh no! Not him! What on earth made you invite him?' George was caught completely off guard and not at all happy. Of all the people Edwin could have asked to come, why on earth would he want to invite Mr Jobsworth?

Edwin held up his hands defensively. 'I know, I know! You two didn't exactly hit it off, but I got chatting to him after that funeral. His car wouldn't start, and we found him stuck in the car park as we were leaving and gave him a lift back to his office. He's only just moved here for the job, and he doesn't know anyone except Brenda – poor sod. And on top of that he's going through a bit of a rough patch – messy divorce by the sound of it. I just felt sorry for him – thought a night out might cheer him up.'

George relented a little. He could almost hear Audrey chiding him for being so churlish.

'Is he fit?' asked Roxy.

George shrugged and looked at Edwin for an answer.

'Fit as in gym-bunny – or gym-buck, I suppose that should be – or fit as in a George Clooney lookalike?'

'Either would be nice, I suppose,' replied Roxy hopefully.

'Judge for yourself,' Edwin said, nodding towards the bar. 'He's the one that's just come in.'

Niall Laughlin was in his early forties. He was not a handsome man, but he had an interesting face. His nose was a little large, but his chin was firm and the eyes behind his spectacles were a soft dark brown. His dark hair was threaded with grey but neatly cut, and his teeth, though slightly crooked, were white and all his own. Overall, Roxy was not disappointed.

Niall scanned the room and Edwin stood up and waved him over to their table. 'This is Roxy, and George you've already met.'

George got up and offered his hand, determined to make amends for their first encounter. 'I'm sorry if I was out of order at the funeral –' he began, but Niall interrupted him.

'No – it's fine. I know you were only trying to help. Those funerals are wretched affairs, and I'd love to try and do something to make them better, but to be honest, it's finding the time. I know it's not much of an excuse, and people like Derek deserve something better, but it's only one part of my job, and I've got my boss breathing down my neck all day insisting that we only do the bare essentials.' He spoke quickly, as though he had prepared what to say and was anxious to get it off his chest.

George nodded thoughtfully. An idea was hatching in his head, but it was too insubstantial for him to share yet, so instead he asked Niall what he'd like to drink.

'No, I ought to buy a round. It's good of you to invite me to come.'

'We're sorted already,' said George, 'but I'm hoping that if I buy you a drink, you might do us a favour.'

Niall looked nervous again but replied, 'I will if I can.'

'Our team's one short, so how do you fancy filling in?'

Before he could answer, Roxy patted the chair next to her. 'Come on, you can sit next to me. It's Edwin's first time too. You're both Duck and Donkey pub quiz virgins, but don't worry, I'll look after you.'

Edwin laughed and Niall blushed, but he sat down, and George went to the bar to buy him a pint. Moments later, Lachie the landlord rang the bell for silence.

'Good evening, ladies and gentlemen! Pens at the ready for the first question – and tonight, we're starting with one for all you sports lovers. Which football teams played in the FA Cup Final in 1974?'

Roxy groaned.

'Liverpool and Newcastle United,' Niall said without a moment's hesitation. 'Liverpool won 3–0.'

Chapter 12

Case no. 63542-7578

Josh knew he was going to score even before his foot made contact with the ball. His instinct was what set him above the other boys on the team. They all had great skills, and they had all put in the hard hours of training. But Josh had something extra – something that made him special. He was a natural. The corner kick from Danno was a bit long, but Josh managed to collect and cajole the ball away from the final defender who stood between him and the keeper, and then he simply launched the ball into the top right-hand corner of the net. The goalie didn't stand a chance – he barely saw the ball as it flew over his head. Josh and his teammates hadn't finished celebrating when the final whistle blew. They had won the Bedfordshire Youth League final 3–0 and Josh had scored a hat-trick.

His parents were waiting for him in the car park when he emerged from the changing rooms, his hair still damp from the shower and his face flushed with excitement.

'Well done, son – we're so proud of you!' his dad said, drawing him into a bear hug.

'You were amazing, Josh!' His mum's commendation sounded dutiful rather than sincere. She wasn't a football fan, and she didn't come to his matches that often. She always complained that it was freezing standing on the sidelines, and if it was wet or windy, she moaned that it ruined her hair. Josh thought that if she wore a proper coat and trainers or boots instead of heels, she might not get so cold, but he never said anything. He sometimes wondered if it was just an excuse and that she wasn't really that interested. But his dad came when he could, whenever his job as a heavy-goods delivery driver allowed.

To have them both there today was really important because not only had his team won the league, but also Josh had some exciting news. It wasn't often that he felt good about himself. He didn't like school much – apart from seeing his mates. He found lessons boring, and his grades reflected his lack of enthusiasm. His mum and dad were always going on at him about the importance of education, but he couldn't see the point. The only thing he cared about was football – and it was football that was going to give him the chance to show his mum and dad who he really was.

'Coach said to tell you that he's going to give you a ring tomorrow,' Josh said, grinning. 'He needs to talk to you about something.'

The expression on his mum's face hardened as she pressed her lips together and narrowed her eyes, oblivious to her son's obvious excitement. 'What about? I hope you're not in trouble, Josh.'

'Of course he isn't – are you, Josh?' his dad said, ruffling his hair.

Josh shook his head. 'There was a scout here tonight from Spurs.' He swallowed, struggling to get the words out. 'He told Coach that he wants me to do a trial for Tottenham Academy.'

He waited a moment for the magnitude of his words to sink in. His dad was a lifelong Spurs fan and had taken Josh to his first home match when he was just six. Josh could still remember the battle-cry roar from the terraces when Spurs had scored the first goal and the sea of waving arms and fists punching skywards. He was too young then to fully understand the fierce, almost feral loyalty that united this tribe of baying fans, but the intoxication of being there in that moment had remained with him ever since. And now, just six years later, he had an opportunity that might lead to him one day playing for the very team that commanded such unconditional devotion.

'Josh – mate – I can't believe it!' His dad picked him up and swung him round and round, whooping with delight.

'Put him down, Steve. You're making a scene!' Josh's mum shook her head disapprovingly. 'Come on, it's freezing standing around here. Let's go and get a pizza to celebrate.'

The Mona Lisa Pizzeria was crowded with families enjoying an early evening meal, but they manged to grab a table in a corner by the window. The restaurant was warm and noisy with chatter and music and the chink of cutlery on plates, and the air was thick with the rich aromas of pasta sauces and freshly baked pizzas. They ordered some drinks and studied the menu. His mum insisted that she wanted only a margarita with a green salad on the side, but his dad ordered a calzone with garlic bread, and Josh chose his favourite, pepperoni. While they waited for their food, his mum started questioning his dad about the academy. How much would it cost? What about Josh's school lessons? Wasn't he too young? Josh allowed their conversation to drift over his head. He was confident that whatever objections his mum raised, his dad would make it happen. There was no chance he would let anything – or anyone – stand in Josh's way when it came to joining the academy. Josh turned to face the window and, with his index finger, he drew the outline of the Spurs cockerel in the condensation. One day, he thought, he would wear it on his chest.

Josh stood shivering in the alleyway that led to the garages behind the flats. It was early November and his thin T-shirt offered little protection against the sharp wind. His feet, in flip-flops, were blue with cold. He wrapped his bony arms around himself and swore. Where the fuck was Weasel? He pulled a pack of cigarettes from the pocket of his jeans, but before he could light one, a car pulled up on the road at the end of the alleyway.

Minutes later Josh was back inside his flat with his little bag of oblivion. Well, not so little today.

'Whatcha done, J? Rob a bank?' Weasel had said when Josh had asked for twice his usual amount.

Not a bank, but he'd lifted the wallet of some suited and booted guy in the corner shop while he was busy arguing with someone on his mobile. Josh had sold the bank cards and kept the cash, which was why he now had a bottle of vodka and enough smack to have an epic one-man party. The flat was just a room with a small bathroom connected. There was a single bed with a soiled mattress, topped with a filthy coverless duvet, and a wardrobe with one door hanging off its hinges. It was impossible to tell if the carpet was patterned or simply covered in stains. The sink and draining board were piled high with takeaway containers colonised by various species of mould, empty cigarette packets and used syringes. The whole place stank of stale sweat, urine and rotten food.

Josh, clutching his goody bag and bottle of vodka, sat down in the single armchair next to a low table. On the table was everything in the world that he needed right now. A large spoon, a syringe, a tea light, a box of matches and the remote control for a stolen TV. It was a still life of his empty existence. Josh unscrewed the lid on the vodka and took a greedy slug before turning on the TV and flicking through the channels. He froze when a football match appeared on the screen. He stared at it for a moment before his mouth curled into an angry snarl. He switched channels and hurled the remote control at the TV.

'Fucking football!' he yelled. 'I fucking hate fucking stupid football!'

He took another gulp of vodka and set the bottle down on the table before lighting the candle.

'Right then. Let's get this party started!'

He held up the bag of white powder and shook it before tipping half the contents onto the spoon. He paused for a moment, considering, and then tipped the rest of it out.

'Fuck it,' he thought. 'It *is* my birthday.'

Josh was twenty-three years old.

Chapter 13

The chatter of children's excited voices rang through the library as a teacher and two classroom assistants shepherded their charges towards the desk where George sat smiling and Roxy appeared to be bracing herself in preparation for some ordeal. Earlier that morning the two of them had set up a large table flanked by display boards in a prominent position in the main room of the library. Year 6 from St Columbanus Academy had been learning about Remembrance Day and had created an impressive collage of pictures incorporating hundreds of poppies, which they had been invited to exhibit at the library. Roxy had gathered a selection of appropriate books on the table, and the children were there to add their artwork to the display. The uncommon level of noise and activity that accompanied the arrival of the children drove Captain to abandon his usual seat and take refuge behind the shelves of the poetry section, where he consoled himself with *The Collected Works of John Betjeman*. Roxy didn't blame him. She was tempted to join him there.

The teacher introduced herself as Mrs Bunney, and Roxy noticed that, as she did so, two boys at the back of the group made ears on the top of their heads with their hands and waggled them before dissolving into giggles. Mrs Bunney turned around and fixed them with a steely smile. 'And just remember, Year 6, that you are here representing St Columbanus and so I expect you to behave sensibly.'

There was a collective shuffling and shushing, and Mrs Bunney returned her attention to George and Roxy.

Roxy leapt in before George could say anything. 'It's lovely to meet you all and we can't wait to see your display. George here will show you where you can put up all your pictures and give you a hand.' She smiled sweetly at George, who narrowed his eyes at her just a little before getting up and leading Mrs Bunney and her pupils to the space that had been prepared.

The children began emptying the carrier bags they had brought with them, and soon the table and floor were awash with tissue paper poppies. One little girl stood holding a painting of a large brown horse, two dogs, a bird of uncertain identity and something that looked very much like a koala bear. The picture was bordered by purple poppies.

'That's lovely!' George told her. 'Did you make it?'

The little girl nodded. 'Purple poppies are to remember all the animals that fought bravely in the war,' she replied. 'Miss Bunney told us about them.'

'I knew about the dogs, and the birds and horses – but what about this one?' George said, pointing to the koala.

'I *think* there were koalas in the war,' the little girl said, frowning slightly. 'But also, I had room for one more animal and koalas are my favourite.'

Thirty minutes and several boxes of drawing pins later, the display was complete, and as everyone stood admiring the fruits of their labours, they were joined by a young woman who introduced herself as Briony Harris.

'I'm from *The Times and Herald*,' she said, 'and I'm here to write something about your wonderful poppy project and take a few pictures.'

By the time the reporter had spoken to Mrs Bunney, George and several of the children, and taken photos of the display and its creators, and Mrs Bunney had gathered her charges together and ushered them out of the door, it was almost lunchtime.

'Thanks for volunteering me!' George returned to his seat beside Roxy and mopped his brow in a gesture of mock exhaustion.

'Well, you dressed for the occasion, so I assumed that you wanted to get involved.' Roxy grinned as she gestured at his shirt, which was a scarlet poppy print on a navy background. 'And anyway, you're so much better with children than I am. You're a dad – and a granddad. I'm not even an aunt. At thirty-nine, I'm virtually an old maid! I'll end up being one of those people who die alone with only Alexa for company and have one of those council funerals that you keep talking about.'

George looked at her, a little unsure now if she was joking or not. Her grin wavered for just a moment, like a flickering lightbulb, before returning to its full beam.

'Go on,' she said, nudging him with her elbow. 'You enjoyed it – admit it! But I'll make you a cup of tea anyway. And I think I'd better get one for Captain too – with a couple of biscuits on the side. He looked pretty horrified when the St Columbanus Massive arrived and he's been hiding ever since!'

While Roxy was in the staff room, George thought about what she'd said. It was true that Roxy lived alone. Her dad had died several years ago, and her mum was now in a local care home. She had been their beloved only child, conceived when they had almost given up hope of being parents. In all the time he'd worked with her, Roxy had never had a serious boyfriend – despite her determined dating. There had been a couple of men that she had seen a few times but nothing that could be called a relationship. He was sure that she must have friends other than the pub quiz team, but now that he thought about it, she rarely mentioned anyone specific. He wondered whom she might contact in those situations that people never liked to think about happening to them: an accident, illness, money problems – emotional problems.

He had always had Audrey, and now Elizabeth. He had friends and he got on well with his neighbours. He supposed that if the worse came to the worst, he also had Roger – his brother. The brother he hadn't spoken to for years and whom he missed desperately, although he'd never admit it. Yes, Roger really would be the last resort. But George knew that if he called him, Roger would be there. So he had options – people upon whom he knew he could rely in an emergency. But did Roxy? Should he ask her? He'd worked with her for over eight years, yet he'd never thought about this before. How could he have spent so much time with her and not know the answers to these questions? He suddenly felt bad that he knew so little about her life outside the library. It was the spectre of those damn funerals again. They had begun to haunt him – the two he had seen and the countless others that he kept imagining. He had assumed that Roxy had only been joking when she'd mentioned having one, but suddenly he wasn't so sure.

'Penny for them?' Roxy plonked a mug of tea and the tin containing the remainder of Mrs Biscuit's biscuits down in front of him. 'Why the face like a wet weekend in Walton-on-the-Naze?'

She sat down next to him and took a sip of her tea. This was his chance – he could ask her now. But how in God's name could he find the right words? *Tell me, Roxy, if something awful happened to you, who would you ask for help? If you were to die suddenly and unexpectedly, do you have anyone who would sort out your affairs and organise your funeral?* He shook his head to himself. He was as likely to start drinking matcha tea and doing hot yoga with Lazarus (George had seen his classes advertised on the library noticeboard and shuddered involuntarily) as he was to come straight out and pry into Roxy's private life.

'Planet Earth to George.'

Roxy was still waiting for an answer, and suddenly one came to him in Audrey's voice.

'For heaven's sake, George, stop stewing about it and do something! If you're serious about wanting to change those lonely funerals, then stop wasting time fretting and come up with a plan!'

Audrey had been a great one for planning. George had put it down to her father being a colonel in the army. But she was right – as usual.

'I'm going to speak to Niall about those public health funerals,' George replied. 'I'm going to ask if there's anything I can do to help him to make them better – more personal. And if he says no, I'm still going to try. Even if all I can do is find out from Edwin when the funerals take place and turn up with some flowers and sing.'

Roxy bit into one of Mrs Biscuit's biscuits, pulled a face and put the biscuit down again. 'I'm sure Niall would be only too pleased to have some help,' she replied thoughtfully.

And if George had been looking at her, he might have seen the slight colouring of her cheeks.

'And if you need another volunteer,' she continued in her more familiar confident tone, 'well, then – I'm volunteering! I can't sing, but I've got a voice that carries, so perhaps I could recite a poem or something.'

At that moment a fierce young woman with cropped hair and navy lipstick presented herself at the desk and gesticulated angrily towards the Saint Columbanus Academy Remembrance Day display.

'It's fucking disgusting!' she pronounced. 'It's just a glorification of war and it has no place in a public library.' She would no doubt have continued her diatribe had she not been interrupted by a low voice that came from behind her.

'And I suppose you think your uneducated opinions do?' It was Captain, and his face looked like thunder. 'Your mouth is clearly bigger than your brain,' he growled. 'It's about honouring the dead. It's about paying respect for all those lives that were lost. Respect!' He fired the word at her like a bullet. 'Something you clearly know nothing about.'

The young woman went to answer back, but one look at Captain's stony face was enough to change her mind. She turned and glared at George and Roxy before flouncing off.

'Well said! That told her.' Roxy beamed at Captain and George nodded in agreement.

'Thanks for the tea,' Captain muttered, retreating into his customary reticence like a tortoise drawing back into its shell.

They watched him walk away.

George turned to Roxy with a wry smile. 'Actually, I quite like Walton-on-the-Naze – even in the rain.'

Chapter 14

George sat nursing his pint in The Duck and Donkey. He had chosen to sit at a table tucked away in a corner so that when the others arrived their conversation wouldn't be overheard. The pub was busier than he would have expected for a Tuesday night. George felt slightly guilty about being out drinking on a school night, but clearly the other customers didn't share his qualms. He grinned to himself. *For heaven's sake, George*, he thought. *Stop being such a stick-in-the-mud! It's about time you learned to live a little – because if not now, when? You've fewer years in front of you than you have behind, so you need to make them count.*

'Evening, George! What's tickled your funny bone?'

He looked up and Edwin was grinning back at him, his nose and cheeks red from the biting wind that was whipping through the streets outside. He set down his own pint on the table and shrugged off his coat.

'I was just thinking that I'm too old to feel guilty about being in the pub tonight when I've got work tomorrow, and that maybe it's time I shook up my life a little.'

Edwin laughed out loud. 'Blimey, George – I hardly think

a couple of pints on a Tuesday night qualifies as debauchery. I can see I've got some serious leading astray to do if you're aiming for something you can feel properly shamefaced about! Still, it's a start, I suppose. And it's funny how thinking about death makes you consider life a bit more carefully.'

George had invited Niall out for a drink to ask him what he could do to help with the public health funerals. He thought it would be easier to chat over a few beers and that, bearing in mind what Edwin had said about Niall being new to the area and knowing hardly anyone, he might welcome a night out. When George had rung him, Niall had proposed the following evening, which suggested that George had been right. He had invited Edwin along for moral support because he was fully in favour of what George wanted to do – and also because George genuinely enjoyed his company.

'Here he is – the man of the moment!' Edwin nodded towards the door where Niall had just come in, wearing a woolly hat and his habitual expression of anxiety. George got up to meet him and asked what he'd like to drink.

Niall pulled off his hat and ran his hand through his hair. 'Thanks, George. I've got work tomorrow so I'll just have half a lager shandy.'

Once they were sitting back at the table, George wasn't quite sure how to start the conversation. He wanted to offer his help, but without any implication that Niall was somehow failing to do his job properly. Perhaps sensing his hesitation, Edwin broke the silence first. 'So, how's it going Niall? How's life at the council treating you?'

Niall sipped his shandy and looked glum. 'I'm finding it a bit of a struggle, to be honest,' he replied. 'It's not that I don't like the work – I do. And for the most part, I know what I'm supposed to be doing because I've worked in environmental health for years. It's just the funerals that I haven't done before. But it's the volume of stuff that I'm expected to deal with – it's completely unrealistic, and I worry that I'll end up not doing some of it properly.'

Edwin nodded sympathetically. 'It's always tough settling into a new job. Have you tried speaking to Brenda? She's your boss, isn't she?'

Clever, thought George as he watched Edwin skilfully nudge Niall into a corner from where he would find it difficult to refuse their offer of help. George knew that Edwin's opinion of Brenda both professionally and personally was hardly favourable and that she was unlikely to be an empathetic boss.

Niall snorted. 'Brenda! All she's interested in is shifting jobs from her desk onto mine. Delegation seems to be a weapons-grade policy with her.' He paused for a moment and took a large swallow from his drink before continuing.

'At my interview, I was promised training and support, but I haven't seen much of that from Brenda. I was sent on a course for a couple of days in my first week which covered the basics of public health funerals. I came back feeling pretty confident and even had a few ideas about how we could improve on what we do at the moment. But when I tried discussing it with Brenda she wasn't interested. She said that there's no point in doing anything except the bare minimum when the only person who's going to benefit is already dead, and that if I had the time to anything extra then I clearly didn't have enough to do.' Niall sighed heavily and drained his glass.

He got up to get a round of drinks in, and when he returned, he had bought himself a pint of lager this time.

'The thing is, I really need this job,' he continued. 'I took it because it's more money than I was earning before, which I need because I've got an almost-ex-wife and teenage daughter to support and the rent on my flat to pay. And I had to move to Bedford because the commute would have been hell and would have cost a fortune. My car's on its last legs and still in the garage waiting to be fixed, and on top of all that I've got Brenda breathing down my neck just waiting for me to cock something up!'

'That woman has no heart.' Edwin shook his head in disbelief. 'But George here has an idea which might just be the answer to one of your problems. Come on, George – tell Niall all about your cunning plan!'

Niall was singing a familiar song from the eighties loudly and with considerable vigour as George and Edwin tried to steer him down the road. His recollection of the lyrics was a little dubious, which was not surprising considering the state he was in, but the tune and pounding rhythm were unmistakable. George and Edwin were supporting most of his weight as best they could with their arms wrapped under his shoulders. Niall's vocals were accompanied by extravagant random gestures as he staggered this way and that without managing to make significant progress in any one direction.

'Bloody hell!' panted George. 'How much did he have?'

'*Stop apologising, I've never done those things!*' bellowed Niall.

'After a slow start, I reckon probably three pints of lager and a Jägerbomb.' Edwin paused for a moment to adjust his grip. 'I saw him down it in one when he went to the bar to buy his last round. I don't think our Niall here is accustomed to strong drink!'

'*'Cause wife is short, and wife is crap, but it's up to me to change the wife called Alice!*' Niall toppled forward precariously but George and Edwin managed to haul him upright again.

'Sang with feeling,' Edwin said with a wry smile. 'Apparently Alice is the name of his soon-to-be-ex-wife. By the way, George – where are we actually taking him?'

'Good question. Do you have any idea where he lives?'

Edwin shrugged. 'Not really. I know he lives close to Russell Park – not far from you, I think. But I don't know his address. Hey, Niall – where do you live?'

Niall frowned for a moment, swaying gently on his feet and then grinned.

Hanging out your nan's old knickers on the fire to dry
It's enough to make you fart and furious when you
stop believing lies
Of a wife called Alice!

'Right!' said George decisively. 'It's freezing out here and he's heavy. Let's get him back to mine, give him some coffee and see if we can get some sense out of him then.'

The walk home from The Duck and Donkey usually took George around ten minutes, but with a Niall-sized ragdoll who was either unwilling or unable to co-operate slung between them, it took considerably longer. By the time they reached George's front door, Niall appeared to be having trouble staying awake. They coaxed him through to the sitting room and deposited him into an armchair, where he promptly fell asleep.

'Do you think he'll be okay?' George asked. 'Should we try and get him upstairs to the guest room?'

'I think he's better off sitting up. We don't want him choking on his own vomit. Just cover him with a duvet or a blanket and leave a bucket next to him.' Edwin shook his head and laughed. 'And there was you worrying about drinking on a school night. It's this poor bugger's chances of making it into work tomorrow I don't fancy!'

After Edwin had left, George brought down the duvet from the bed in the guest room and laid it gently over Niall, who was now sound asleep and snoring. Remembering Edwin's words of warning, George fetched a plastic bucket from the kitchen and set it down on the floor by Niall's feet.

Upstairs in his own bed, George lay awake in the dark mulling over their evening in The Duck and Donkey. Niall had been cautiously receptive to his offer of help. He was worried about what Brenda might think, but nonetheless clearly grateful. George sensed that his gratitude was about more than just the funerals. He couldn't imagine what it must be like to be in Niall's position because he'd never been there. He'd had a long and happy marriage, a wonderful daughter, a job he thoroughly enjoyed and was blessed with a group of loyal friends. Niall was alone in a strange town going through tough times both at work and in his private life and no one had his back. What Niall needed was some friends.

Chapter 15

The following morning, what Niall really needed was a couple of paracetamol and some very strong coffee. George had already shaved and showered and was eating his breakfast by the time Niall made an appearance in the kitchen. His eyes were bloodshot, and his face had a waxy pallor. He shuffled in and slumped down onto the chair opposite George. He propped his elbows on the table and dropped his head into his hands.

'I feel like death warmed up,' he groaned.

'You look like it too!' George replied cheerily. 'Would you like some breakfast?'

Niall made a pitiful sound that implied he most definitely would not.

'Right,' said George briskly. 'You'll feel better with something inside you, so I'll make you some scrambled eggs and toast.'

At the mention of scrambled eggs, Niall scrambled to his feet with his hand over his mouth and rushed off to expel whatever was left inside him from the previous evening. George turned up the volume on the radio a little to cover the sound of Niall's retching. He gave up on the eggs but made some toast and boiled the kettle. When Niall returned, he looked a little better.

'I'm so sorry,' he said quietly. 'I don't know what to say.'

George patted him on the shoulder and smiled. 'You don't have to say anything. We've all been there. Now sit down and try to eat some toast. The received wisdom is that coffee is good for a hangover, but I must admit that I prefer tea – what about you?'

Niall sat down and gingerly pulled the plate of toast towards him. 'Tea, please. Strong with milk – no sugar.'

George made him a mug of builder's tea and handed it to him with a couple of painkillers. He glanced up at the clock on the wall. 'I'm going to have to get going' he said. 'I need to get to the library. Will you be okay to let yourself out? The back door's locked so just shut the front door behind you.'

Niall swallowed the tiny piece of toast he was chewing and closed his eyes. 'Shit!' he exhaled in a desperate whisper. 'Shit! Shit! Shit!'

George raised his eyebrows, trying not to smile. 'Brenda? What time are you supposed to be at work?'

'In about twenty minutes. But I'll have to go home first, have a shower and get changed. She's not going to be happy,' Niall added glumly.

George pulled his mobile from his pocket and began texting Roxy.

Can you hold the fort for a while? I'm going to be a bit late. All good but just helping out a friend in need! See you soon.

The reply came almost instantly:

Okay, but you owe me one. Also – you'll be making all the teas/coffees this week.

George replied with smiley face and thumbs-up emojis.

'Right – that's sorted,' he told Niall. 'Drink your tea and I'll give you a lift home. I'll wait while you get yourself sorted and then give you a lift into work. If we get a shift on, you'll only be about an hour late. You can give Brenda a ring on the way and tell her why you've been held up.'

Niall stared at George incredulously. 'What – tell her that I got drunk last night and woke up in someone else's house with the hangover from hell and vomited in their toilet while they made me breakfast?'

George shook his head. 'I didn't say you had to tell her the truth. Tell her …' He paused for a moment, trying to come up with something plausible that she couldn't blame on Niall. 'Tell her that your key broke off in the lock as you were leaving your flat this morning and you're waiting for the locksmith, who should be here any minute. You're terribly sorry but obviously you can't leave your flat unsecured and you'll be there as soon as you can.'

Niall's face brightened a little. He forced himself to swallow another mouthful of toast and then drained his mug of tea, washing down the painkillers. George handed him his coat and they headed outside. Just forty-five minutes later, George pulled up outside the council offices and a clean and slightly clearer-headed Niall climbed out of the car.

'Thanks, George. I really appreciate this.'
'No problem. What are friends for?'

After work, George took his car home and set off on foot in the direction of Sid's shop. The bitter wind of the previous evening had blown itself away, and although it was still chilly enough for a hat and gloves, it was a bright and sunny afternoon and, in the distance, George could see Captain and his dog striding briskly through the park. George would normally have passed the shop on his walk back from the library, but this morning he had driven straight to work to save time after dropping off Niall.

Roxy had been very inquisitive about their meeting at The Duck and Donkey and had questioned George about it closely. She had laughed out loud – enough to make several people turn and frown disapprovingly from the library floor – when George had told her about Niall's singing and their team stagger back to his place. But when he had told her about the state Niall had been in when he had finally surfaced, George could have sworn that he glimpsed a flicker of concern in her expression, despite her sardonic snort of amusement. He wondered if his pierced and purple-haired colleague might be developing a soft spot for Nervous Niall. It seemed an improbable match. And given Niall's current domestic situation, it was unlikely that he would even consider embarking on a new relationship. George made a mental note to watch out for Roxy. He didn't want her to get hurt. He had told her that Niall had agreed to let both him and Edwin try to help with the public health funerals – and that was the very reason why he was now on his way to Sid's shop.

Sid was standing outside in a proprietary pose – emperor of his emporium – watching the world go by and swigging tea from a tin mug.

'Good afternoon, young man!' he regaled George. Sid referred to almost every customer or potential customer as 'young'. He called Mrs Brunetti 'young lady' whenever she came in to buy jars for her home-made pickles, and she had recently celebrated her eightieth birthday and even brought him a piece of her birthday cake. 'What can I do for you today? Are you after something specific or are you just here to browse and see if anything takes your fancy?'

George considered how best to answer him. He was beginning to realise that putting his plan to help Niall into action was going to involve some rather unusual conversations. 'Well – something specific, but not in the sense that I can tell you precisely what it might be.'

Sid raised his eyebrows. 'Can you at least give me a clue?'

'You remember that day when you almost dropped that box from the house clearance, and the little poodle ornament broke, and you let me take the tin of photos?'

'I do. I sold the crystal vase the very same afternoon.'

'And you told me that you've got a contract with the council to clear out places when someone dies and there's no one else to do it?'

Sid nodded slowly, clearly wondering what was coming next.

'I was wondering if next time one of those house or flat clearances comes up, you could let me know so I can have first look at whatever you clear out?'

Sid frowned. 'Are you thinking of setting yourself up as some kind of dealer, George? Thinking of taking a stall at antiques fairs and trying your luck? Because if that's the case, I'm afraid you'll just have to take your chances with my other customers. I can't have you cherry-picking the stock before it goes on the shelves – especially not if you're going to be selling it on to make a profit. I don't mind letting you know when I've got new stuff in, but that's it.'

George shook his head. 'No, it's nothing like that. It's about …' He paused. It was pretty hard to explain in a few sentences exactly what it was all about – but he had to try. He had to try and get Sid onside. 'It's about honouring the dead when there's no one else to do it.'

George went on to explain about the public health funerals and how he was hoping to help Niall make them more meaningful. 'That tin of photographs was a portal into the lives of two people. I don't know who they were, but those photos showed me some of the places they went, the people they cared about and the things that made them smile. The pictures made them and their lives more real. I think that maybe if I can see what's left behind when someone dies alone, I might be able to get a better idea of who they were and what kinds of lives they led, and then we might just be able to make their funerals a bit more personal. I'm not quite sure how, just yet, maybe with a reading or a poem, or just a piece of music that meant something to them. But to make it work, I need to know something about them and so – anyway, I thought you might be able to help. Elena at the florist's has already kindly agreed to provide some free flowers for any of these public health funerals that I get involved with,' George added persuasively.

A slow smile split Sid's face. 'If I had a hat, George, I'd take it off to you. I think it's a great idea. Slightly weird, but very kind nonetheless – and, yes, of course I'll let you know when the next job comes in.'

They exchanged phone numbers and Sid promised to be in touch.

'So not so much would-be antiques dealer,' he added with a wink, 'but more George McGlory – Death Detective!'

Chapter 16

Allegra Monteverdi lay seemingly lifeless on the tiled floor of the hallway. Even in this most unfortunate of circumstances, she had retained her customary dignity. Her limbs were elegantly sprawled as though they had been positioned quite deliberately, like a well-to-do corpse on the set of an Agatha Christie movie. Her clothing had been insufficiently disturbed to afford unflattering glimpses of substantial old-lady hosiery and underwear with in-built incontinence protection – if indeed Allegra Monteverdi ever wore such things. It seemed unlikely, Briony would reflect much later that evening when she returned to her flat. But for the moment, having just walked in the front door, she was more concerned about whether Allegra was alive or dead. She dropped her bag and rushed over to kneel by her neighbour's side.

'Allegra,' she whispered fearfully. 'Allegra, it's Briony. Can you hear me?'

She touched the older woman's cheek with her fingertips. The skin felt smooth and cold, like marble. Allegra's eyes snapped open like a doll's.

'I can see and hear you perfectly well, thank you.' Allegra

winced as she attempted to push herself up into a sitting position, and Briony placed an arm around her shoulder to support her.

'What on earth happened?'

Allegra tipped her head to one side and arched an eyebrow. 'I thought I'd take a moment to lie down and admire the very fine cornicing on the ceiling.' She sighed heavily. 'I slipped. I came out to see if I had any post and the next thing I knew I was on the floor. New shoes.' She pointed accusingly at the impeccable lilac suede pumps on her feet. 'The soles are far too smooth.'

'Are you hurt?'

Allegra raised her hand and touched her temple tentatively. 'I think I may have banged my head, but it doesn't feel too bad.'

One at a time, she slowly stretched out her arms and legs, assessing each for functionality and pain. 'Well, nothing's broken,' she announced, 'but I expect I'm going to have some fairly impressive bruises tomorrow.'

Briony helped Allegra to her feet and walked her slowly back to her flat. 'I really think we ought to speak to someone about that bang on your head,' she said once Allegra was comfortably settled in her own sitting room.

'What on earth for? There isn't even a lump. I'm perfectly fine.'

Briony shook her head doubtfully. 'But you lost consciousness – so you might have concussion.'

Allegra flapped her hands at Briony dismissively. 'I most certainly did not! It had only just happened when you came in. I had simply closed my eyes for a moment to gather my thoughts. If you'd got home a few minutes later, I would have been back in my flat and you'd have known nothing about it.'

Briony chewed her lip thoughtfully, debating with herself whether or not to call the NHS helpline for advice. But as she glanced up at Allegra and their eyes met, the woman's defiant look warned that she had better not. Instead, she tapped the word *concussion* into Google on her phone and scanned through the list of symptoms.

'Have you got a headache?' she asked Allegra.

Allegra shook her head impatiently. 'It's just a little sore where it collided with the floor. But then so are my elbow and my knee. It's hardly surprising, is it?'

'Do you feel sick or dizzy?'

Allegra rolled her eyes in exasperation. 'No and no. I'm grateful for your help, but there's no need to fuss. I'm fine.'

Briony didn't bother to ask if Allegra was feeling groggy or confused. 'Well, if you do start to feel unwell in any way, just give me a shout. I'll leave you my mobile number. Now, shall I make you a cup of tea?'

Briony wanted a reason to stay with Allegra for a bit, just in case she should have any delayed reaction to her fall. Allegra looked at her and narrowed her eyes.

'Don't think I don't know exactly what you're doing' she said sternly, but there was a hint of amusement in her expression. 'I'd prefer a martini, but' – she checked her watch – 'I suppose it is a *bit* early. Come to that, what are you doing here in the middle of the day? Have you been dismissed from your employment?'

'No such luck! I'm working from home this afternoon.'

Allegra told her where to find the tea things in the kitchen and instructed her to use a teapot and loose-leaf lapsang souchong. Briony brought everything back on a tray, including a quartered lemon and a small jar of honey with a spoon. Allegra stirred the leaves in the teapot, and once she was satisfied that the liquid had attained the optimum colour, she poured two cups. She offered one to Briony and gestured for her to help herself to lemon, but then her face took on a scandalised expression as the tea in Briony's cup turned opaque.

'I'm afraid I take mine with milk. I helped myself from the fridge,' Briony said apologetically.

Allegra smiled. 'I'm only teasing. You should drink it exactly as you like it. Never apologise, never explain!' She squeezed lemon into her own cup, added a little honey and then sniffed the contents appreciatively. 'If you really hate your job that much, why don't you look for something else?'

Briony sighed. 'Because I really want to be a journalist – and junior reporter jobs are as rare as unicorn droppings! Mostly, all that's on offer are unpaid internships, and I need to earn money to pay my way. I'm lucky to have this job, I know that – I just wish it wasn't so, well, crap, really. And to add insult to dodgy sandwiches and weird vegetables, my boss, Mr Bollock –' Allegra frowned and Briony grinned sheepishly '– Mr Bullock, has just dumped the births, marriages and deaths columns on me as well. I'm surprised we even bother doing them any more. Most people do that stuff on Facebook these days.'

Allegra sipped from her cup and set it down. 'I *always* read the obituaries. I find them completely fascinating! Granted, they're mainly commonplace, but every now and then there's a tantalising detail – a chink of light that reveals just a little something about the person and the life so briefly summarised in a few lines of text. Sometimes it's an unusual name – I still recall Xavier Enrico MacNamara and Minnie Pook. Occasionally it's a reference to a specific event – a woman called Francesca once mentioned "our terrifically memorable day" in her husband's obituary, and I often wonder what happened on that day to make it so terrifically memorable. And then sometimes it's how they died. Keith Baxter – the actor – died "aged 90, while swimming in the sea off his beloved Corsica" according to his obituary. Another man, whose name escapes me, died altogether less serenely during a pie-eating competition in Hartlepool.'

'But are they really relevant nowadays?' Briony argued. 'Aren't they just an old-school formality that's gradually dying out?'

Allegra gave a wry smile. 'Death will never die out. It's the only thing that unites us all – the certainty that each of us will face it in the end. And I believe it's important to mark it properly – to turn the final page and close the book. The rituals surrounding death are the acknowledgement of a life. Besides, an obituary is a way of letting people know who can't be reached in other ways. People who have lost touch with the deceased but may still be interested in their demise and might even wish to attend the funeral to pay their respects.'

'Well, at least, thanks to you, now I know I'll have one reader!'

Allegra offered her more tea and Briony held up her cup.

'What is it that you would really like to write about?'

Briony shrugged. 'I don't mind as long as it's a proper story. Something that people care about, that affects them ...' She trailed off, uncertain how to articulate the passion that she felt about her writing.

'Well, perhaps you need to be more proactive. Instead of waiting for a story to fall into your lap or for Mr – your boss to assign you one, go out and find one. Find something that intrigues you, infuriates you or ... breaks your heart – and write about it. And make it so brilliant that he has to publish it.' Allegra leaned back in her chair, as though satisfied that she had solved Briony's problem.

Briony looked unconvinced. 'How are you feeling?' she asked.

'Stop changing the subject. I'm fine.'

They sat in silence for a moment, and Briony recalled that the first time she had been inside this flat she had thought to herself that Allegra's life might be a story worth investigating.

'On the subject of work,' she began tentatively, 'do you mind me asking what you did for a living?'

Allegra smiled her inscrutable smile. 'I don't mind you asking, but I may choose not to tell you,' she teased. She pointed towards the shelf of the bookcase that housed the photograph albums. 'Pass me one of those, would you? Any of them – it doesn't matter which.'

Briony handed her one of the albums, and she opened it to reveal pages of picture postcards. There were numerous scenes of Paris along with ticket stubs for theatres and various tourist attractions, menus, even miniature matchbooks. As Allegra turned the pages, the scenery and mementoes recalled the Côte d'Azur – Cannes and Nice – and then on to Monte Carlo.

Allegra passed the album back to Briony for her to study more closely. 'This was my working life.'

Briony looked up at her in astonishment. 'But what did you do? Were you a travel writer? Did you test out luxury holidays?'

'Not exactly. My work involved extensive travel, but I can't really talk about it in too much detail. I suppose you could say that I worked in communications.'

Briony continued to turn the pages, fascinated by the contents of the album. A photograph album which contained not a single photograph.

Chapter 17

'Joshua Fullbright – now why does that ring a bell?'

Gordon Bullock was leaning – too closely – over Briony's shoulder and peering at her laptop as she formatted that week's obituaries column. She could feel the warmth radiating off his body and smell his ineffective deodorant, stale sweat and coffee breath.

'Not sure,' she replied, pushing back into her chair, hoping to force Gordon to retreat from her personal space. 'It's a notification from the council, not the family or funeral directors. Apparently, he died of a drugs overdose and there's no next of kin to make the arrangements. It's just a basic announcement – name, date of birth, date of death and details of the funeral.'

Gordon stood up straight and stretched, pressing the palms of his hands into the small of his back. 'I'm sure I know that name from somewhere. Maybe we ran a story on him once.'

Gordon had an almost encyclopaedic memory for news items that had appeared in *The Times and Herald* since he had taken up his post almost fifteen years ago. Briony opened the newspaper's archive files on her screen, tapped the name into the search bar and hit the return key. Two items appeared on screen. She opened the first and a photograph appeared of a football team and their coach. The boys all looked to be around twelve or thirteen years old and were grinning proudly. One of the boys and the coach stood in the centre of the shot holding a large silver cup between them. She read the caption beneath.

'That's him,' she said, pointing at the boy holding the cup. 'Joshua Fullbright. He scored a hat-trick in the Bedfordshire Youth League final in 2014.'

Gordon snapped his fingers. 'Now I remember him! He was something of a football prodigy at the time. Went off to play for the Spurs youth academy. I reckon it was me that interviewed him and his parents about it.'

Briony opened the second item from the archives and there was Gordon's piece, along with a photo of Josh and his parents.

Gordon peered at the screen. 'That's it. He was a nice enough lad, as far as I recall, despite the fact that he and his dad were raving Spurs fans.' Gordon was a die-hard Arsenal supporter, a Gunner through to his marrow. 'But his mum' – he tapped his finger on the sharp face of the woman in the photo – 'there was something about her that I didn't like. She was a hard-nosed bitch.'

Briony leaned in closer and studied the photograph. The man looked proud as punch of his boy, his arm flung around his shoulders in an affectionate gesture. The woman sat slightly apart, her pose carefully angled towards the camera. With her fixed smile, she looked almost bored. But Josh's fresh face shone with joy. He looked so young and so eager to take on his life and follow his dreams – as though he could barely sit still long enough for the photo to be taken. His energy was almost palpable. And now he was dead.

'I wonder what on earth happened to him?' Briony just couldn't reconcile the death announcement with the beautiful boy in the photograph.

Gordon wandered back to his own desk and slumped down in his chair. 'Life!' he declared. 'That's what happened to him – real life, instead of the fairy tale. He probably didn't make the grade at the academy, never got into the senior team and then had to come back home with his tail between his legs.'

'But what about his mum and dad?'

'Who knows? Families fall apart all the time. Anyway, serves him right for supporting such a crap team in the first place.'

Briony scowled at him in horror at his callousness and he threw up his hands in the air. 'Only joking! There's no need to give me the death stare!'

Briony returned her attention to her laptop, and Allegra's words echoed in her head. If she was going to stay here and put up with Gordon's bollocks, she had to find something decent to write about.

'Maybe there's a story there,' she suggested tentatively. 'Maybe I could do some digging around and find out what really happened.'

Gordon snorted. 'I've told you what happened, and I'd bet good money that I'm right. So don't go wasting your time on it. And anyway, nobody wants to read about a failure.'

In that moment Briony hated Gordon so much that she had to grip the arms of her chair to prevent herself from marching over to his desk, punching him in the face and telling him where he could stick his job. But she knew that if she did that, he would have won. She had to stay and work out a way to be better than him – not just as a human being, but as a journalist. For Briony, failure was not an option.

Chapter 18

George's thoughts turned to Roxy as he sat in The Duck and Donkey sipping his pint. He was there earlier than usual for a Thursday night as he was meeting Niall to talk about a funeral before meeting the others for quiz night. Edwin had cried off because it was his wedding anniversary and he was taking his wife out to dinner, so Niall was a substitute team member again.

George had noticed something different about Roxy at work that morning, but he hadn't been able to put his finger on it. He was worried that it might have been something he was supposed to have noticed and maybe complimented her on. Audrey had always said that he was the least observant man on the planet when it came to certain things. He had rarely noticed when she wore a new dress or had her hair done, and when she had remonstrated with him, he had always said that she looked lovely all the time. Audrey had, more often than not, laughed off his glib platitudes with good humour, but now he wished that he had been more attentive. He regretted not telling her more often that she was beautiful, and funny and clever, and that he loved her, instead of taking it for granted that she knew. That horse might have bolted now, but at least George could learn from his past mistakes and behave differently in the future. It was another valuable lesson that grief had taught him. Roxy often commented on his crazy shirts and always noticed when he wore a new one. He was determined to reciprocate from now on.

'I'm not late, am I?'

George looked up to see Niall standing next to him, shrugging off his coat.

'I've got you a pint in.' George gestured to the glass on the table. 'But I'd take it easy tonight if I were you – maybe stay off the Jägerbombs,' he added with a wink.

'Never again!' Niall shook his head. 'And I'll be sticking to shandy after this one,' he said, raising his glass. 'Cheers!'

He pulled something from his coat pocket and passed it to George. It was a sheet of paper covered in handwritten notes.

'His name's Joshua Fullbright,' Niall began in a low voice, glancing around to make sure no one was listening. 'According to the coroner's report he died of a drugs overdose – most likely accidental but impossible to say for sure. There were no personal items in his flat other than a few clothes. His neighbours said they didn't really know him – only that he was a junkie. In fact, one of them said "Good riddance!" when I told him Joshua was dead.'

George shook his head in disgust, but Niall continued.

'To be fair, George, you can't judge him for that. Have you ever lived next door to an addict – drink or drugs?'

George shrugged.

'They can be bloody awful neighbours. Noisy at all hours of the day or night. Messy, dirty, bringing their mates back to join in the "fun", and often involved in petty – and sometimes not-so-petty – crime. That's no joke if you live next door and want a normal life, your kids to be safe and a decent night's kip because you have to get up for work in the morning.' Niall paused a moment, seemingly for his words to sink in, before he continued. 'Anyway, I managed to trace a next of kin – his mother, Michelle Butcher. She's in Brighton.'

'So isn't she coming to the funeral?' George asked.

Niall shook his head. 'She's in Brighton, Adelaide – Australia. And she said that even if she were in the UK she still wouldn't come. Apparently, Joshua's dad died when he was fifteen, and according to Michelle, he became a bit of a handful after that. And when she remarried, Joshua didn't get on with his stepdad and things went from bad to worse. That's when the drugs started, and Joshua began stealing money and things from home to sell to fund his habit. Michelle said that she had been at her wits' end and frightened of what he might do next. She even went so far as to say that he was ruining their lives. Eventually, they felt they had no choice but to throw him out, and after that, they lost contact. Two years ago, her husband was offered a job in Adelaide and off they went.'

'But how did she react when you told her that her son was dead?' George couldn't conceive that any parent wouldn't be devastated to learn of the death of their child.

Niall sighed. 'She said she wasn't surprised. She said that she'd tried everything but he was beyond help, and that she'd lost her son years ago. So if you meant what you said about wanting to make public health funerals better, it seems like Joshua Fullbright's is an ideal place to start. It's in a couple of weeks.'

George sipped his pint dolefully. This wasn't going to be as easy as he had, perhaps naively, thought. Joshua's short life sounded so bleak. How on earth was he going to mark his death with anything uplifting or positive?

'There was one other thing,' Niall added, interrupting George's train of thought. 'I did a quick Google search, and it seems that Joshua was a bit of a football star when he was a kid. His team won some county youth league cup back in the day. I didn't get a chance to study the details because Brenda landed something else on my desk that she didn't want to do herself, but it might be worth checking out. Now – can I get you another drink?'

While Niall was at the bar, Roxy arrived and sat down. 'Nice shirt, George! That's one of my favourites.'

It was a purple print of clouds and wild horses. George studied her, trying to figure out what had changed. She looked – nicer, softer somehow. But he knew better than to say that. It might sound horribly sexist.

'Have you done your hair differently?' He hazarded a guess.

Roxy frowned. 'No. Why?' she demanded defensively.

'You look different – in a good way. You look nice.'

'Meaning I don't usually?'

George was beginning to wish that he had kept quiet. 'No, of course not. I only meant –'

She cut him off with a wave of her hand and a wicked grin. 'I'm only teasing! And thank you for noticing.'

George was relieved, but still none the wiser about what it was that was different about her.

Niall returned from the bar, and as he sat down the bell rang for the start of the quiz.

The following morning, Roxy had been in high spirits at work despite the fact that they'd only managed third place in the quiz. There had only been one question on football – which Niall had answered correctly – but rather too many on rap music, online gaming and *Game of Thrones*, subjects with which none of them were at all familiar. George had told her about Joshua Fullbright's funeral, and she had suggested that he take a look on social media to see if he had any accounts, which might then show if he had any friends. Now George was at home and, after a lunch of tuna mayonnaise sandwiches, he was about to take on his first case as a death detective. He smiled to himself, remembering Sid's words. He only hoped that he could do Joshua justice.

After just twenty minutes at his laptop, he was already feeling pessimistic. There was no trace of Joshua on Instagram, Facebook or any of the other platforms Roxy had suggested. Then George remembered what Niall had said and tried a Google search. He was immediately rewarded with several hits from the local newspaper, *The Times and Herald*. There were two old articles relating to football and a very recent entry in the obituaries column. George scoured the first two stories for any information that might be helpful and discovered that Joshua's football coach had been a man called Martin Hobson. He appeared in one of the photographs that accompanied the articles and looked to be in his mid to late thirties, which would make him pushing fifty now, George calculated. Might he still be coaching football? It didn't take George long to find the website of Joshua's old football team, and he slapped the palm of his hand down on his desk in triumph when he read that the contact person for all enquiries was none other than Martin Hobson. George composed a carefully worded email. He included his phone number and stated that he would be very grateful if Mr Hobson could call him as a matter of some priority. He hit 'send'. Now all he could do was wait.

But as it turned out, he didn't have to wait very long. His mobile rang early that evening, just as he was clearing away his dinner things. It was an unfamiliar number and an unfamiliar voice on the line when he answered it.

'Hi. Is that George McGlory? It's Martin Hobson.'

'Yes – I'm George. Thank you so much for calling me.'

While George explained to Martin why he wanted to speak to him, he sat down, picked up his pen and pulled his notepad towards him.

There was a shocked silence on the end of the phone before Martin replied. 'It's such a waste! I can't believe that Josh is dead. He was always Josh, by the way. No one called him Joshua. He had such talent, so much promise. He would have gone straight to the top – I've no doubt about that. He wasn't just a brilliant footballer – he had the right attitude as well. He was willing to work harder than any of the other lads.'

'According to his mum, it all started to go wrong when his dad died. Do you know anything about that?'

'That's right. It was tragic, really. Josh's dad supported him all the way. He was his biggest fan and proud as anything when Josh started playing at Spurs Academy. Josh had been with them a couple of years when his dad was diagnosed with a brain tumour. It was a very aggressive form of cancer and the tumour was inoperable. Three months later he was dead.'

George blew out a breath. 'That poor lad. No wonder he didn't keep playing. He must have been heartbroken.'

'Oh, he was,' Martin replied. 'But he was desperate to keep up his football. He knew it was what his dad would have wanted. It was his mum who pulled him from the academy. She said she couldn't keep up with all the travelling and was worried about the cost of everything.' He was silent for a moment and George could hear the bitterness in his voice when he resumed. 'Personally, I think she was just making excuses. She never wanted him to play at the academy in the first place, and once Josh's dad died, it would have all been down to her and it was too much trouble. Josh came to me and begged me to talk to her and try and change her mind.'

'And did you?'

'I spoke to her – but it didn't do any good. I can still remember how hard-nosed she was. Quite prepared to sacrifice her son's dreams for her own convenience. The academy contacted her too, but she was adamant. I tried to stay in touch with Josh after that, but he wasn't interested, and I can't blame him. Anything to do with football just reminded him of what he'd lost. After his dad died, football could have been his lifeline, but his mum snatched it away and … well, here we are now talking about his funeral. I hope she's happy!' he spat angrily.

'She won't be going to the funeral, that much I do know,' George told him. 'But will you come?'

'Of course. It's the only thing left that I *can* do for Josh.'

Chapter 19

Briony checked her appearance in the mirror and was satisfied that she would pass muster. She hadn't been sure what might be appropriate for the funeral of someone whom she had never met and knew very little about. She had settled on her best jeans and a navy sweater with her smart winter coat on top. But what finished the outfit off was a beautiful cashmere scarf the colour of primroses which Allegra had loaned her for the occasion. Briony had confided in Allegra that she planned to attend the funeral, though she had been at a loss to explain why she felt so strongly about going.

'Perhaps your instinct is telling you there's a story there that needs to be told,' Allegra had suggested, and maybe she was right. Briony hadn't told Gordon, mindful of his instructions not to waste her time, but his callous summary of the young man's life as a failure had ignited a fury in her that had flared into defiance. All she knew was that she needed to be there, and if Gordon didn't like it then he could go to hell!

Elena flipped the sign on the door and turned the key in the lock. She had decided to close the shop for a couple of hours so that she could attend the funeral. It was the first one that George had organised, and she wanted to be there to support him. Elena was very fond of George. He always brightened her day when he came into the shop, and she often considered what a lucky woman Audrey had been to have had him as her husband. Elena had left her own unfaithful and now ex-husband behind in Croatia. He was about the same age as George, but that was the only thing they had in common. She thought it was a wonderful thing that George was doing, and she was very happy to be a part of it. She had given him a candle he could light at the service, and that morning she had taken a spray of blue and white flowers to the funeral director so it could be placed on top of the coffin for the journey to the crematorium. The arrangement had included roses, larkspur, giant thistles and chrysanthemums interspersed with eucalyptus. George had asked for blue and white because apparently these were the colours of the young man's favourite football team. Elena hoped that she had done his request justice. She checked her watch. She had just enough time to go home and get changed before the service.

———

Martin Hobson took the newly purchased Spurs scarf from the passenger seat of his car, removed its cellophane wrapper and placed it around his neck. It looked at odds with his dark suit, but it was the perfect accessory for the occasion. He checked his pocket for the piece of paper on which he had written the tribute that he had agreed to deliver at the funeral. He only hoped that he would be able to say the words without choking on his emotions. In the days since he had learned of Josh's overdose, he had struggled to come to terms with what had happened – not just Josh's death but the events of years ago which had undoubtedly set him on his fatal trajectory. Martin couldn't help but wonder if he could have done more to support him. If he could have tried harder to make Josh's mum change her mind. Probably not was the conclusion that he had come to – but it didn't make him feel any better. So now all he could do was pay his respects. He started the car and set off for Josh Fullbright's final fixture.

Roxy checked the clock on the wall behind her and sighed. The service would be starting soon. It was strange, she thought, to be disappointed at missing out on a funeral, but she was. She couldn't really have asked for time off work to go to the funeral of a stranger. But she had been so involved, so invested in the preparations George had made, that she felt cheated that she would not see their efforts come to fruition. George had asked her to find a poem he could read. They had decided to avoid anything too religious, so Roxy had suggested 'Do Not Stand at My Grave and Weep' by Mary Elizabeth Frye. The idea that a young man who had died alone in a filthy bedsit, addled by alcohol and drugs, might metamorphose into diamond glints on snow, and gentle rain, and sunshine and stars felt like a miraculous redemption worth wishing on Josh Fullbright.

Edwin gently placed the spray of flowers Elena had prepared on top of the coffin next to the large wreath with its distinctive centrepiece of the Tottenham Hotspur cockerel. The wreath had been sent by the Spurs Academy, who had heard of Josh's death from Martin Hobson and had wanted to contribute something in memory of their former player. The highly polished hearse gleamed in the sharp winter sunlight as it set off at a dignified pace towards the crematorium. Edwin had decided to drive today. The flowers on the coffin made it look like any normal funeral, he thought. No one seeing the hearse on its stately journey would guess that this was a public health funeral. The wreath and the roses said that somebody cared. That this person would be missed. Edwin nodded in reply to an elderly couple who bowed their heads as the hearse passed by them. It used to be a common practice – a mark of respect that came as naturally and readily as a reflex – but these days it was rarer. But when it happened, it always warmed Edwin's heart. *The way we treat our dead is a measure of our own humanity.* These were his father's words and the mantra he had ingrained in Edwin from his first day working for the Bury family firm. It had become the underpinning tenet of his professional life and a personal value that he held dear. He had even introduced it as part of the company insignia. For Edwin, being a funeral director wasn't a job, it was a vocation. As they turned onto the long and winding drive of the crematorium, Edwin glanced in his mirror at the coffin.

'Here we are then, Josh. It's time for kick-off.'

George stood with Elena, Niall and Martin Hobson at the door of the crematorium chapel waiting for the hearse to arrive. George had made the introductions and thanked Elena and Martin for coming before they had all lapsed into silence. They watched a car pull into the car park, and a young woman wearing a yellow scarf got out and began making her way towards them. As she came closer, George thought that she looked vaguely familiar but couldn't place her. Before he could speak to her, the sound of wheels crunching on gravel betrayed the arrival of the hearse, and when it turned into view each of the spectators felt that strange frisson peculiar to the moment at a funeral when the guest of honour arrives. The chapel manager ushered Elena, Martin and the young woman inside to take their seats, leaving George and Niall to follow the coffin.

The service began by George lighting Elena's candle, which stood in a large brass holder next to a wooden stand on which was propped a picture of Josh. It was an enlargement taken from the photograph that had accompanied one of the articles in *The Times and Herald*. The photo had been Roxy's idea.

'Only one of you at that service will have seen Josh alive,' she had said. 'And the funeral needs to focus on the person, not the body in the box.'

The quality of the image wasn't great, but Josh's face shone with pure joy. George turned to face the tiny congregation and announced that they were here to remember and honour the life of Josh Fullbright, son of Steve and Michelle. He then invited Martin to deliver his eulogy. Martin stood up and adjusted his jacket nervously. He walked to the front of the chapel, placed his sheet of paper down on the lectern and then took a deep breath.

'I first met Josh when he was just nine years old,' he began. 'He was a happy, lively little boy with a cheeky smile and a passion for Spurs which he shared with his dad, Steve. They used to go to matches together, and Josh would come back full of stories about the players he had seen and the goals they had scored. But Josh himself was a brilliant footballer. Even at nine years old, I could see that he had the potential to play at the highest level. Josh didn't just have an amazing talent: he also had the determination to succeed. He worked harder at his game than any boy I've ever known – and I've been coaching football for longer than I care to remember now. But Josh was more than just a brilliant footballer. He was a team player – always watching out for his mates and never once getting too big for his boots – excuse the pun,' Martin added with a sad smile.

'Steve supported him all the way. Josh was the apple of his eye and I know how very proud Steve was when his son was offered a place at the Spurs Academy. Josh's dream was, one day, to play for Spurs, and after that to play for his country.'

Martin paused for a moment and smoothed out an imaginary crease in his piece of paper.

'Very sadly, Josh's dreams didn't come true.' Martin's voice cracked a little, but he swallowed hard and continued. 'Steve died suddenly when Josh was just fifteen, and the changed circumstances at home meant that Josh was no longer able to continue at the academy.'

Listening to this, George couldn't help but admire Martin's restraint and discretion, knowing as he did how much Martin despised Michelle Butcher for her treatment of Josh. George had felt obliged to name her at the start of the service, but wasn't at all sure she deserved such further consideration.

'I didn't see much of Josh after Steve died,' Martin continued, 'and in recent years we had lost touch completely – something that I now very much regret. Josh died far too young and in tragic circumstances which we will never be able to understand properly. But we are here today to remember the real Josh as he was before life conspired to break him. The person whom I consider it an absolute privilege to have known and coached. We are here to shine a light on the bright, cheeky, ridiculously talented young man who loved football, Spurs, cheese and crisps sandwiches – and fishing. Outside of football, Josh enjoyed fishing – also with his dad. They used to go off on their bikes and sit by the river for hours watching their floats bobbing in the water. I'm not sure if they caught much. Josh's fishing tales always seemed to be about "the one that got away". And it seems today that Josh himself is the one that got away. So let's hope that now he's found his dad and that somewhere they're sitting by a river and fishing together again.'

Before returning to his seat, Martin took the Spurs scarf from his neck and laid it carefully on the coffin. 'God bless,

Josh,' he whispered as he allowed his hand to briefly brush the polished wood of the lid.

Next to George, Elena muttered 'Amen' and dabbed at her eyes with a tissue. George got up and patted Martin's shoulder as their paths crossed.

'Next we're going to listen to a song by Chas and Dave called "Wonder Where He Is Now",' George announced. 'Martin told me that Josh and his dad were Chas and Dave fans, not least because of their association with Spurs, and we chose this song because it's about old friends who used to go fishing together.'

By the end of the song, there wasn't a dry eye in the chapel. Even the young woman whom George had yet to identify looked tearful. To end the service, George read the poem that Roxy had suggested and then led a communal recitation of The Lord's Prayer – permission for which had been granted by Niall after it was discovered that Josh had been christened as a baby. The chapel was silent for a moment, and the coffin began to disappear behind the curtains. As all eyes returned to the photograph of Josh, the orotund tones of Louis Armstrong floated upwards to the rafters. 'Smile', he sang.

Chapter 20

The mood outside the chapel was an odd mixture of melancholy and elation. The flowers and the wreath from the coffin had been brought outside and they all admired them, praising Elena for her artistry and Spurs Academy for their thoughtful gesture.

'Well done, George – and Niall. You did the lad proud sorting this out!' Edwin told them. 'And your speech was just right,' he said, turning to Martin. 'You helped us see Josh as he really was and not just as a stranger. Anyway – I can't stand here chatting. I must get the car back. We've got another funeral in an hour. See you on Thursday, George.'

With no wake to attend, those who remained were soon overtaken by a vague sense of deflation and aimlessness and began to drift away. Elena went off to reopen the shop, Niall said he'd better go or else he'd have Brenda on his case, and Martin shook hands with George, thanked him for getting in touch and then said goodbye. The young woman who had been inspecting the message on the wreath also went to leave, but George called after her.

'Excuse me,' he said. 'Did you know Josh? Were you a friend of his?'

The young woman's face reddened slightly, and George suddenly remembered where he had seen her before.

'You're a reporter, aren't you? You work for *The Times and Herald*. You came to the library where I work to do a piece on our poppy display.'

She nodded. 'Yes – I'm Briony. Briony Harris.'

George frowned. 'So are you writing a story about Josh? Is that why you're here?'

Briony shook her head. 'I came, in part, I suppose, to spite my boss.'

George's frown deepened and Briony replied with a wry smile. 'I've been landed with the births, marriages and deaths columns at the paper. My boss saw Josh's obituary and remembered he had written a piece on him and the Spurs Academy. When he found out that Josh had died of an overdose, he basically wrote him off as a worthless failure. That's typical of him. He's such a heartless …' Briony hesitated, and George raised his eyebrows in amusement.

'Don't mind me,' he said. 'Would "bastard" do – or were you thinking of something stronger?'

'He's such a heartless bastard!' Briony enunciated the word with deliberate relish. 'Anyway – I wanted to come partly to say "Up yours!" to him, but mainly because I thought it was so sad that someone who seemingly had an amazing life ahead of him ended up with such a horrible, lonely death. I couldn't help but feel there must a reason for it, and I can't really explain it, but I just had to come.'

George considered whether or not he should share Josh's story with this woman who had come to his funeral for such dubious reasons. 'If I tell you, you're not going to write about it are you?'

Briony hesitated before replying. 'To be honest, I did think about it initially. But now, it just feels wrong. My bastard boss said that I shouldn't waste my time on it because no one wants to read about failure, but it's not that. I'm trying to make something of my career instead of just doing the stuff that I get given – which is mainly dross. A friend of mine advised me to go looking for stories worth writing about instead of waiting for them to fall into my lap. But I don't think it would be right to use Josh's story, whatever it is, for my own ends.'

'I agree. Today was all for Josh – to give him a decent send-off and to remember him with affection and respect,' George replied, before giving Briony a brief account of Josh's life and untimely death.

They began walking back to their cars.

'So how did you know Josh?' Briony asked.

'I didn't.'

Briony stopped and stared at George, her faced crumpled into a puzzled expression. 'Then what were *you* doing here?'

George smiled. An idea was beginning to form in his head: a small collection of component thoughts – related but not yet collated into a coherent whole.

'It feels odd that there was no wake, doesn't it?' he said. 'Look, I just need to say hello to my wife – she's buried here – and afterwards can I buy you a cup of tea and maybe even a piece of cake? Then I'll tell you all about what I was doing here. I've a feeling there could be a story in this for you after all.'

That evening, George sat with his elbows on the kitchen table, having just finished the fish and chips supper he had picked up from the shop around the corner. He let out a long, satisfied breath of contentment. Fish and chips were a treat he rarely allowed himself, mindful that his waistline was increasing with his age. But it had been quite a day, and he was exhausted, both physically and emotionally. His brain, however, was still ticking over relentlessly. It had gone well, he thought. And now at least he had some sort of blueprint for future funerals. The photograph and the candle had worked beautifully – and the Spurs scarf that Martin had brought had been a lovely touch. He had asked Edwin to keep the scarf until he could think of what best to do with it.

He wondered if Michelle Butcher, halfway across the world, had thought about her son at all today. He knew Niall had informed her of the date of the funeral, just in case she changed her mind. Perhaps they had judged her too harshly. It couldn't have been easy for her when her husband died, leaving her to bring up Josh on her own. But then George remembered Martin's anger when he had spoken about her and pictured for a moment what Josh's funeral would have been like if it hadn't been for his own intervention. Perhaps she deserved their disapprobation after all.

His conversation with Briony had been cautious. Her enthusiasm when he had told her what they were hoping to do with public health funerals had alarmed him a little. She had been full of ideas and offers to help. She had suggested setting up a memorial website for those people who died alone, which could provide more information about the deceased than a headstone or plaque. It could also provide a permanent point of reference for anyone searching for a lost friend or relative after the funeral had taken place. She had also, of course, wanted to write a story about what they were doing, which, she had said, might encourage other people to come forward and volunteer to help. And hadn't this been exactly what George had wanted when he had offered to take her for a cup of tea? It had – but he just wished he had thought it through properly first. They had only done one funeral. But if he turned down Briony's offer of help? The words 'gift horse' and 'mouth' sprung to mind. He had, at least, made her promise not to do anything – or write anything – until he had spoken to Niall. He was just tired, he told himself – and a little overwhelmed. He'd feel better in the morning.

He cleared the table and went through to the sitting room where he collapsed onto the sofa. He was just about to turn on the TV when his mobile rang. It was Elizabeth.

'Hi, Dad. It's me.'

Elizabeth spent a few minutes telling him about Lil's 'dreadful' new boyfriend, a possible promotion that was in the pipeline for Nick and the book she had just read for her book club. But George had the distinct impression that this was all just a preamble to what she really wanted to say.

'Have you thought about what you want to do for Christmas this year, Dad?'

And there it was.

'Not really, love. It's only November.'

'It'll be here before you know it.' There was a pause before Elizabeth continued. 'We'd love you to spend it with us, but we were thinking about going away this year – to Dubai, actually. And of course, you're very welcome to come with us, but we need to book and so on.'

George couldn't think of anything worse but refrained from saying so. 'It's really nice of you to offer, but I'd just as soon stay here.'

'But, Dad, we couldn't possibly leave you on your own at Christmas.'

He could hear the guilt in her voice. 'Don't be daft! I won't be alone. I've got lots of friends here. In fact, I've had two invitations to Christmas dinner already,' he lied. 'You go,' he said. 'You'll have a wonderful time.'

'Well – if you're sure …'

George was completely sure. Completely sure that he'd dodged a bullet. Christmas in Dubai – God forbid!

'And what have you been up to?' Elizabeth sounded more cheerful now.

George told her about Josh's funeral. His account of the day's events was met with a stony silence.

'Are you still there, love?' George asked.

'I'm still here,' she replied, but her tone was considerably cooler than it had been. 'I'm just a bit surprised that you went to all that trouble for a stranger, but you couldn't do the same for your own father. You didn't even *go* to his funeral.'

Chapter 21

Overnight the temperature plunged to well below freezing, and the next morning George had to pour boiling water from the kettle into the bird bath to melt the ice. The robin – *his* robin, as George liked to think of his gardening companion – hopped at his feet, fluffed up against the cold into a ball of feathers, chirping for food. George loaded the bird table with porridge oats and sunflower seed kernels and left the robin, a blackbird and a squabble of starlings to their breakfast. He decided to walk through the park to work. Elizabeth's words from last night still rang in his ears and had stirred up memories that he worked very hard to keep buried. He needed to clear his head. The grass, bristled white with frost, crunched beneath his feet. He pulled his scarf up higher to cover his mouth and his hat down lower to cover his ears, so that only a slit of his face was exposed to the biting cold.

Approaching him from the opposite direction, George recognised a familiar figure preceded by a large dog who was clearly impervious to the weather and prancing this way and that, chasing and catching an orange ball. As the distance between them decreased, the dog seized the ball, ran up to

George and dropped it at his feet. He looked up at George, his tail wagging furiously, with a pleading expression on his face. George picked up the ball and flung it across the grass and the dog set off in hot pursuit to retrieve it.

'You'll never get rid of him now,' Captain said as the dog returned with the ball and dropped it at George's feet. 'You've got a job for life.'

George threw the ball again. 'He's a beauty,' he said. 'What's his name?'

'Sailor.'

'It suits him. I can just imagine him dancing a hornpipe!' George joked.

Captain almost smiled.

'This is the last time,' George told the dog as he picked up the ball and threw it once more. 'Well, I must get going or I'll be late for work. Enjoy the rest of your walk. Perhaps I'll see you later at the library?'

Captain looked puzzled and George realised that, with his face largely obscured, the man hadn't recognised him. He pulled down his scarf a little.

'I'm George,' he said. 'I work at the library with Roxy.'

Captain nodded, threw Sailor's ball and carried on walking.

At work, Roxy was eagerly awaiting a full account of the funeral. It was quieter than usual in the library, with the weather perhaps deterring people from venturing out, and as they sat at the desk together, George told her everything that had happened, including the appearance of Briony and her wanting to write a story about what they were doing. He also confided the misgivings which were still nagging him, even though he could barely articulate precisely what they were when she questioned him.

'I suppose I thought it would be a simple thing to do. Just turn up at the funerals, say something appropriate, maybe have a few flowers, some music – but if Briony writes about it, it could become a much bigger deal.'

'And what's wrong with that?' Roxy asked. 'Surely it would be great to get more people involved? To raise awareness that these funerals actually take place – and why?'

George sighed. 'I just don't want it getting out of hand and turning into some sort of vulgar circus. And I certainly don't want to get Niall into trouble with Brenda.'

'Of course not!' Roxy replied with feeling at the mention of Niall's name. 'But it doesn't have to be like that. Honestly, George, I think you're overthinking it. It was your idea, and you organised what happened yesterday. All you need to do is work out some sort of master plan that you follow for each of the lonely funerals and agree it with Niall. That way, it can't get "out of hand". If other people want to help or volunteer, you can decide in advance what they can – and can't – do.'

George brightened. Thank goodness for Roxy. She might have purple-streaked hair, but she also had an uncommon amount of common sense. But it also dawned on George that he didn't want to do this alone – and there might be times when he couldn't.

'I know I started this, but other people are already involved now, so I think it's only fair that they should be consulted. Niall, of course, and Edwin. And Elena, who's very kindly agreed to provide flowers and a candle for each funeral.'

'And me,' Roxy added. 'I found the poem. I could find more poems and readings.'

'Right. How about we all get together one evening at The Duck and Donkey and put our heads together?'

Roxy grinned. 'Perfect. The inaugural meeting of The Funeral Society!'

'And what about Briony?' George asked.

Roxy considered for a moment. 'I think we *should* invite her. That idea about the memorial website sounds like a good one, and as long as she agrees not to write anything until we give her the nod, with her connections and access to information she could be really helpful.'

'You're right, as usual. What would I do without you?' George exclaimed.

'Make your own coffee,' Roxy replied smartly.

George got up at once and came back minutes later with two steaming mugs. On his way to the desk, he passed Captain, who had just come in. He greeted George with his customary curt nod, making no concession for their more genial encounter in the park earlier. George handed Roxy her coffee and sat down.

'Good morning!' Mrs Biscuit approached the desk with the pile of books she was returning in one hand and a biscuit tin in the other. She dumped the books on the desk with a dramatic sigh. 'And what a morning I've had so far! Firstly, my Norman lost his mobile. He's always losing his mobile!

And instead of looking for it, he comes and finds me and tells me he's lost his mobile, as if I'm psychic and can see it with my third eye or magic it out of thin air. Well, normally I just ring it on *my* phone, and we follow the theme music from *Mission Impossible* because that's his ring tone, but this time it didn't work because his phone was still on silent from when he went to the dentist yesterday afternoon. Norman put it on silent because he didn't want it going off and startling the dentist while he was drilling Norman's tooth, but then he forgot to put it on again when he came out. So I told Norman to retrace his steps from when he got home yesterday after the dentist and, eventually, he found it in the laundry basket under my second-best bra. Then my bus into town was seven minutes late and the couple sitting behind me were having a row about Nigel Farage. Personally, I've never liked him. He always looks like he's broken wind and got away with it.'

By this point, there were several people waiting in a queue behind Mrs Biscuit, and Roxy looked past her and said, 'I'll be with you in a minute.'

Mrs Biscuit took the hint and handed the tin to George. 'These are my latest for you to try,' she said. 'Chocolate chip, chilli and chestnut. And I'll have my other tin back, if I may, before I go.'

Chapter 22

Case no. 63542-7579

Claire and her mother, May, stepped off the coach into the bright, golden sunshine of a perfect July morning. They walked along the pavement a little way before looking around to get their bearings, so as not to block the stream of passengers alighting behind them.

'What a glorious day!' May said as the sea breeze whipped at their skirts and threatened to steal her sun hat. 'What shall we do first? Cup of tea, paddle, look round the shops or have a go in the amusement arcade?'

Claire, wearing enormous sunglasses, her long auburn hair swept back with a silk headscarf, smiled and shrugged. 'I don't mind,' she said in a soft voice. 'You choose.'

'Right then – let's fortify ourselves with a cup of tea and a cream doughnut, and we can plan the programme for the day.'

The streets of Hunstanton were busy with day trippers and holidaymakers, but not heaving as they soon would be once the schools broke up and family holidays began. Today's tourists were mainly men and women of post-retirement age with walking sticks, comfortable, cushioned-soled shoes and small yappy dogs. They found a café and sat outside to drink their tea and eat their cakes. If she had been alone, Claire would have chosen a table inside and out of the way, but she knew that wouldn't be her mother's preference and she didn't want to disappoint her on their big day out together. Besides, with her mother to follow, Claire was better able to navigate her way in the company of others.

'We've got to make the most of the sea air!' Claire said. 'And anyway, out here, we can watch the world go by.'

Claire knew that May loved nothing more than sitting outside a café and people-watching, particularly on a sunny summer's day in an English seaside town. But what she didn't appreciate was May's constant hope for something more for her daughter than merely watching the world go by – her hope that Claire would become more participant than observer. Claire was thirty-two now and still lived with May in the house where she had been born. She had done well at school, passing eight O levels with top grades, but hadn't wanted to stay on at school or go to college. She was a talented artist and earned her living designing illustrations for greetings cards – work that she could do from home. For variety, she had recently turned her hand to composing the suitably sentimental verses contained within the cards, which had proved surprisingly easy and had virtually doubled her income.

A wasp buzzed greedily above Claire's doughnut, and she wafted it away with an elegant hand. A couple walked past them on the pavement, and Claire saw the blatant glance of admiration the man shot in her direction.

'He fancied you!' May teased, nudging her with her elbow.

She nudged her mother back, giggling. Claire was an extremely attractive woman, and she knew it – but simply as an empirical fact measured by the societal standards referenced in films and magazines, rather than something she was proud of and used to her advantage. She took care of herself and her appearance in the same way one might a cherished car, maintaining both beauty and functionality with equal attention. Her motivation was purely egocentric and had no regard for the opinions of others. Claire had never had a boyfriend or felt any interest in the opposite, or her own, sex in a romantic sense and it didn't bother her in the slightest. Those kinds of relationships weren't something she aspired to or particularly valued. But she did feel bad for her mother. She knew May had always longed for grandchildren, and now that the Queen had just become a grandmother again, May was always talking about 'that lovely Prince William' and showing Claire pictures of the royal baby in newspapers and magazines.

They finished their tea and made their way across the grass in front of the pier onto the promenade where a row of motorbikes was parked, their polished chrome and paintwork glinting in the sunlight. The bikers were standing together in various huddles eating fish and chips from paper wrappers, and several of them glanced up at Claire and winked or smiled as she and May walked by. But Claire was more interested in the bikes than the bikers. Objects that she found attractive or intriguing or ingenious were far more appealing to her than any person could be. She loved her mother, of course, and she had loved her father until he had died the previous year. But she had grown up witnessing and experiencing their devotion for her and each other every day, so perhaps the capacity to feel love for them had been acquired by osmosis from her parents. What was certain was that she had never experienced the same or similar feelings for any other living creature. She understood the concepts of courtesy, kindness and compassion, and was able to practise them appropriately, but in the same way that others might speak a foreign language when in a country that was not their own. She did so because she knew it was the right thing to do and not because she was motivated by any feelings of empathy.

'That Harley's gorgeous!' she said to her mother, admiring a black and silver mechanical beast, oblivious to the bike's owner who was not so bad himself, May thought.

They carried on down to the beach where they discarded their shoes and skipped squealing in and out of the breakers that frothed onto the sand and then slunk back in sibilant retreat. The warmth of the sun on their faces and the icy water tickling their toes were such simple sensations but in combination brought such joy. It reminded May of all the seaside holidays they had spent together as a family when Claire was young. She had been such an easy child, quite happy paddling, building sandcastles and collecting shells – secure and content in her own company. May had often worried that her daughter had no friends. She would politely but firmly reject any overtures made by other children when she was playing on her own. But Claire had always appeared to be perfectly happy. It seemed then, as now, that for Claire, alone was not at all the same as lonely.

Soon, the lure of the arcade on the pier with its flashing lights and bells and buzzers proved too strong for Claire to resist. The amusement arcade had been a holiday highlight for her as a child, and she would save her pocket money for weeks beforehand to feed the greedy machines that still fascinated her so. Claire and May changed some silver at the kiosk and then, armed with little plastic pots full of coppers, they each chose a machine. From behind her penny pusher, May watched her daughter's rapt expression as the coins she dropped bounced down their zig-zagging descent, and then jangled and clinked as they landed. Next came the tantalising shove and the teasing teetering of coins on the edge of a precipice, promising but rarely delivering a clattering avalanche of treasure. Claire gasped with delight as a sequinned heart key ring and a scattering of twopence pieces dropped down into the metal tray.

That evening on their homeward journey, as they sat side by side on the coach, Claire examined the baubles that were laid out on her lap. As well as the key ring, the machines had eventually surrendered a tiny pink unicorn, a miniature pack of cards, a glittery rubber ball and a plastic toy tiger. Their wander round the shops after lunch had been fruitful too, and whilst May had bought some sticks of rock for her friends and a souvenir tea towel, Claire had settled on a snow globe containing a mermaid and a quantity of turquoise glitter for her dressing table.

She looked up from her precious trinkets for a moment and gave May a dazzling smile. 'We've had a brilliant day, haven't we, Mum?'

THE LIGHT A CANDLE SOCIETY

Claire was in her observation seat in the sitting room waiting for the last of that day's deliveries. The small Edwardian villa she had shared with her mother until her death fifteen years ago, and where Claire now lived happily alone, was at the bottom of a cul-de-sac, and her habitual vantage point in the window provided a perfect view of all the comings and goings in Windermere Close. Claire felt a prickle of anticipation as a white Transit came into view and pulled up outside her house. The doorbell rang and, as usual, she watched until the delivery man had returned to his van and driven away before she got up from her chair to collect her parcels. The postwoman and all the regular delivery drivers knew that Miss Considine never came to the door unless she absolutely had to. The standing instructions registered with the Royal Mail and all the other companies that Claire dealt with – including the supermarket delivery firm – were that all deliveries that didn't fit through the letterbox should be left on the small table in the enclosed porch. Once the coast was clear, Claire retrieved her parcels from the porch and took them through to the kitchen. The table was already piled high with packages, and the kitchen floor a Lego landscape of boxes piled into haphazard towers of varying heights. Some of the boxes were open but not unpacked, and others remained sealed – their secrets yet to be revealed. Claire squeezed her latest parcels onto a corner of the table and clicked on the kettle. While she waited for the water to heat, she sliced open the tape on one of the boxes and opened it to reveal a quantity of brightly coloured silk scarves individually wrapped in cellophane. She riffled through them without unpacking them and sighed with satisfaction.

'Beautiful!' she declared and then turned back to the kettle as it boiled.

She made herself a mug of tea, selected another parcel from the latest delivery and made her way back to the sitting room. It was 5 pm and late September, and stealthily but steadily the nights were drawing in and getting colder. Claire pulled the curtains closed and lit the gas fire. She sat down in the only other chair that was empty – an armchair close to the hearth. The sofa was crammed with packages and parcels, spilling over the cushions like a deranged domestic sorting office. More box towers lined the walls of the room, with some of their disparate contents disgorged in piles across the floor. Claire took a couple of tablets from the foil blister pack in her pocket and swallowed them with her tea. She wouldn't normally bother taking painkillers for just a headache, but this one was so tiresome. She set down her mug and picked up the parcel, resting it on her lap. She had no idea what it contained. In the years since her mother's death, online and telephone shopping had become Claire's main occupation. It had started as a hobby and finished up as an Olympic sport. She had no desire for human interaction and gained nothing from the company of others, which was why she almost never went out except for her daily walk around her garden. But buying was her passion and obsession. The very act of shopping was both exhilarating and relieving, like some sort of retail bloodletting. When Claire felt a nameless threat or terror building inside her, serious shopping would vaporise it as surely as the rising sun on morning mist. She tore the tape that sealed the parcel and pulled back the flaps of the brown cardboard box. Inside was an electric luxury foot spa and massager which promised to relieve pain and stress in overworked feet and promote blood circulation in lower legs.

'Interesting!' said Claire, examining it briefly before putting the box down on the floor and closing the lid.

She picked up the remote control and switched on the TV. The woman on the screen gave Claire her brightest smile. 'Welcome to The Shopping Channel!'

Chapter 23

'Right,' said George, looking round the table in The Duck and Donkey. 'Now everyone's here, let's get started.'

'Everyone' was George, Roxy, Elena, Edwin, Niall, Briony and Sid, who had heard about it from Elena and offered to come along.

'The inaugural meeting of The Funeral Society!' Roxy pronounced.

Elena frowned. 'No, no. I don't think we should be called that. It sounds too sad, and what we're doing isn't sad. We're trying to make things less sad.'

'Blimey, George,' said Edwin with a mischievous grin. 'You'd best get a grip! There's dissension in the ranks already!'

'It doesn't really matter what we're called, does it?' George replied, eager to move on to more important things. 'It's what we do that counts.'

Briony wondered if she should keep quiet for the moment. She felt like a probationer, still to earn her place in the group and therefore not entitled to express an opinion just yet. But then there was no point in her being here if she didn't get involved.

'That might not be strictly true,' she ventured. 'If you're hoping to spread the word about what you're doing and perhaps get other people involved, then it would definitely help if you had a memorable name.'

'I think The Funeral Society's pretty memorable,' said Roxy, a little tetchily.

'It is – but it sounds a bit … morbid,' Briony replied. 'Maybe go for something a bit more positive?'

'The trouble is,' Edwin chimed in, 'people like you and me, Roxy – we're not fazed by death. We're not afraid to look it in the face and call it by its name – instead of talking about people passing away, passing over, being lost, falling asleep, dropping off their perch or skipping over the rainbow bridge. But most people prefer to look the other way and euphemise the bejesus out of it. They want to pretend it doesn't happen – right up until it does. So if we want to get the support of these delicate death-shy folk, we mustn't scare the horses. Softly, softly catchee monkey and all that.'

'Shouldn't that be pony?' Roxy said with a wry smile. 'It sounds like we're trying to recruit a menagerie.'

George was beginning to feel as though he was trying to herd cats. 'Okay – so does anyone have any suggestions about what we might be called?' he said in an effort to move things forward. 'Preferably something that doesn't include the words death or funeral.'

'I think we should be called The Light a Candle Society,' Elena suggested. 'George lit a candle at Josh's funeral to shine a light on his life – and that's what we're trying to do for all these people who die alone. George should always be the one who lights the candles because it was his idea in the first place, and so we should be The Light a Candle Society.'

'I think that could work really well,' said Briony, imagining it in a headline for the feature that she was already drafting in her head.

'What about everyone else?' George asked, looking round the table. There was a general nodding of heads.

'I think it's perfect,' Edwin replied. 'And a gold star goes to Elena!'

'Thank goodness for that!' said George, picking up his pen and pulling his notepad towards him. 'And now let's get on with deciding what we're actually going to do.'

Elena repeated her offer to provide floral tributes and candles, and Roxy agreed to find appropriate readings or poems. 'I might even have a go at writing something myself if I feel inspired,' she added.

'That sounds great,' said Niall and Roxy smiled – a little bashfully, George thought.

'Well, I'll be sorting out the order of service, organising who's doing what during the funeral itself, and then acting as a sort of master of ceremonies, I suppose,' said George. 'I'm also happy to write and deliver a short eulogy if no one else turns up to do it. But one thing I did want to raise was funerals of different faiths. We might need to do something different for, say, a Muslim, Sikh or Hindu funeral. And what about Jewish ceremonies?'

'I don't think we need worry about that,' Niall replied. 'I asked Brenda about it when I first got the job, and she said that in the fifteen years she's been dealing with public health funerals she'd never done a single Muslim, Sikh, Hindu or Jewish ceremony. Some communities, it seems, are much better at caring for their vulnerable members and making sure they never end up on their own. They even have community funds to pay for the funerals of those who can't or don't have anyone else to foot the bill.'

'Which is exactly why we must do better,' George replied firmly.

'I'll be doing all the admin as usual,' said Niall, 'but I told the staff at the crematorium what you were planning to do, and I think they were genuinely touched. Steve, the chapel manager, and Lee and James, the two cremation technicians, suggested creating a memorial display cabinet which could be erected somewhere in the cemetery. The cabinet would contain a small object relating to the deceased, labelled with their name and their dates of birth and death. They came up with the idea because at lots of funerals families place something relevant to the deceased on the coffin for the service. They don't always claim them again afterwards, and the things that are left behind are kept on a shelf in the cremation area.'

'That's a beautiful idea!' exclaimed Elena.

'And it would be the perfect home for Josh's Spurs scarf,' added Edwin, recalling that he still had it for safekeeping.

'I'm sure I'll be able to help you find the right sort of cabinet,' said Sid. 'You want something like one of those old shop display fittings, or even one of those Victorian cabinets where they used to keep all their weird and wonderful specimens and collections – although I'm not sure how well they'd last if they were outside and exposed to all the elements.'

'There's a covered area with a seat that faces the ornamental pond in the cemetery. I think that's where they were hoping it could be located,' said Niall. 'But it might be a good idea to meet up with one of them and take a look yourself, so you can get an idea of how big and robust it needs to be. If you give me your number, I can pass it on and get one of them to call you.'

'Right-ho. And I might be able to help with some of the contents of the cabinet too,' Sid added looking quite pleased with himself.

Edwin drained his glass. 'I'll be doing what I normally do at every funeral,' he said, 'but I'll be liaising with George and Niall, and if anything else is required I'll do my best to deliver. And right now, I propose to deliver another round of drinks. What does everyone want?'

George accompanied Edwin to the bar and insisted on paying. He had called this meeting, he said, and he was grateful that people had turned up and were being so generous with their support. They returned to the others with a laden tray. The drinks were distributed, and packets of crisps in a variety of flavours were dumped in the middle of the table for communal consumption.

'Ooh, George – you're spoiling us!' teased Roxy, tearing open a packet of cheese and onion. And then turning to Briony she asked, 'What is it exactly that *you're* proposing to do to help us?'

There was a barely discernible edge to her voice, which nonetheless told George that she had not quite forgiven Briony for the 'morbid' comment.

Briony smiled in response. 'Well, firstly, I want to thank George for inviting me tonight. I was so moved by Josh's story and the funeral you gave him. I'd really love to help – and I think there's several ways that I can, if you'll let me, of course.'

She paused for a moment and George nodded encouragingly for her to continue.

'We could set up a website with links to social media platforms to help with the search for friends and relatives when someone dies alone. I know this is Niall's responsibility, and the last thing I want to do is tread on his toes, but I'm sure the time he has available to spend on these searches is limited, and the website could supplement what Niall does. It could also be a good way of finding out more about the person who has died from former friends and acquaintances. They might not want to come to the funeral, but they may be able to provide us with information that would help us get a better picture of the person who's died. Maybe stuff about the person's childhood, schooldays or any hobbies, sports they used to play – that kind of thing.'

'That sounds promising – and it would give us a way of reaching more people to let them know about the funeral in case they *did* want to come,' added George.

'The website could also have permanent memorial pages,' Briony continued. 'Each person could have their own entry which would record all the information that we have about them – a virtual headstone if you like. That way, if anyone comes looking for them after they've died, there will always be a memorial to them on the website that anyone can view.'

'And you'd be prepared to set all this up – for free?' Roxy asked, sounding a little sceptical.

'Well, there might be some minimal costs involved – buying a domain name for the website, for example – but I'd certainly give my time for free and be happy to get it up and running. And the other thing I could do – with your agreement – would be to run a story about the funerals and The Light a Candle Society – spread the word and encourage more volunteers to join us. And then we could also consider ways of fundraising to help with covering the costs.'

George glanced around the table, trying to gauge the reaction to Briony's proposals.

Niall was the first to speak. 'I'll need to speak to Brenda, my boss, before I agree to anything going in the press, but in principle I'm happy with all of it. I've got to be honest, I was a bit put out when George gatecrashed my first public health funeral, but I think I was worried about what Brenda might say more than anything else. These days I'm more inclined to think "Bugger Brenda" – particularly after a couple of pints,' he said, raising his glass with a grin, 'but we do need to get her onside somehow.'

'Bugger Brenda, indeed!' added Roxy. 'She must be a right miserable baggage if she can't see the good in what we're trying to do.'

'You leave Brenda to me and Briony,' said Edwin. 'I've known Brenda for a while now, and though I say so myself, I reckon she's got a soft spot for me.'

Sid gave a low wolf whistle and Niall looked faintly horrified.

'Over the years,' Edwin continued, 'I've worked out what makes her tick. She's a terrible jobsworth, but if she can take the credit for something without having to put the work in, she's more than happy. I'll tell her that *The Times and Herald* have contacted me because they want to run a story about public health funerals, and I've told them to speak to her because her department does such a brilliant job. I'll convince Brenda that it's all down to her because she appointed Niall who, inspired by her commitment to provide the best possible services to both the living and the dead, had the innovative idea of enlisting the help of The Light a Candle Society. All Briony has to do is mention her in passing in her article.'

'And do you really think you'll be able to persuade Brenda to agree,' asked Roxy, 'even though it's absolute bollocks?'

'She'll be putty in my hands,' replied Edwin with a wink.

George lay awake in bed that night, his eyes wide open in the darkness, wondering what he had started. He listened to the familiar sounds that were part and parcel of the fabric of the building where he had lived for so long. The gentle creak of a wooden floorboard, the occasional rattle of a window frame and a soft gurgle in a water pipe. It was as though the house was settling itself down to sleep. But sleep was proving to be elusive for George as he chased a relentless stream of doubts and possibilities around in his head. He tried to focus on the positive. He was doing a good thing. They were all doing a good thing.

But not everyone thought so. Elizabeth had said no more about the funerals during their subsequent phone conversations, but George could sense the disapproval sharpening her words and weighing down the silences between them. Unlike George, Elizabeth *had* been to her grandfather's funeral, and she had sat in the front pew with George's brother, her beloved Uncle Roger. Roger with whom George had no contact save for the exchange of Christmas and birthday cards. The last time they had met in person had been at Audrey's funeral and they had barely spoken. As boys, they had been close and had remained so as men until Roger had traced their father, who had been absent since George was eleven and Roger six. That betrayal by his brother had been more than George could bear, and the schism wrought that day had remained irreparable ever since. Because however hard he tried, George couldn't think of a way out of the corner into which he had painted himself. Elizabeth's censure of his behaviour towards both his father and Roger was born of ignorance. But George was too afraid that the truth would break his brother's heart, just as staying silent for all these years was breaking his.

Chapter 24

Briony took one more shot of the two women dressed in hedgehog costumes smeared with red paint lying in the middle of the road, and their fellow protesters brandishing 'Save Our Hedgehogs' banners. Then, waving her thanks, she made her way back to her car. *Another day, another groundbreaking report from ace journalist Briony Harris,* she thought. The residents of Little Odell wanted 'Caution Hedgehogs Crossing' signs erected at either end of the main road that passed through their village to protect their beloved hedgehog population from road traffic accidents, and Briony had every sympathy with their cause. She was very fond of hedgehogs. But she was never going to make a name for herself writing about them. It had been a week since the meeting of The Light a Candle Society in The Duck and Donkey, and she still hadn't heard from George about whether or not she could write her story. Perhaps Brenda had been impervious to Edwin's charm after all.

She threw her things onto the passenger seat and started the car. Her mobile rang. Damn! She kept meaning to get one of those phone holders that fixed to the dashboard. She switched off the engine and grabbed her bag, rummaging inside it to retrieve her phone. By the time she found it, the caller had hung up. She checked the number. It was George's. She called him back and he answered immediately.

'Sorry, George, I was driving, and I don't have one of those Bluetooth thingies in the car. What can I do for you?' She tried not to sound too eager.

'Briony – thanks for calling back. I saw Edwin this morning and Brenda's agreed that you can write a story about the public health funerals. I've just spoken with Niall to double-check that we can go ahead, and it seems that we can.'

Briony bit back a whoop of joy. She didn't want to ruin her reputation as a serious journalist before she'd even earned it. 'That's brilliant news, George!' *Literally*, she thought to herself. 'I'll get to work drafting some ideas straightaway, and I'd like to attend at least one more funeral if that's okay?'

'That's fine,' George replied. 'I'll be in touch as soon as I know there's going to be another one. In the meantime, if you need anything, give me a ring or pop in and see us at the library.'

George hung up and Briony sat there for a moment taking in the significance of his call. This could be, at last, her chance to write something really worthwhile – something that people would actually want to read. It was a story with numerous possible tributaries. She could write not just about the funerals and The Light a Candle Society, but also about the reasons why people end up dying alone – their backgrounds, their histories and how, even in this day and age, someone can die in their own home and remain undiscovered for weeks or even months afterwards. Briony knew this really happened because she'd tapped one of her contacts in the police. At least, that's how she liked to think of it. She'd actually asked the guy who lived in the flat opposite hers when she had bumped into him in the corner shop, and they had walked back to the house together. Having discovered from Allegra, who knew something about everyone living in each of the flats, that he was a police constable, Briony made a point of speaking to him whenever she saw him, judging him to be a potentially useful source of information. He had been a little surprised when she had raised the topic of undiscovered corpses as they strolled home with their respective groceries. But when she reassured him that she was only asking as part of her research for a story, he had told her that he had recently been called to a house where a woman had been dead for some time.

'The only reason anyone noticed was down to the smell,' he had said. 'The postwoman caught a whiff of it when she pushed open the letterbox.'

Briony started the car again and set off towards home, her mind whirring with ideas about what she was going to write. For the moment, she was refusing to acknowledge, let alone address, the giant Gordon-shaped elephant in the room. She had offered to write this story, and she had intimated strongly that its publication would benefit George's and The Light a Candle Society's cause. But what she hadn't told them was that she had no official authority from the newspaper. And even if she went ahead and wrote the story, without Gordon's knowledge or permission the chances of it being published were as slim as the cigarette papers he used for his roll-ups. She pulled up outside the flats and went in. As she rifled through the post on the table in the hall, Allegra's front door opened, and she greeted Briony with a graceful wave.

'Good evening, dear. Have you had a good day?'

Briony smiled. 'Yes – I think so.'

Allegra raised one eyebrow quizzically. 'I'm intrigued. Would you like to join me for a drink and then you can tell me all about it?'

'I can't think of anything nicer,' Briony replied. 'Let me just dump my stuff upstairs first.'

'Martini?'

'Perfect!' said Briony, taking the stairs up to her flat two at a time.

Allegra had taken to inviting Briony to join her for a drink in the early evening on a regular basis a couple of times a week. Briony had begun to look forward to these occasions, as she enjoyed the older woman's company, but during their conversations she had discovered little more about Allegra and her life before she came to live in her flat. Allegra was better at asking questions than answering them. She would have made a good journalist, Briony often reflected. She was so accomplished that she was able to elicit confidences as easily as if her subject were under hypnosis.

By the time Briony pushed open Allegra's front door and joined her in the sitting room, her martini was waiting for her on the table beside her chair.

'Cheers!' she said, raising her glass to Allegra.

Allegra reciprocated. 'Now, tell me all about your day.'

Briony told her about the hedgehog campaigners and the two women in paint-smeared costumes lying in the road.

'Sounds marvellous! I hope they get their signs. I believe we may have hedgehogs in the garden here. I'm sure I hear them sometimes, snuffling about in the evening. Perhaps I should put some food out for them.'

'And then I had a call from George,' Briony continued. 'He's got permission for me to write the story about the public health funerals and George's group of volunteers, who are calling themselves The Light a Candle Society.'

Briony had told Allegra all about Josh's funeral and the meeting of The Light a Candle Society, and Allegra had agreed it would make a wonderful article for the newspaper.

Allegra studied her critically. 'Well, you don't look very pleased about it. I thought this was going to be your breakthrough story. You should be delighted – so why are you not?'

Briony sighed. 'Because I don't have Gordon's permission to write it. I haven't even discussed it with him. And if he doesn't like it, then there's not a cat in hell's chance that he'll publish it.'

'Permission!' Allegra expostulated. 'I have never in my life sought a man's permission to do anything and neither should you.'

'But he's my boss,' Briony replied, a little taken aback by Allegra's vehemence.

'He's your employer, not your master. You may write about anything you choose, so long as you carry out your official assignments too. It's a brilliant story, so write it brilliantly.

Make it so brilliant that he can't refuse it, and fight your corner until he publishes it.'

'If only it was that simple. You make it sound easy.'

Allegra fixed her with a cool stare. 'Very little worth having in this life is easy. But if you truly want it, there's usually a way of getting it. So the question is, Briony, how badly do you want it?'

Chapter 25

'Now, there might be a bit of an odd smell inside,' Sid warned George as he parked his van outside the house at the bottom of Windermere Close. 'The old dear who lived here wasn't found straightaway. Apparently, she'd been dead for a few weeks before anyone noticed.'

They climbed out of the van and walked down a path to the side of a slightly overgrown, but clearly once well-kept, garden to the forest-green painted front door with pretty stained-glass panels.

'She died in the sitting room,' Sid continued, 'and the gas fire was on. So by the time the police were called the body was a bit … ripe. But the specialist cleaning team have been in, so it shouldn't be too bad.'

George was beginning to wonder if it had been such a good idea to agree to accompany Sid on his preliminary visit after all. Perhaps he should have waited until Sid had cleared the house and then just gone through the contents at Sid's shop. He hadn't really thought about what it might be like to step inside the home and life – and in this case death – of a stranger. Niall had already been to the house, conducted the required search and collected the necessary paperwork. He had then contacted George to let him know that Miss Considine would be having a public health funeral. Thankfully she had left a will, and the funeral would be paid for from the proceeds of her estate, with the rest going to various charities. But it seemed she had no family or friends and so hers was to be The Light a Candle Society's first official funeral.

As Sid dug his hand in his pocket to find the front door key, George admonished himself for his cowardly queasiness. If he really wanted to give Claire Considine the funeral she deserved, then what better way for him to get to know her than seeing how she had lived inside her own home? It was a privilege to be given the opportunity and he should treat it as such. Once Sid had unlocked the door, they entered the narrow hallway and stood for a moment in respectful silence, almost as though they were waiting to be invited in. The chime of a clock sounded from upstairs on the landing.

'Must be a self-winder,' said Sid, taking a notebook and pen from his pocket. 'I'm going to have a wander round and make a note of everything so that I can give Niall a quote for the clearance. Why don't you have a look and see if you can find anything you can use for the funeral?'

Sid headed off upstairs and George opened the nearest door and stepped into the sitting room. The first thing he saw was the chair. It was loosely covered in a clear plastic cover, but a large stain was still visible. There was a similar mark on the carpet which the cleaners had been unable to erase completely. The room smelled of cleaning fluid with a faint undertone of something sweet and rotten.

'Oh, Claire,' George breathed. 'I'm so sorry.'

Niall had told George that Claire Considine had died in her armchair in front of the gas fire. According to the coroner's report, a post-mortem had revealed that she had died of carbon monoxide poisoning. A completely preventable death, if only she'd had her fire serviced regularly or had a carbon monoxide alarm. Since Niall had shared this with George, he had bought two extra alarms for his own house and recommended to Roxy that she do the same.

The state of the room was a peculiar contradiction. The ornaments on the mantelpiece were neatly placed, the books in the bookcase were all in order, and a selection of framed photographs on a sideboard were in a tidy row. But the walls were lined with cardboard boxes stacked in ramshackle towers. Additional boxes were piled in a disorderly heap on the sofa and several, with their contents spilling out, lay upturned on the floor. From what George could see, the contents were brand new and resembled the stock of a wildly eclectic market stall. There were sumptuous silk kaftans, soft toys, costume jewellery, beauty products, posture-correcting neck pillows, Christmas jumpers and, in the box nearest the chair, what looked like some sort of foot spa machine. It was clear from the boxes that they had all been purchased from several well-known mail order shopping companies. Claire Considine had clearly had a serious habit, but that wasn't something he would particularly want to mention at her funeral.

He inspected the framed photographs. One was taken in the front garden of the house in Windermere Close. A man and woman stood just in front of the porch, with a younger woman between them. It looked like a happy family group – they were all smiling. Their clothes indicated that the picture had been taken in the 1970s. (George remembered well those brightly patterned slim-fitting shirts with enormous collars! As a teenager he had loved them, and it was then that his passion for colourful shirts had been ignited.) The young woman – possibly Claire – had long auburn hair and was wearing flared jeans and what looked like a cheesecloth shirt. She was beautiful but somehow remote, the coolness in her eyes seeming to express a warning to the observer to keep their distance. George glanced at the back of the photo frame just in case anything helpful was written there. It wasn't. But then he had the idea to remove the picture from its frame and was rewarded with the following words neatly inscribed on the reverse of the print.

Me (May), Ronald and Claire. Windermere Close, July 1974

George could check with Niall that Ronald and May were Claire's parents, but it seemed very likely, and the photo would sit well on her coffin. Her parents would be there with her.

'How are you getting on?' Sid came in, still scribbling in his notebook, and gave the chair a wide berth.

'I've found what I think is a family photo – Claire and her parents.' He held it out for Sid to examine. 'But it doesn't tell me much about Claire other than the fact that she was beautiful.'

'She was a stunner, all right!' Sid exclaimed. 'It makes you wonder why she never got married.' He started rummaging through the boxes. 'I think we can safely say that Claire liked a bit of retail therapy.'

'Hmm,' replied George, lost in thought. 'But I wonder what started this off. It's as though she was trying to fill some unbearable emptiness in her life.'

'Well, she was certainly filling up her house,' Sid replied distractedly, as he jotted down notes and figures.

George turned his attention to the cupboards at the bottom of the sideboard, where he found a number of old lever-arch files. Inside the first ones he took out were page after page of original illustrations, each one signed in the lower right-hand corner with the initials C.C. in copperplate script and numbered on the reverse. Some were delicate floral arrangements in pastel colours, others were landscapes or sporting scenes, and some were comical cartoon figures like the pictures once used in children's books. The illustrations seemed vaguely familiar to George – none of them specifically, but as generic examples of something he recognised but couldn't name. Further investigation of the contents of the sideboard gave him the answer. One of the files contained correspondence, including invoices and receipts, and several shoeboxes contained samples of greetings cards. The illustrations on the front of them were Claire's. He pulled a card from one of the boxes, and as he studied it, he felt the hairs prickle on the back of his neck. A pair of silvery bells wreathed in roses and forget-me-nots. The bells were tied with white ribbons held in loops and swags by a pair of flying bluebirds. This very card hung on the wall of the bedroom that he had shared with Audrey for so many years and where he now slept alone. Audrey's parents had sent it to them on their wedding day, and Audrey had liked it so much that she had framed it as a keepsake. The card meant that Claire Considine was no longer a complete stranger. She had a totally unexpected but exquisitely poignant connection to George and one of the happiest days of his life, which made him all the more determined to honour her death.

Chapter 26

George had just come in from the garden, where he had been feeding the birds, when the phone rang.

'Hello, Dad – it's me, Elizabeth,' said his daughter, quite unnecessarily considering that George only had one child.

'Hello, love. I thought you were off on your holidays today?'

'We are. But I just wanted to check that you were okay before we left. I still wish that you were coming with us.'

'I'll be fine. I've got lots of nice things planned – and I'm also going to put my feet up, eat and drink lots of things I shouldn't and watch old films. I'm looking forward to it!'

'But where are you going on Christmas Day?'

'I'm going to the cemetery first thing to see your mum, and then I'm going to The Duck and Donkey for Christmas dinner. Roxy is going too – she's on her own now her mum's in the care home – and I expect there'll be some other people there that we know. I'll get a proper slap-up meal without having to do the washing-up afterwards!'

'It's still charging in the kitchen where you left it!' Elizabeth yelled in response to a shouted query from Gus, who was obviously searching for his phone. 'And hurry up – the taxi will be here in a minute! Sorry, Dad – you were saying, dinner at The Duck and Donkey?'

George was itching to get off the phone. He needed to have a shower and get ready. And the irony was that he knew full well Elizabeth didn't really want to be chatting to him right now either, and she had only rung him to assuage her completely misplaced guilt before she flew off on holiday with Nick and the kids. She obviously remained unconvinced that the plastic palaces of Dubai held no attraction for George whatsoever.

'Elizabeth, I promise you that I'm going to be absolutely fine. I'm having Christmas Day with my friends, but I'm also going to be having a bit of time to myself to do whatever I like, or to do nothing at all. You go and have a wonderful holiday – and you can tell me all about it when you get back. Take lots of photos and bring me back a souvenir tea towel!' he joked.

After a quick shower, he dressed in his navy suit and a dark blue shirt scattered with pale blue flowers. He had been thrilled to discover the shirt with its forget-me-not print that would coordinate so well with the floral tribute Elena had created for the occasion. He picked up his car keys and grabbed a soft woollen scarf from the coat rack in the hall, which he wrapped around his neck. He had promised to pick Roxy up on his way. It would be Christmas Eve tomorrow, and both he and Roxy had finished work for the festive season, which meant that Roxy was able to come to the service. She was waiting on the street when George pulled up outside her house. She was wearing a sunshine yellow coat with a scarf the green of new leaves in the spring.

'You look very nice,' George told her as she climbed into the car.

'Thank you. I've dressed to match the poem I'm going to read.'

The funeral was at 3.45 pm and already the day was darkening. A bank of slate-coloured clouds was skulking low on the horizon, backlit with the purples and pinks of the impending sunset, and fairy lights on Christmas trees in the windows of the houses that they passed made pops of colour in the gloom. Briony was waiting for them in the foyer of the crematorium chapel, and they were soon joined by Elena and Niall. Elena handed George the candle she had chosen for Claire.

'It's rose scented,' she told him, 'to match the flowers.'

George checked his pocket for the lighter. 'I'll just take it in and put it on the stand,' he said, nodding towards the chapel.

When George returned, Sid was with the others, wearing a very smart black suit and a black trilby with a purple band. 'I thought I'd come and swell the numbers a bit,' he said with a grin. 'Are we having any hymns? I've got a good loud singing voice!'

Niall had found a christening certificate for Claire amongst the papers at Windermere Close, so they had agreed that a hymn would be acceptable at the service.

'Just the one,' said Niall, 'so give it your best shot!'

The wreath on the coffin was a simple circle of white and pink roses, ivy and forget-me-nots. Once the pallbearers had settled the coffin onto the catafalque, Edwin placed the objects George had selected in front of the wreath: the framed photograph of Claire and her parents, the sample greetings card with the silver bells and forget-me-nots, and a red sequinned heart key ring he had found on her dressing table. Briony discreetly took a couple of pictures on her phone before the service started.

George stepped up to the front of the chapel and lit the candle. 'We are here today to celebrate the life of Claire Considine,' he began.

'Claire was the much-loved daughter of May and Ronald and a generous supporter of charities that help the homeless, and rescue donkeys and horses.'

Niall had told him these were the charities that would benefit from Claire's will, so it seemed like a pretty fair extrapolation.

'She was also a talented artist,' George continued, 'who designed greetings cards for a living. Through her work, she touched the lives of so many people whom she never knew. We all understand how much it means to receive cards from friends and loved ones – whatever the occasion. Over the years, Claire's cards must have brought so much joy on birthdays, anniversaries, Christmases. Their messages of "Good Luck", "Thank You" and "Get Well Soon" must have been very much appreciated, and their expressions of condolence must have brought comfort and perhaps a little consolation to those who were grieving. My lovely wife, Audrey, and I received one of Claire's cards on our wedding day and I still have it – a precious memento of a wonderful day. Claire's gift was not simply her art, but the way in which it was shared to spread joy, support and solace amongst so many people – and that is her incredible legacy.'

They sang 'Abide with Me', and Sid's rich baritone resonated inside the almost empty chapel. His voice was powerful and true, making him the soloist and the rest of them his backing singers.

Next, Roxy introduced her reading. 'I've chosen this poem for Claire,' she said, 'because it's about drawing on memories of something beautiful to make yourself feel better when you need to. And I think that Claire's cards would have held happy memories for the people who received them long after they were sent.'

She then read 'Daffodils' by William Wordsworth.

The service ended with a simple blessing led by Elena, and as Claire's coffin disappeared from view, Morecambe and Wise sang 'Bring Me Sunshine'. It was another reference to the happiness that Claire's cards had spread. Roxy had suggested 'Return to Sender' sung by Elvis Presley, and although George and Niall had both laughed out loud, they had decided that Brenda might not approve. George thanked Steve, the chapel manager, and wished him a merry Christmas and then followed the others outside.

'Now, after Josh's funeral we didn't have a wake,' he told them. 'And I couldn't help but feel that just leaving the chapel and going our separate ways afterwards seemed a bit odd. It felt somehow unfinished. So as we've agreed, from now on, when possible, we're going to pop in at The Duck and Donkey and raise a glass to our new absent friend. And I wanted to let you know that Lachie, the landlord, has heard about the funerals and offered to provide us with a few light refreshments on the house.'

'What's all this about light refreshments?' Edwin had joined them, carrying the flowers and the things from Claire's coffin. He laid the flowers down in the display area for floral tributes.

'Just a reminder about the wake we're having for Claire at The Duck and Donkey,' George replied.

'I'll see you there in a bit, then,' Edwin replied with a grin. 'I've got to get the hearse back and put to bed, and then I'm done for the day. Would you like me to keep these safe with Josh's scarf?' he asked, nodding at the photo, card and key ring he was holding. 'Just until Sid sorts out a display cabinet?'

'Thanks, Edwin. That would be great,' George replied.

'And on that subject, I think I may have found something to fit the bill. I just need to check that the good folk here are happy with it,' Sid interjected. 'And you too – of course!' he added, doffing his hat in George's direction.

It was almost 5.30 pm by the time they reconvened in the pub, and The Duck and Donkey was crammed with people who had finished working for the Christmas break and were celebrating. But true to his word, Lachie had reserved a couple of tables for them, and when he saw them come in, he sent one of his bar staff over with plates of sandwiches and savoury snacks and some small metal baskets containing hot chips. Niall and Sid went to the bar to get a round of drinks, and when they returned, George raised his glass to propose a toast.

'To Claire,' he said. 'Our absent friend. Safe journey to wherever!'

'To Claire!' they all repeated.

'And also, to all of you,' George added, smiling round at everyone, 'for your kindness and generosity in helping to make my crazy idea work. I really appreciate it.'

'And I'd like to propose a toast, as well,' said Niall, clearing his throat a little nervously. 'I'd like to thank George for coming up with this bonkers – but brilliant – idea in the first place and for convincing me to go along with it, even when I was too scared to rock the boat with Brenda. And for not minding when I was sick in his toilet.'

Roxy snorted with laughter and lifted her glass, but Niall waved it back down.

'And I'd also like to thank Edwin,' he continued, 'for all his help and support – both at work and in getting me back to George's when I was too drunk on Jägerbombs to stand up.'

Elena was staring at George wide-eyed, with a mischievous smile on her face. 'And I thought you lived such a quiet life!' she joked, waggling an egg and cress sandwich at him.

'And so we both did until Niall led us astray,' said Edwin, raising his glass. 'Come on, the man's proposed a toast – to George and me!'

'To George and Edwin!' they all chanted.

'And seeing as everyone's at it,' Edwin continued, 'my toast is to Brenda – because it's Christmas, and she agreed to the funerals and to Briony's story.'

'Teacher's pet!' Roxy mouthed at him with a grin. 'Come on, Elena. We can't let the men make all the toasts. It's your turn.'

Elena frowned, thinking for a moment. 'To Josh,' she said finally, 'because he didn't have a wake.'

'To Josh' sounded more like a prayer than a toast, as they all remembered how short his life had been.

After a brief silence, George turned to Briony. 'And what about you? What's your toast?'

Briony would have loved to raise a glass to getting the better of Gordon Bollocks, but she hadn't shared with anyone here the fact that she still hadn't got permission to write her story about the funerals, so she stuck to something simple. She helped herself from one of the metal baskets. 'To chips!' she said. 'My favourite food!'

'A woman after my own heart,' said Niall, raising his glass.

George saw the expression that clouded Roxy's face. 'Roxy – what about you?' he asked. 'You haven't made a toast yet?'

Roxy pushed back her chair and got up. 'I need to go to the loo,' she said.

———

In the ladies, she stared in the mirror critically. She had removed all her piercings save for two earrings and softened her make-up in the past couple of weeks. She thought she looked better, more attractive. But no one else had noticed. She didn't care, she told herself. She hadn't done it for anyone else's benefit. As she made her way back through the pub, the crowd shifted, and through a gap she saw a familiar figure tucked into a corner, his face turned away from curious glances. Roxy went to the bar and bought a packet of crisps and then wove her way through to the corner where Captain sat with his large grey and white dog.

'Hello,' she said. 'I thought it was you. I hope you don't mind me interrupting, but I just wanted to wish you merry Christmas.'

Captain looked up at her, his face impassive, and said nothing, but the dog stood up and gently pushed his wet nose against the back of her hand.

Roxy shrugged ruefully. 'And yes, okay, I also wanted to say hello to your gorgeous dog.'

Captain rubbed the back of the dog's neck with his fingers, and his face wrinkled into a slow smile. 'He's a grand lad,' Captain muttered. 'I wouldn't be without him.'

'What's his name?'

'Sailor.'

'Sailor,' Roxy repeated, and at the sound of the familiar word, the dog ducked and pushed his head under Roxy's hand, demanding to be stroked. Roxy looked at Captain, who nodded his consent.

'Does he like crisps?' Roxy asked as she stroked his soft fur.

Captain grunted. 'They'll make him fat.'

'But what about just a couple?' Roxy persisted but didn't open the bag. 'As a special festive treat?'

She met Captain's impenetrable gaze with a warm but determined smile. After a long moment of stalemate his eyes softened, and he nodded once more. Roxy ripped opened the packet before he could change his mind and fed the delighted Sailor a couple of crisps. And then a couple more.

'Last one,' she said to the grinning dog as she fed him a cluster that had stuck together. She folded the top of the bag over and set it down on the table beside Captain's drink. 'For Ron,' she said.

Captain raised his eyebrows, clearly puzzled.

Roxy grinned. 'For Ron,' she repeated. 'Later-on.'

She scratched Sailor's chin one last time and then turned to go. 'I should get back to my friends,' she said. 'It's nice to see you both.'

Captain briefly touched the peak of his cap and then turned back to his drink.

The words 'Merry Christmas' that followed in Roxy's wake were spoken so low that she wasn't sure afterwards that she hadn't imagined them.

Chapter 27

'Merry Christmas, love!'

George squatted down by Audrey's grave and groaned as his knees protested. He adjusted the wreath of holly and ivy tied with red ribbon that he had brought with him so it leaned perfectly straight against her headstone.

'I wonder what Elizabeth and her lot are up to now.' He checked his watch. 'They're four hours ahead of us, so they're probably just about to sit down to their Christmas dinner. I bet they won't be having turkey, though. Or maybe they're having a leisurely dip in the pool and won't be having dinner until this evening.'

George shifted uncomfortably. 'I'm sorry, love – I'm going to have to stand up.'

He struggled to his feet and placed one hand on Audrey's headstone. 'Well, whatever they're doing, I hope they're enjoying themselves. I'm only glad I'm not there with them! Christmas in warm weather just isn't natural. You couldn't wear a Christmas jumper in Dubai, could you?'

George was sporting his own Christmas jumper ready for his dinner in the pub. 'What do you think?' he said, opening his coat to reveal a sweater with two penguins on the front kissing under a sprig of mistletoe. Audrey had always loved penguins. He rebuttoned his coat. It was cold and damp enough to need one, but too mild for festive frost or snow.

'Claire's funeral went well, and we put the card that I told you about – the same one your mum and dad sent us on our wedding day – on the coffin. I still can't believe it was one of Claire's designs. Talk about coincidence! Elena reckons it was a sign, but you know what I think about all that hocus-pocus stuff.'

George waited for a woman with a little boy carrying a snowman decoration to go by before continuing. 'Sid turned up, which was good of him. He's got a lovely singing voice, you know. And this time we had a little wake afterwards, which was nice. It gave us all a lift – ended the day on an upbeat note. We could have done with that after Josh's funeral. Honestly, Audrey, everyone's been so kind and generous – the last thing I want is for them to go home after one of these funerals feeling sad and depressed.'

George paused for a moment and a thought struck him. 'You know, love, in a funny way, I think that by having a get-together afterwards we're not just celebrating the lives of Claire and the others, but also our own. Having a drink and a chat and a laugh with friends – reminding ourselves how lucky we are that we still can.'

A couple passing by with a bouquet of red roses smiled at George and wished him a merry Christmas.

'And to you too!' he replied.

'I'm a bit worried about Roxy, though,' George continued, once the couple with the roses were out of earshot. 'I think she might have a bit of a thing for Niall. She hasn't been on any dates recently, and she acts differently when he's around. But he's still going through his divorce, so I'm not sure he's ready for another relationship.'

And I'm also not sure Roxy is his type, George thought – but he kept it to himself. He didn't want to say it out loud, not even to Audrey. It felt disloyal, even disparaging somehow. Maybe he could find out more about how she felt over Christmas dinner and after a few glasses of Prosecco. The cemetery was getting busy now, with lots of families arriving to pay seasonal respects to their loved ones.

'Well, I'd best be off now, love.' George patted Audrey's headstone affectionately.

He picked up the other wreath that he had brought with him and made his way across the grass and along the gravel path that led him behind the chapel to the place where the cremation remains from public health funerals were buried. He stood for a moment and looked around the garden. To call it a garden seemed like an extravagant misnomer at this time of year. It was a dull and drab patch of land – a dreary palate of browns and greys. Even the lawns were more mud than grass, and the rose bushes only clusters of sharp, bare brown sticks that looked like claws pushing up through the earth. Beyond this place, the cemetery was awash with colour. Christmas wreathes and flowers glowed red and green and gold on graves and tombs and columbaria. George looked down at his wreath and wished that it was bigger, brighter – better. But it *was* better. Better than nothing. He wondered how many lonely souls were huddled together in this soil. How many earthly remains had been returned to this earth with no one to mourn them and no one to bring flowers? The card on the wreath George had brought with him bore only four names.

In memory of Kathleen, Derek, Josh and Claire.

He set the wreath down at the foot of the sundial. *It's not going to happen any more*, he vowed to himself. *Not on my watch*. No one else would be buried here and forgotten. Soon there would be the memorial cabinet and the virtual headstones on the website. In future, every life would be acknowledged and remembered.

George shivered. It wasn't that cold, but he'd been standing still for too long, and it had started to drizzle. His thoughts turned to The Duck and Donkey – turkey and all the trimmings, pulling crackers, paper hats and terrible jokes. Maybe even a sing-along with the pub piano if Lachie decided to play. He was going to call for Roxy on the way and they would walk there together – and hold each other up on the way home, Roxy had joked. George turned away from the sundial and headed off towards the car park. Just before he left the garden, he glanced back to look at the wreath that he had laid. The circle of deep green leaves and red berries woven with scarlet ribbon was a small but conspicuous beacon in a bleak landscape. It was a promise of things to come. And there, in the barren dirt beneath a rose bush, was another flash of colour, a feathered spark of life. The robin paused for a moment, his blackcurrant eyes fixed on the prize. Then he pecked at the earth to seize his Christmas dinner.

Chapter 28

George began to button his coat as the train slowed on its approach towards St Pancras Station. Sunlight flashed off the window he was sitting by for a moment before being snuffed out as they trundled into a tunnel. It was 4 January and George's birthday. He was meeting Elizabeth, Nick, Angus and Amelie for lunch at a restaurant between St Pancras and King's Cross, which was where their train from Edinburgh came in. They were staying in London overnight and seeing a show in the West End later in the day. They had invited George to go with them, but he had politely declined. He didn't think *Mamma Mia* would be quite his thing – and besides, Roxy had organised a birthday drink with the others at The Duck and Donkey, as there was no quiz that evening. Amelie and Elizabeth were huge ABBA fans, but George wondered whether Angus and Nick were quite so keen.

The train pulled in to the station and the doors opened with a hiss. George took the escalator up into the station concourse, where the scent of hyacinths from the flower stall and the aroma of fresh coffee greeted him. The crowds were thinner than usual, but early January was a quiet time of year. People were resting after the Christmas and New Year celebrations, and their bank accounts were recuperating from strenuous seasonal expenditure. He turned left and was soon outside again, in brilliant sunshine and a spiteful wind. He checked his watch. He was a little early. He could go inside and wait for Elizabeth and the others at their table, but he decided to have a stroll around – do some window shopping and watch people coming and going.

He was heading away from the restaurant when he heard voices that he thought he recognised. He turned to see Amelie and Angus coming out of King's Cross Station, squabbling over a beanie hat that she had clearly snatched from his head. George was about to call out to his grandchildren when he saw Elizabeth and Nick behind them. There was someone else with them. George turned and walked away, his heart punching against his chest. His face grew hot, and he could feel the blood pulsing frantically around his body as though his veins had suddenly constricted.

A young woman wearing headphones stopped and looked at him with a concerned expression as he grabbed at the back of a bench and managed to sit down. She uncovered her ears and touched him lightly on the shoulder. 'Are you okay?'

George took a deep breath. And then another. He managed to summon up a fair impersonation of a smile. 'I'm fine, thanks.'

The young woman frowned, clearly uncertain whether to believe him. 'You sure? You look a bit – weird.'

George smiled again, more convincingly this time. 'That's normal for me.'

The young woman grinned, replaced her headphones and went on her way. George sat very still for a moment and then tentatively glanced round in the direction of the restaurant. There was no sign of his family. They must have gone inside. George considered what to do next. His shock was subsiding, driven away by a surge of emotion so intense that it surprised him. This was Elizabeth's doing, he was sure. She had poked the bear. Her arrogance and naivety were infuriating – but more than that, hurtful. She was perfectly aware of how he felt, but she had gone ahead and created a situation she knew damn well would cause nothing but trouble. And pain – she had no idea how much pain.

The best thing he could do, George thought, would be to walk straight back into St Pancras and catch the next train home. He didn't want a row in public, nor did he want to endure a meal accompanied by awkward, insincere but doggedly civil chit-chat. He certainly didn't want to ruin the day for Amelie and Angus. But before he left, he couldn't resist taking a look – like sipping tea that you know is too hot and burning your tongue anyway. He sidled up to one of the large leadlight windows, doing his best to look casual, and peered into the restaurant. It took a while for him to spot them, but there they were, talking and laughing, drinks already in hands.

The sight of his brother provoked a contradictory mess of emotions: a visceral pang of loss followed by the bitter memory of betrayal; love and the instinct to protect inextricably shackled to resentment and anger. At sixty-two Roger was still handsome enough to attract admiring glances. He had never married – through choice – but had never lacked female companionship when he wanted it. He was clearly recounting some entertaining anecdote, as all eyes at the table were on him. Only Elizabeth looked slightly distracted as she checked her watch and then glanced towards the door. George moved away from the window, tears stinging his eyes. He had almost forgotten that they were still waiting for him. That this was his birthday celebration.

Once he was safely back inside St Pancras, he took out his phone and brought up Elizabeth's contact details. He would have to text the lie he was about to tell her. He couldn't trust himself to speak to her and sound credible. But what on earth could he say? *Keep it simple*, he thought.

> So sorry, love, but I'm not going to make it today. Felt a bit rough when I woke up, but thought I'd be okay. Got as far as Harpenden on the train but was sick in the toilet and had to go back.

George smiled to himself, in spite of everything, remembering Niall's toast in The Duck and Donkey.

> Home now, so DON'T WORRY and enjoy the show. Probably something I ate. I'm off for a lie-down. I'll text you later. Dad xx

He didn't wait for her to reply but pocketed the phone and headed off to catch his train.

'What did she say to that?' Roxy asked him. They were sitting in The Duck and Donkey waiting for the others to arrive. George took out his phone and showed Roxy the message.

> Why didn't you text me sooner? We've been waiting for you. The kids are so disappointed, and we had a surprise for you. It's such a shame. Text me later. Hope you feel better soon xx

'Had you been really ill, I'd say that was a bit harsh,' Roxy said with a mischievous grin. 'Do you think she believed you?'

'I'm not sure. I must admit that the time-lapse before I texted her does seem a bit suspect, but it was the best I could think of at the time.'

Roxy sipped her drink thoughtfully before addressing the elephant in the room. 'So, tell me to mind my own business if you don't want to talk about it, but what's the big deal with your brother? I know you don't get on, but you've never said why. And why would Elizabeth bring your brother to your birthday lunch without telling you, knowing that you don't want anything to do with him?'

George winced at the oversimplification contained in those last words. He desperately wanted his brother back in his life, but he couldn't find a way to make that work. He couldn't reconcile himself to a reconciliation that didn't involve the truth. And although the truth might exonerate George to some extent, it would shatter illusions that were precious to Roger. He was damned if he did and damned if he didn't. George wasn't sure if it was pride, love or guilt that made him choose to deal with their past alone rather than inflict an honest account, and the pain that would inevitably accompany it, on Roger.

'It's a long and not very original story, but the gist of it is this. Our dad was a difficult man. When he was sober, he was great – funny, kind, loving. Everyone thought he was the perfect husband and father, including me and Roger. Mum always used to say that he could charm the apples off the trees and turn them into cider, like Jesus turning water into wine. She always said it with a smile, but by the time I was eleven or twelve, I understood the bitterness and pain behind that smile. He loved to drink, and when he drank, he forgot that he loved us. He spent more time in the pub than he did at home, and when he did come back, to be honest, I was scared of him. Roger was too young to understand, and between us, me and Mum made sure he didn't see the worst of it. We came home from school one day and he was gone. She said he'd gone away for work, and after that she never talked about him. I didn't know if she'd thrown him out or he'd left of his own accord, and truthfully, I didn't care. We were better off without him.'

George paused for a moment and took a deep draught of his beer.

'God – I'm sorry I asked, George. I haven't exactly cheered you up on your birthday, have I?'

George shook his head. 'It's fine, Roxy. To be honest, after what happened today, I'm grateful to have the chance to talk about it. Anyway, some years ago, after Mum died, Roger took it into his head to find Dad. He joined one of those ancestry sites online and, lo and behold, he turned up the old man like a bad penny. He didn't tell me about it until after they'd met a couple of times. He tried to convince me to see him too. Said that Dad hadn't got long left and that whatever had happened in the past wasn't important any more. But he had no idea – how could he? All I knew was that I could never betray Mum after all she went through, so I point-blank refused. And that's it – that's what we fell out over.'

Before Roxy could say anything, a brightly coloured foil balloon emblazoned with the words 'Happy Birthday!' was thrust in George's face. An enormous, elaborately decorated cake covered in candles was set down in front of him, and Edwin, Niall, Elena and Sid stood grinning around the table.

'Happy birthday, George!' Elena said, kissing him on the cheek.

'Happy birthday to you!' the rest of them chorused loudly.

Edwin slapped him on the back and gave Roxy a hug. 'Right then,' he said. 'Who wants a drink?'

Chapter 29

'And how is everyone today?' asked Mrs Biscuit, handing over the books she was returning. She peered at George and narrowed her eyes. 'You're looking a bit of a funny colour this morning. You almost match that shirt you're wearing,' she joked.

George was wearing the shirt Roxy had bought him for his birthday – a white horses print on a pale sage background.

'He's fine,' Roxy replied on his behalf. 'He just had a few too many lemonades in the pub last night, celebrating his birthday.'

George smiled wanly.

'If I'd known it was your birthday, I'd have made you some special biscuits!' declared Mrs Biscuit. George's stomach gurgled threateningly at the thought.

'As it is, I've only got these,' she said, passing a tin to Roxy. 'But they have got ginger in them, which is supposed to be good for settling the tummy. Ginger and prunes.'

'They sound excellent,' George muttered doubtfully as Mrs Biscuit left them and went to peruse the shelves in search of this week's reads.

'They sound lethal!' said Roxy once Mrs Biscuit was out of earshot, moving the tin out of sight as charily as though it were an unexploded bomb. She glanced at George and her grin softened into a sympathetic smile. 'Can I get you anything? Paracetamol? Lucozade? Hemlock?'

'A cup of tea would be lovely.'

Roxy nodded and headed off towards the staff room, leaving George to contemplate his hangover. He had gone to bed last night feeling pleasantly tipsy and decidedly cheerful. He had had a wonderful evening with his friends, old and new. They had drunk and laughed, and George had marvelled at how lucky he was to have such amazing people with whom to celebrate his birthday. He had lain in bed, allowing random thoughts to float through his mind like clouds in a summer sky. How thoughtful it was of the young woman with headphones to check that he was okay. How delicious the birthday cake was that Elena had made, and how kind it was of her to take so much trouble. Was his car tax due this month or next? What would he take to work for lunch tomorrow? How strange it was that other people's deaths had made his own life so much better by bringing him new friends.

And then this morning he had woken up feeling and looking – according to Mrs Biscuit – like one of the walking dead.

'I can't hold my drink like I used to,' he told Roxy as she returned with their tea.

'That's because you're so old now,' she replied cheerfully. 'But that means it's cheaper and quicker for you to get drunk. Every cloud …'

'Speaking of weather,' George replied, nodding towards the doors, 'here comes The Shipping Forecast.'

The Shipping Forecast was another of the library's Habituals. His real name was Fitzroy Cromarty, hence his epithet. Roxy and George had speculated whether his parents had been sailors or meteorologists or had simply heard the two words broadcast daily on Radio 4 and decided that in conjunction they would make a splendid name. Either way, their son was neither weatherman nor mariner. He was short and slight with ears that were too large and long for his narrow face. Softly spoken, he had a shuffling gait and hesitant demeanour that caused him to look constantly bemused. His passions were the books of John Steinbeck and medieval cuisine. Roxy thought they should introduce him to Mrs Biscuit so they could write a recipe book together.

By lunchtime, George was feeling much better, and as he and Roxy sat in the staff room eating sandwiches and soup respectively, their conversation returned to the events of the previous day.

'Have you heard from Elizabeth today?' Roxy asked.

George shook his head. 'I texted her this morning to say that I was feeling much better – ironic, really, because I was actually feeling much worse – and asked if they'd enjoyed the show.'

'Karma can be a bitch,' Roxy teased.

'Anyway, I've heard nothing since.'

Roxy blew on a spoonful of soup. 'Are you going to ring her and confess?'

'Confess what? That I had a few too many and ended up with a hangover?'

Roxy rolled her eyes. 'Seriously, though. What are you going to do?'

'I had thought I might just brazen it out and stick to my story.'

'But what if she does it again? She's bound to, now that she's got the idea in her head. She won't stop just because it didn't work this time.'

George sighed. 'I'll cross that bridge when I come to it.'

The silence that followed stretched through comfortable to uneasy before Roxy put down her spoon and sighed. 'Why can't you just tell him?' she demanded. 'Roger's a grown man now, not a child. You don't need to protect him any more.'

George looked up at her, surprised at her outburst. 'I might not need to protect him, but perhaps I want to. He still has fond memories of his dad. I wish I did. I don't want to rob him of them,' he said quietly.

'But his memories of your dad are based on lies – or at least the deliberate concealment of facts. Doesn't he have the right to know the truth? Doesn't he have the right to know what your mum – and you – went through and then make up his own mind what he thinks about your dad?'

George could feel the anger rising within him. He tried to control it, but his voice was just a bit too calm and perilously close to patronising. 'I know it must be difficult for you to understand. Your dad was a lovely man. But mine ripped our family apart, and if I tell Roger the truth now, what would have been the point of everything that Mum and I did to keep it from him?'

'Look, George, I understand why you felt the need to protect a little boy, but what you're doing now isn't fair. You blame

Roger for betraying you and your mum by contacting your dad and for being with him when he was dying. But how can you judge Roger for that when he never knew how bad your dad was? When he never knew because you never told him? You say your dad ripped your family apart when you were a kid. Well, guess what, he's still doing it – and you're letting him by covering up what he was really like.' Roxy was clearly angry too now, and she wasn't finished either. 'Bloody hell, George – you can't have it both ways! Don't you see? It's so hypocritical!'

George stood up and threw the remains of his lunch into the bin. He couldn't cope with Roxy speaking to him like this. She was supposed to be his friend. She was supposed to have his back. What the hell did she think she knew about his family anyway?

'I know you're only trying to help, and you're entitled to your opinion, but it's my family and I'll deal with it the way I see fit,' he said sharply.

Roxy slammed her palms down on the table in exasperation. 'You're a better man than this, George. You're not a hypocrite or a martyr but that's exactly what you look like right now!'

'Well, either way, it's none of your damn business!'

He picked up his coat and bag and slammed the door on his way out.

By the time her lunchbreak was over and Roxy returned to her desk, she felt a little more composed. But she was still frustrated that George couldn't see how unfair he was being and upset about the way he had spoken to her. Yes, she had pushed him hard and asked the questions he didn't want to answer, but she had only done it because he was being an idiot. George was the one who was tearing his own family apart now. Elizabeth, and especially Roger, didn't need his protection and it was patronising of him to assume they did. And George might think she was interfering, but what she was trying to do was to be a good friend. Because that's what good friends do, isn't it? They tell you when you're being an idiot. It's called 'having your back'.

Roxy became aware of someone standing at the desk in front of her, the sense of their presence falling over her like a shadow. She looked up to see Captain.

He studied her face and frowned. 'You okay?' he muttered gruffly.

'Fine, thanks,' she replied with false brightness.

His expression hardened a little and his eyes lost their gentle enquiry and returned to neutral.

Roxy realised her mistake. 'No, actually, I'm not. I've had a row with George.'

Captain raised his eyebrows. 'Serious?'

'He thinks I'm interfering, but I'm just trying to stop him being a complete numpty.'

'Let's hope he listened,' Captain replied, poker-faced but with a wink that made Roxy smile.

'How's that gorgeous dog of yours – Sailor?'

Captain shook his head. 'He's getting fat. Too many crisps.'

Chapter 30

Case no. 63542-7580

Arthur tried to think of something nice to say as his little sister, Susan, paraded proudly up and down the kitchen in a white dress their Auntie Ella had just brought round. The dress was made of puffy material that stuck out at Susan's waist, making her look like Doris – the name they had given to the doll with the big skirt that their Grandma Nell used to cover the spare roll of Izal toilet paper in her outside privy.

'You look like Doris,' he said.

Susan stuck her tongue out at him, and Arthur's mum clipped him round the ear. 'Don't be rude to your sister. She looks beautiful. Ella, you've done a lovely job – hasn't she, Bob?' said his mum, turning to his dad who was sitting at the table cleaning out his pipe.

Arthur's mum fluffed up the frills of the skirt and stroked the big silky bow that was stitched on the waistline at the back of the dress. 'You'll have the prettiest dress in church next week, Susan. What do you say to your Auntie Ella?'

Susan ran over to her auntie and flung her arms around her.

'Thank you, Auntie Ella. It's the best dress ever! It'll be nicer than Beverley Parker's, even if her mum did buy it from her catalogue.'

Arthur was growing bored now. He was itching to go outside and play. He couldn't remember there being all this fuss over the suit he had worn for his big day in church just over three years ago.

'Of course it will!' exclaimed his mum. 'Your Auntie Ella's the best seamstress I know! And there's no way I'd be sending my daughter to her first communion in a dress from a catalogue that anyone can buy. Now go and get changed before you get it dirty.'

'Well, I'm glad you like you it,' said Auntie Ella, sitting down at the table next to her brother-in-law and pulling a packet of cigarettes from her handbag. 'But how long do I have to wait before anyone offers me a cup of tea around here?'

Arthur's mum put the kettle on to boil and fetched the biscuit tin from the pantry.

'Can I go out to play now?' Arthur asked, prising the lid off the tin and helping himself to a digestive. He was planning to go to the woods. Some older boys had tied a Tarzan rope to one of the trees beside the stream and Arthur had been longing to swing on it.

'Can I go too?' Susan had reappeared wearing shorts and a T-shirt and her most appealing smile.

'No!' said Arthur. 'You're too little. You won't be able to keep up with me.'

'Why not? Where are you going?'

Arthur ignored her question. 'Why don't you stay here and play with your dolls?'

He only said it because he knew it would wind her up. Susan wasn't keen on dolls, and despite the delight she had shown for her communion dress, she was more of a tomboy when it came to the games she liked to play.

'Muuummm ...' Susan began, dragging the word out into a whine.

'Take your sister with you, son. You can always dunk her in the stream if she misbehaves,' his dad said with a wink. 'You know how much your mum and auntie love to gossip, and it's bound to be about something unsavoury. We don't want Susan hearing anything she shouldn't and being corrupted – especially not just before her first communion.'

'Watch your cheek, you!' Arthur's mum said to his dad, setting a cup of tea down next to him. 'Me and Ella are going to be discussing the buffet for the party next week after the service. Father Dougal himself might put in an appearance, and we don't want him thinking that we can't lay on a decent spread.'

Arthur's dad stood up, pipe in hand, and picked up his tea. 'In that case, I'll go and listen to the cricket on the wireless and leave you to decide on the sausage rolls and sandwich fillings!'

Outside, the air was warm and still – but expectant rather than tranquil. It was as though the world was holding its breath, waiting for something to happen. A portly bumble bee buzzed lazily on the honeysuckle that sprawled over the wooden fence separating the garden from the fields beyond, and a pair of wood pigeons dozed in the branches of the apple tree. Arthur and Susan climbed the fence and set off across the fields, galloping over the meadow grass scattered with cowslips and daisies. The sky above them was swollen with billowing clouds that looked like giant grubby sheep, and as the children ran, they could smell the rain coming. The first fat drops fell just as they reached the cover of the woods, followed by a distant rumbling growl. Susan turned to her brother with shining eyes.

'Brilliant!' she said. 'It's going to thunder and lightning!'

At the stream, Arthur claimed first swing on the rope. 'I'm the eldest – and I have to check it's safe,' he told Susan, full of big-brother authority. Susan stood and watched with growing impatience until Arthur finally relented and helped her onto the rope.

'Hold on tight!' he instructed, then pulled her back and released her.

As she sailed through the air above the stream, spinning and kicking her legs, a crack of thunder rang out and Susan squealed with excitement. Arthur watched her from the bank and smiled. She wasn't too bad really – for a girl.

———

Arthur hung his coat up in the hall and went through to the kitchen to make himself a cup of tea. He flicked the switch on the kettle and then changed his mind and flicked it off again. What he really fancied was a glass of whiskey, and given the circumstances, what did it really matter if it was only three in the afternoon? In the sitting room he took the bottle of Jameson from the sideboard and poured a generous measure into a tumbler. He swirled the golden liquid around the glass and inhaled its sweet, spicy aroma. Nectar! He sat down in his armchair and took a deep swallow. *Just one*, he thought. Just one before he wrote the letter. After that he would get himself something to eat – a last supper – and then, who knew?

He had been to see Marie at the care home just to make sure, one more time, that she would be all right. She had been watching a quiz programme on TV, smiling at the screen, uncomprehending but seemingly perfectly content nonetheless. She had had no idea who he was, as usual. Her husband of over fifty years was a perfect stranger to her, but she had tolerated his presence in the same way one would a fellow passenger sharing a seat on the bus. Marie would be fine. The care home was a good one. The fees were taken care of, and she wouldn't notice if he visited or not. Arthur's relationship with Marie had never been a grand passion – more of a friendship that had eventually, almost imperceptibly, deepened into something more. But theirs had been a good marriage. They had had their ups and downs, like most people, but they had stayed the course. The death of a child sometimes broke a marriage apart, but not theirs. When their John had died in that car accident, grief had bound them together, each a splint for the other until they were both healed enough to face the world again. John had been twenty-two – hardly a child – but he was still their boy. Arthur's life with Marie had been steady and contented, and he considered himself lucky. He had kept the vows he had made on his wedding day until there had come a time when he could no longer care for Marie at home. And by then, she was barely Marie any more. He hoped that God would understand.

Arthur closed his eyes for a moment. He was tired. His body ached from the physical exertion of that afternoon's outing. He had walked back from the care home through the park, watching children playing on the swings, a couple of dogs chasing after a ball and a scrum of pigeons squabbling over a discarded sandwich beneath a bench. The whiskey was making him pleasantly drowsy. But that wouldn't do – not yet anyway. He pushed himself up out of the chair and went over to the stereo. Marie had eventually persuaded him to get a CD player, but he had always preferred vinyl, and now he lived alone the CD player had been banished to the loft. He dropped an album onto the turntable. The mellow bluesy tunes of Earl Humphrey and His Footwarmers were a perfect accompaniment to the Jameson. Now he was up, he might as well get on with the letter. He collected his glass and went back through to the kitchen, leaving the door open so he could still hear the music. The notepad, pen and envelope were waiting on the table. He'd never been much of a letter writer. Even birthday and Christmas cards, and the odd holiday postcard, had all been Marie's department. He picked up the pen and began.

Dear Susan

As he put down in words what he was going to do and why, he tried not to think about how angry his sister would be. She had no right to condemn him, however strong her faith was. It was his decision and one that only he had the right to make. He had thought long and hard about it. He had examined every possible route by which he could reach the inevitable destination, including the one via the clinic in Switzerland. The cost of that was well beyond his means, but he could get to where he was going just as effectively flying economy class. Arthur was not going to allow himself to finish up like Marie – a grotesquely diminished version of himself at the mercy of strangers. For Marie there had been no other option, and she was, at least, mercifully unaware of her own decline. But Arthur would have to suffer the knowledge of each and every step of his own humiliating disintegration – the agony of a sound mind trapped in a decomposing body. Already, writing was becoming difficult, the loss of strength in his right arm and hand causing his pen to slip between his fingers. And so, he had made his choice. And it had brought him not only relief, but also inestimable peace. He was leaving on his own terms, and if Susan didn't like it, then she'd just have to live with it. He finished the letter with the words

Your ever-loving brother, Arthur xxx

and then he folded it neatly and pushed it into the envelope which was already addressed to his sister.

He drained his glass and went back into the sitting room to refill it. He was hungry now and telephoned a local takeaway, The Codfather, to order a fish and chips supper for delivery. He had been using up the contents of the kitchen cupboards over the past few weeks, and his fridge was empty save for half a pint of milk and a couple of carrots. When the doorbell rang a little while later, Arthur collected his food from the door, tipping the driver with a pound coin. He debated whether to eat his supper straight from its paper wrapping but decided against it. It was the way fish and chips ought to be eaten outside, particularly by the sea, but indoors a plate felt necessary. The cod was moist and the chips crisp and delicious, and Arthur enjoyed them immensely. He was, he thought, preternaturally calm considering what he was planning for dessert. He wondered if he had gone into some sort of shock. But he felt perfectly lucid and strangely serene. He was ready and it was time.

Arthur washed his plate and knife and fork, dried them on the tea towel and put them away. He wanted to leave things nice and tidy. Finally, he took the note he had written earlier and pinned it to the front door. It was dark now, and no one would see it until the next day. Back in the sitting room, he turned the record over, and Earl Humphrey began playing 'Please Don't Talk About Me When I'm Gone'. Arthur smiled. It was strangely fitting. He picked up a framed photograph from the sideboard and several boxes of pills from one of the drawers and put them down next to his glass on a side table beside his chair. As he popped the pills from their foil packets, he gazed at the three smiling faces in the picture. Marie, Arthur and John. Going, going, gone.

Chapter 31

Briony swore as the printer beeped and flashed its annoying red light that signified that the ink cartridge had run out. She was trying to print a copy of her article about The Light a Candle Society in the office and had taken the opportunity to do so while Gordon had 'popped out to get a sandwich'. By which he usually meant an enormous hot sausage roll from the bakery next door, which he would smother in tomato ketchup and eat at his desk and the office would reek of it for the rest of the afternoon. Briony exchanged the empty cartridge for a new one and waited impatiently while the printer whirred and rattled and the digital display told her that it was 'processing'.

'Come on! Come on!' she muttered, keeping an anxious watch on the door. Gordon monitored the use of the printer with a gimlet eye and would be bound to ask what she was printing if he caught her. She managed to snatch the final page from the machine just as Gordon returned, brandishing his malodorous meat pastry.

Briony was still trying to work up the courage to pitch her story to Gordon and attempt to persuade him to publish it. But she hadn't been idle in the meantime. In fact, her procrastination had caused her to be so productive in other related areas that she had to admit to herself, at least, that dealing with everything other than Gordon had become a delaying tactic that she really needed to quit. She had set up the memorial website and linked it to a Facebook page. Neither were live yet but they were ready and waiting for George's and Niall's approval. The website had a home page explaining The Light a Candle Society and what they did, a link to a contact form for people who wanted to volunteer or contribute in some way, and memory pages for Kathleen, Derek, Josh and Claire. That just left her article. She had worked on it over the days between Christmas and New Year, when she had returned from spending Christmas Day and Boxing Day with her parents and brother back home in Essex and the office was still closed.

Briony had worried about leaving Allegra on her own for Christmas, but when she had mentioned it to her, Allegra had announced she was spending Christmas and New Year at The Savoy, as she had done for the past ten years. On her return, she had invited Briony in for martinis and asked what progress she had made with her big story. When Briony had admitted that, although she had drafted it, she still hadn't approached Gordon, Allegra had thrown up her hands in exasperation.

'What in heavens name are you waiting for?' she had said. 'Do you truly want to be a proper journalist? Because if you do, you need to show a good deal more gumption than this!'

Suitably chastised, Briony had told Allegra all about the website and the Facebook page, but Allegra had refused to be fobbed off. She had offered to read the draft and provide constructive criticism, which was why Briony had printed a copy.

That evening, Allegra must have heard Briony's car pull up on the drive because she was waiting for Briony in the hall when she came in. Allegra gazed at her expectantly, like a teacher waiting for homework to be handed in.

'I've got it!' Briony said, pulling the sheets of paper from her bag.

'Excellent!' Allegra replied, taking them from her. 'You go upstairs – freshen up and get changed – and then join me for a martini. And then we can talk about your story.'

Briony had a quick shower, pulled on some jeans and an old sweatshirt, and trotted back down the stairs. She let herself into Allegra's flat and found her, drink in hand, still poring over the printed pages. Briony sat down and took a sip from the martini Allegra had prepared for her. They sat in silence for what felt to Briony like an age, but her watch testified to being a little over two minutes.

'It's not too bad,' Allegra finally declared. 'You've covered all the facts, but I think it needs more of a human focus.'

Briony frowned. 'But it couldn't be more human. The whole story is about the only inevitable human condition – death!' she declared a little testily.

'I'm not questioning what it's about – I'm suggesting that a different approach to the subject matter might have a greater impact. What you've written is simply factual reporting. It needs more heart – more emotion to engage your readers and make them want to read on.'

Briony had worked hard on the story, and she was proud of it. She wondered for a moment what qualified Allegra to appraise her work and whether she should listen to her. Perhaps, she reflected ruefully, because Allegra was an intelligent and erudite woman who had a good deal more life experience than Briony, although exactly what kind of life had proffered this experience she had still to discover. The galling thing was that Briony knew that Allegra was right. She had recorded all the facts about the funerals, and the people who had died, and what The Light a Candle Society did, but in studiously avoiding anything that might be regarded as mawkish, she now realised the story had lost its heart.

'Perhaps it should begin with George,' she said, thinking aloud. 'I could start it off as an interview with him and then move on to the rest of it.'

'That sounds much more promising,' agreed Allegra. 'George is your leading man – just an ordinary chap, a widower and part-time librarian, who's taken it upon himself to do an extraordinary thing for people he's never met who have no one else to remember them. And what's more, he's persuading others to join him. People love an unexpected hero.'

Briony began rewriting in her head. Suddenly, she was desperate to get back to her laptop. She drank her martini as quickly as she dared on an empty stomach and then got up.

'Do you mind if I go, Allegra? I just want to get this sorted while it's fresh in my mind.'

Allegra smiled. 'Of course not. You're a journalist – your writing should come first.'

Briony retrieved the printed draft and practically galloped back up the stairs to her flat.

It was a little after 2 am when she finally leaned back in her chair and stretched her arms above her head. There was a satisfying if rather painful click, followed by a series of bony crunches as she rolled her shoulders to release the tension in her neck and back. At last, it was done. She decided that she would send it to Gordon tonight – except it was now this morning. She would email her pitch and her story and give him a chance to think about it before she had to face him. Her first assignment of the day was to interview a woman who was self-publishing a book about the life of her grandmother, a Mrs Euphemia Perkins. According to the brief Briony had been given, Euphemia – known as Effie – had been a seamstress and self-appointed wise woman who had practised natural healing. She had allegedly been able to treat varicose veins, bunions, gout and constipation with admirable success, and her wart-charming skills had been the talk of the town. Briony was going to visit the author at home to conduct the interview, so she wouldn't be in the office until late morning, by which time Gordon would hopefully have read her email.

Briony wasn't a smoker. She had been in her first year as a journalism student, mainly for effect – and to fit in with her peers. But the cost of smoking soon became prohibitive, and as Briony could take it or leave it, she decided to leave it. So now she was a non-smoker. Pretty much. She kept a pack of 'emergency' cigarettes in the flat and smoked on average around three a year. This morning, she was going to smoke her first of this year. She didn't know if it was a reward for finishing the story or an incentive to encourage her to send it to Gordon. It wasn't even that she enjoyed the smoking itself much – it was more the ritual. The taking a little time to herself to deliberately and defiantly do something that was largely frowned upon these days. It was a tiny act of rebellion that made her feel reckless and slightly naughty for just a few moments. She found the packet tucked away at the back of her underwear drawer and removed a single cigarette. She let herself out of the flat and tip-toed downstairs. It was cold outside, and she shivered, but you couldn't put on a coat to sneak outside and have a fag. Such a sensible precaution would spoil the whole spirit of the thing. She stood by the hedge, trying to look both insouciant and inconspicuous as she lit her cigarette and took a cautious drag. At that moment a car pulled onto the drive, and she was caught in its headlights. The lights went out and the driver door slammed shut.

'I didn't know you smoked.' It was Zach, her 'police contact' who lived in the flat opposite hers.

'I don't,' Briony replied. 'It's just a rare aberration.'

Zach checked his watch. 'It's almost 2.30 am. I've just finished my shift – what's your excuse?'

'I've just finished writing a piece for the paper – the one I told you I was researching.'

'So when will I be able to read it in *The T and H*?'

Briony shrugged and flicked the ash from her cigarette. 'Maybe never. I've got to persuade my boss to run it yet.'

'I know some dodgy sorts I could get to lean on him if you like,' Zach replied with a grin.

'Thanks for the offer, but it's a good story and I have to make him see that myself. I need to get him to take me seriously.'

She stubbed out her cigarette, and they made their way inside and climbed the stairs. On the landing outside their respective flats, they each paused for a moment.

'I don't suppose you fancy a beer, seeing as you're awake?' Zach asked. 'I always have one to wind down a bit after a shift before I eat and go to bed, and it would be nice to have some company for a change.'

Briony was tempted but she shook her head. 'I have to get this story sent off – accompanied by a professional and extremely persuasive email – and I don't think a beer would help my concentration.'

'Fair enough. Well, good luck.' He sounded disappointed.

Briony pushed her key into the lock, and then turned back to Zach. 'But maybe another time. That would be nice – for a beer, I mean.'

Zach nodded. 'Yeah, it would.'

Back at her desk, Briony steeled herself for her final task before she went to bed.

The email was a strong and succinct pitch for a feature article that Gordon really ought to publish, Briony assured him, because people would definitely want to read about – 'The Man Who Lights the Candles'.

Chapter 32

George removed the dead dahlias from Audrey's headstone and replaced them with some white roses and alstroemeria.

'I feel like a pariah!' he told his wife as he rubbed at a mark on the black marble with his finger.

That morning at the library, Roxy had been polite but no more and had largely kept out of his way. The atmosphere between them had been decidedly frosty, and George was desperate to effect a thaw but clueless how to go about it without a full capitulation on his part. He *was* sorry for upsetting her, and he knew he could have expressed himself more civilly, but was she right? Was he being hypocritical and behaving like a martyr?

'You know full well she is!' Audrey's voice was loud and clear in his head. *'I told you that you were being unreasonable about Roger, but you were always so stubborn about it! In the end, I kept quiet, hoping you might eventually come to your senses.'*

George busied himself arranging the fresh flowers, pretending not to hear her. He had decided against telling

Elizabeth the truth about his absence from his own birthday lunch, sticking to his story of a twenty-four-hour bug, from which he had fortunately made a swift recovery. He had glossed over the details and remembered not to mention his night out at The Duck and Donkey when he had spoken to her on the phone last night, concentrating instead on questioning her solicitously about her stay in London and the musical they had seen. But he was conscious that all he had done was buy himself some time and that he would have to face the music at some point. George was certain that Elizabeth wouldn't let the matter drop and would simply arrange another 'surprise' for him. He could hardly refuse to meet up with his daughter and her family indefinitely. As he pondered this conundrum, his mobile rang. It was Niall.

'How was your weekend, George?'

'Good, thanks,' he lied, having spent most of it worrying about his row with Roxy and his lies to Elizabeth. 'What about yours?'

'Hmm. Interesting. My daughter came to stay and I'm not sure I really understand teenagers.'

'Nobody does, mate. Except other teenagers. What can I do for you?'

'There's going to be another funeral – but this one's a bit complicated. If you want to do something for it, do you fancy meeting up in The Duck and Donkey one night after work and I'll tell you all about it over a couple of shandies?'

'I'd love to,' George replied, only too glad to have the prospect of something to take his mind off his own problems.

They settled on Thursday night and agreed to meet an hour

before the quiz. Niall had planned to stay afterwards and cheer on George's team, but when he arrived at the pub, he told George that he would be acting as a substitute for Roxy. 'She texted me earlier to say she wouldn't be able to make it and would I like to stand in for her. Didn't she tell you?'

George stared gloomily into his pint. It hadn't been an easy week. 'I'm afraid that Roxy and I are barely on speaking terms at the moment.'

Niall raised his eyebrows. 'Anything you'd like to talk about?'

'Maybe later. But let's get this funeral sorted first.'

Niall pushed a folder across the table towards George. 'I've made some notes for you, but I'll just run through the basics. It's a chap called Arthur Chambers and he was seventy-six. I'm waiting for the official word from the coroner, but it's pretty much certain that he took his own life. He left a note on his front door, hoping that someone would see it. The postman found it and did what the note instructed him to do. He called the police. When they came, they broke in and found the place all neat and tidy and Arthur sitting dead in his armchair. On the table beside him were an empty glass of whiskey and several packets that had contained prescription drugs. He'd also left a note for his sister, which the police read before passing on to me – the coroner needed to see the contents. The police informed the sister of Arthur's death and I spoke to her subsequently.'

'But if he has a sister, why will you need to arrange his funeral? Surely she will want to do it?'

Niall sighed heavily. 'It's a really difficult situation. Arthur's sister, Susan, is a devout Catholic. It seems they were both brought up in the faith, but for Susan it's the cornerstone of her life. In her view, Arthur's suicide is unforgivable – a mortal sin.'

'I thought the Church took a more lenient view these days?'

'It does. But it appears that Susan does not. When I spoke to her, the poor woman was devasted. But I couldn't tell what had hurt her the most – her brother's death or the fact that he had killed himself. At the moment, she's refusing to have anything to do with the arrangements and says she won't come to the funeral. Arthur also has a wife, Marie, but she's in a care home and in the final stages of Alzheimer's. Apparently, she hasn't recognised her husband or anyone else for the last year or so. The care home tells me that Arthur paid her fees in advance for the next six months and she's unlikely to live any longer than that. The only other close relative was their son, who was killed in a car crash back in 1998. So unless Susan changes her mind, which seems unlikely, I'm afraid I have to take her at her word and proceed as though Arthur has no family. I can't force her to do anything.'

'Do we have any idea why Arthur did it?'

'That's the saddest thing of all. I reckon he had a very good reason. Arthur had been diagnosed with motor neurone disease. He said in his letter that he knew exactly what he was doing because he was not prepared to become trapped in his own body and completely dependent on the care of strangers. He wanted to die under his own steam with his dignity intact.'

'He was clearly a brave man.'

'I think so too, but his explanation only convinced Susan of his sin – her word, not mine. You see, the fact that he consciously decided to die and then took his own life are proof to Susan that he deliberately, knowingly disobeyed God. Well, her God at least. Had the balance of his mind been disturbed or he'd been suffering from mental illness, both the Church and possibly Susan might be more forgiving. From what I can understand, the Catholic Church these days has a few more caveats regarding suicide which are open to interpretation and would quite probably save Arthur's soul from eternal damnation, but Susan is immovable.'

George sipped his pint thoughtfully. Arthur's fate put his own problems firmly into perspective. 'Well, of course we'll do something for him,' he said. 'What else do we know about him?'

'I've got some photos, so we can use one of those at the funeral. But as Susan has said she wants nothing from the house, I'll have to arrange for it to be emptied. Thankfully, Arthur left a will which was pretty straightforward. The proceeds of his estate are to be used to pay for a basic funeral for himself and to support Marie in the care home. What remains after she dies and her funeral is paid for goes to Susan. I've spoken to the firm that Arthur used, and his solicitor is named as an executor along with Susan, who, unsurprisingly, has flatly declined the role. The solicitor has given me the go-ahead, so I'm going to ask Sid to do the house clearance. I thought maybe you could arrange to go with him and see what you could find that might help us get to know Arthur a bit better and give him a suitable send-off?'

'I'll pop in and see Sid tomorrow,' George replied.

'I get the impression that Arthur was a really decent man,' said Niall, turning his glass round and round on a beer mat and studying its contents. 'He made sure that everything was in order before he died – almost as though he wanted to cause as little trouble as possible. He went to see his wife – presumably to say goodbye – and paid her fees in advance. He left a note on his front door so that no one other than the police would walk in and find his body. He covered the chair he was sitting in with a waterproof picnic rug, and George, he'd even emptied his cupboards and fridge of any perishable food. He thought of everything. I reckon he truly deserves a proper funeral.'

'And we'll make sure he gets one. I wonder if he had an idea how Susan would react?'

'I'm sure it must have crossed his mind. But maybe he thought that, given the circumstances, she might show him some mercy, so to speak.'

There's still time for that, George thought to himself.

'Good evening, gents! Can I get anyone a drink?' Edwin shrugged off his coat and hung it over the back of a chair. 'I hope you've got your lucky shirt on, George. I reckon it's going to be a tough one tonight!'

Chapter 33

It had taken Gordon Bullock almost a week to get round to reading Briony's story. He had acknowledged her email the morning after she had sent it and simply said that he would take a look when he got a moment. Briony knew he was doing it on purpose to wind her up. During that week he had found plenty of moments to discuss the merits of Arsenal's new centre forward with Dave 'Dosh', the accounts manager, and to play Wordle on his phone and to book a weekend break in Paris online for his wife's upcoming birthday, all on the paper's time. Finally, on Friday morning he called her name across the office without getting up from his chair and beckoned to her to join him at his desk. She sat down without waiting to be asked, and she saw his mouth twitch with annoyance.

'I've had a look at your candle man story.'

Briony detected a slight inflection on the words 'candle man' and couldn't decide if it was intended to be disparaging.

Gordon wrinkled his nose which had the effect of dilating his pudgy nostrils, giving Briony an unwelcome view of his unkempt nasal hair. 'I'm not altogether sure it's the kind of thing that would appeal to our readers.'

'Why not?' Gordon's procrastination had worked in winding Briony up and her frustration made her bolder. Less Briony, more Allegra. 'It's a human-interest story. It's exactly what you always say I should be writing about. Let me see – "extraordinary stories about ordinary folks". Isn't that what you said? Isn't that what you have always told me our readers love?'

Gordon pushed out his chest, and consequently his belly, and huffed. 'It's a bit morbid – writing about people dying alone and their sad little funerals. It isn't exactly going to cheer anyone up, is it?'

'Oh, so we can only write happy news, is that what you're saying? Funny that, because I could have sworn we covered a manslaughter trial last week and an armed robbery the week before that.'

Gordon leaned back in his chair. '*We* didn't cover an armed robbery and a manslaughter trial. Simon did.'

Briony shook her head in disbelief. 'So what you're saying is that I can only cover the fluff, whilst he gets to do the serious stuff? Isn't that a bit sexist?'

Gordon closed his eyes for a moment and sighed deeply. 'Why is it that you women always claim discrimination if you don't get your own way? It's got nothing to do with sex and everything to do with experience. Simon is our senior reporter.'

'But how am I supposed to get experience if you won't let me write about anything other than misshapen fruit and vegetables, sponsored cross-stitch-athons and frivolously litigious supermarket shoppers?'

'I'll let you cover more stories when you're ready. You've only been here a few months. Don't try to run before you can walk.'

'I've been here over a year,' Briony replied icily.

Gordon smiled at her, and she could have slapped him. 'Look, I'm not saying there isn't a story there, with that chap George and his cronies. I just think it needs a different approach.'

Briony's face was red with fury. She wasn't giving up, but she was stepping away from the fray for the moment, before she said something unprofessional and quite probably offensive. She got up and started back towards her desk.

'Briony,' Gordon called after her in a placatory tone. She turned and he smiled at her again. 'Just leave it with me. I'll have a think about it.'

At lunchtime, Briony went to the café across the road from *The T and H* office. She normally ate something at her desk, or in her car if she was out on an assignment. But today, she couldn't bear to be in the same room as Gordon for any longer than was strictly necessary. She ordered a bowl of soup and took a seat by the window, where she proceeded to tear a paper napkin into shreds. Not only was she furious with Gordon for belittling her story, but she was also mortified at her failure to deliver what she had promised to George and the others. Yes, she had set up the website, but it would be much harder to publicise it without the article in *The Times and Herald*. She was going to look like a complete fool. And to top it all, Allegra was going to be disappointed in her. Allegra, the woman whom she had come to admire so much and whose approbation she held so dear. *Shit!* she thought to herself as she ripped another strip off the napkin. *Shit! Shit! Shit!* A waitress brought her soup, and Briony burned her mouth on the first spoonful. As she gulped down some water in an attempt to soothe the pain, she heard her mobile ringing in her bag. She fished it out and answered. It wasn't a number she recognised.

'It's Edwin. Are you all right?' he asked. 'You sound a bit funny.'

'I just burned my tongue on my soup.'

'You should have blown on it first.'

'Thanks, Edwin. What's up?'

'I'm not sure. But it could be something fishy.'

Briony was already intrigued as to why Edwin should ring her, but now there was something fishy as well.

'Have you written your story yet?'

'Yes – I have,' replied Briony slowly, 'but I'm not sure when it's going to be published yet.' It wasn't a lie.

'Well, it seems you're not the only one wanting to pick my brains about public health funerals. Yesterday a man rang here asking about exactly the same thing. Our receptionist gave him some basic information, but he was pretty keen to speak to me too, so she asked him to call back this morning when she knew I'd be in. This chap told me he'd heard about something called The Light a Candle Society and asked if I had anything to do with it. I asked him why he wanted to know, and he said he was a journalist and he was just doing some research for a piece he was thinking of writing. It all seems a bit dodgy to me. I reckon he's trying to steal your story.'

Briony drew a sharp intake of breath. 'Who was he? What was his name?'

'Simon. Simon Sinclair.'

Fifteen minutes later, Briony had spoken to George and Elena and left a message for Niall. According to Elena, a man had been in her shop asking questions about The Light a Candle Society and Elena had told him that he would need to speak to George. Simon had rung George that morning and left a message, but George had been at work and had only just listened to it when Briony rung.

'I won't ring him back,' George promised. 'It's your story. And if he calls again, I won't answer.'

Briony had always liked Simon. He had been kind to her when she had first started at *The T and H*, showing her the ropes and including her in conversations at tea and lunch breaks before she knew anyone. But over the past months she had seen less of him, as they were both frequently out of the office on assignments and working more from home. Would Simon really knowingly have stolen her story? Could he possibly have heard about The Light a Candle Society from somewhere else and be pursuing it without any knowledge that she had covered it first? There was only one way to find out. She punched his number into her phone. To her surprise, he picked up straightaway.

'Briony. Hi, how are you?'

He didn't sound like a man who had done the dirty on her.

Briony cut straight to the chase. 'Simon, are you writing a story on a man called George McGlory and The Light a Candle Society?'

'I am. Why – do you know him?'

'Of course I know him – I've even been to some of the funerals! But more importantly, I've already written an article about them. I showed it to Gordon, but he said he wasn't sure if it was the kind of thing our readers would be interested in.'

There was a brief silence before Simon replied, his tone hardening. 'I'm so sorry, Briony. I had no idea. That duplicitous bastard! He told me he'd heard about this guy who had started going to the funerals of complete strangers who had no family, and he'd started a group of volunteers called The Light a Candle Society to make the funerals more meaningful. He said it would make a great piece for the paper and asked me to get cracking on it straightaway. He completely failed to mention that it was your idea and you'd already pitched a story to him. I always knew he could be a bit of an arrogant dickhead, but to do this is a fucking disgrace!'

For a moment, Briony wondered if it might not be better to let Simon write the story. He was, after all, the senior reporter. Gordon clearly thought he would make a better job of it, and at least it would get published, which was surely the most important thing for George and Niall and the others.

'Maybe you *should* write the story,' she said quietly. 'Gordon will never print mine.'

'No – absolutely not! And don't be so sure about Gordon. I can be very persuasive. Are you in the office tomorrow morning?'

'Yes. Why?'

'Send me over your story now – including any photos. And make sure you're at your desk for 10.30 am tomorrow.'

THE LIGHT A CANDLE SOCIETY

Briony was at her desk ready and waiting when Simon breezed in the next morning, went straight over to Gordon's desk and sat down.

'Morning, Gordon. How's things? Did you get that story I sent over about The Light a Candle Society?'

Gordon glanced over at Briony, who stared hard at her laptop, pretending to be engrossed in something on her screen. 'I did,' Gordon replied in a much quieter voice than his usual bray. 'Let's go and get a coffee and we can have a chat about it,' he said, pushing himself up out of his chair.

Simon waved him back down. 'No time, I'm afraid, Gordon. I've got another job on this morning. Just tell me if you're happy with it or if you want any changes?'

'No, no. It's fine as it is. Great.' Gordon nodded a little too vigorously and shuffled some papers on his desk.

'What do you think about the title – "The Man Who Lights the Candles"? I was pretty chuffed with that.' Simon also seemed pretty pleased with himself as he watched Gordon fidget uneasily in his seat.

'Yes. Very good.'

'So when will we be running it? If you're happy with it as it is, there's no reason why it can't run next week. I've probably given you too many photos, but I'll leave it to you to decide which ones to use,' Simon added generously.

'Yes – let's say next week then,' Gordon replied briskly.

'Great,' said Simon, getting up. 'Hi, Briony – how's it going?' he asked, as though he had only just noticed her.

She raised her eyebrows and Simon winked at her. When he reached the door of the office, he turned back. 'Oh, and Gordon ...'

His boss looked up at him, irritation written all over his face.

'That story is Briony's – she wrote every word. So make sure it's her name on the byline.'

Chapter 34

'What do you reckon?' Sid asked, patting the side of the handsome wooden cabinet that was loaded onto his van. 'This should do the job nicely!'

The cabinet was a good six inches taller than George and had glass panels on three sides so that anything inside it could be easily seen.

'It's perfect!' George agreed. 'But will it be okay outside in all weathers?'

'It'll be fine. The wood's been treated with preservative, and in any case, it's going to be under cover in that sheltered spot by the ornamental pond that Niall mentioned. You'll see for yourself in a minute.'

George raised his eyebrows. He had been under the impression they were going to Arthur's house to begin the clearance.

'I thought seeing as I've got some extra manpower for the afternoon, you could help me drop it off at the cemetery. James, the cremation technician, and Jack – he's the gravedigger – are meeting us up there, and they'll give us a hand to unload it and shift it into place.'

An hour later, after a good deal of huffing and puffing and manoeuvring this way and that, the cabinet was in position and the four men stood back to admire it.

'I suppose it'll look better when it's got something in it,' said Jack doubtfully.

'Of course it will!' declared James. 'I think it's a great idea. The funerals of those people are so sad. I always say their names out loud before I wish them "bon voyage and God bless" and push their coffins into the burner. I make sure I look after them as well as everyone else who comes in here. But I can't help wishing they had someone there, on the other side of the curtain in the chapel, to see them on their way. Someone who cared that they had been in this world and made their mark, however small, before they left it.'

Jack shrugged. 'But I don't see how this cabinet full of odds and ends is going to help.'

'It's a memorial,' explained George. 'Each thing in the cabinet will be a permanent reminder of the person who owned it. Each object will say about that person "I was here, and I mattered".'

Sid handed a small key each to James and George. 'I thought it best that we keep it locked. We don't want anyone pinching anything.'

Arthur Chambers had lived and died in a narrow Victorian semi with bay windows, a pitched roof porch and a small front garden that consisted of a neat square of gravel and clusters of potted plants. A passageway shared with the neighbours ran down the side of the house, giving access to the back garden. Sid drove his van slowly down the street trying to find somewhere to park.

'It's always a bugger doing clearances around here,' he told George. 'These houses weren't built for people with cars, and those bloody passageways are a nightmare for getting furniture in and out. I once got a piano completely stuck in one of them.'

'How did you get it out?'

'I had to chop it up. Good job it was a house clearance rather than a removals job.'

George laughed. 'It's like that song – "Right Said Fred".'

Sid frowned. 'What – that one about I'm too sexy for my shirt?'

George shook his head in mock despair. 'I'm showing my age now! No, the song about shifting a piano by Bernard Cribbins.'

Sid managed to squeeze the van into a space at the top of the street and they walked back down to Arthur's house. Sid had to force the front door a little to push back the post that had accumulated on the floor. Inside, the house smelled fresh and clean, and each room they passed through was neat and tidy. It felt almost as though the occupants had left it like that before going away for a while – perhaps on holiday – so that it would make for a pleasant welcome on their return. But Arthur would not be returning, thought George. And somehow the pristine state of the house – the result of Arthur's meticulous planning, preparation and execution of his ending – was even more poignant than the gentle chaos George had encountered in Claire's home.

'I'm just going to nip back to the van to get a few boxes,' Sid said, having finished a quick tour of the premises. 'I'm not going to be shifting any of the big stuff until I can park nearer to the house, but I can pack up some of the smaller stuff today.'

George began his quest for the man whom Arthur had been in the sitting room. The first thing that caught his eye was the large collection of vinyl records. As he searched through the albums it occurred to him that he and Arthur had very similar taste in music. There was Motown, old-school R&B, some Northern Soul and even some David Bowie and Rolling Stones. There was an album on the turntable. This must have been the last record that Arthur had played. George lifted it up gently with his fingertips and inspected the label. Earl Humphrey and His Footwarmers. They were new to George. He replaced the record on the turntable and pushed the play button. He tried to imagine for a moment what it would feel like knowing that this was the last music you would ever hear. In this life, at least. He wondered if Arthur had chosen it specifically and if it had some special meaning for him, or whether it was simply an old favourite selected as a comforting soundtrack to his final scene. George's reverie was interrupted by the sound of the door opening. Sid strode into the room grinning from ear to ear and brandishing a newspaper he had nabbed from the delivery boy in the street.

'Well, George,' he declared, 'it looks like you're famous!'

Sid opened the latest copy of *The Times and Herald* and pointed to the lead article on the second page, where a photograph of George standing outside the chapel at the crematorium was printed under the heading 'The Man Who Lights the Candles – by Briony Harris'.

When George got home, he brewed himself a cup of tea and sat down to make a phone call that he had been putting off for several days now. The visit to Arthur's home and the story in *The Times and Herald* had given him the motivation – or perhaps the courage – to speak to Susan Blacklock, Arthur's sister. Niall had asked him if he would make a last-ditch attempt to persuade her to come to Arthur's funeral. He had been obliged to ask Susan's permission before sharing her phone number with George, and she had surprisingly consented. The service itself wouldn't take place for a couple of weeks yet, which could give Susan time to reconsider her hitherto adamant stance if only George could think of something to say that might make her change her mind.

The phone rang several times before a woman answered. 'Hello. Who's this?' she asked warily.

George tried for his friendliest tone. 'Hello, is that Susan Blacklock?'

It was.

'My name's George McGlory and I'm –'

'I know who you are,' Susan replied in a friendly tone. 'I've just been reading about you in the paper, and that nice man from the council, Mr Laughlin, told me that you might ring.'

'Then perhaps you also know that I'll be helping Niall – Mr Laughlin – to organise Arthur's funeral?'

George paused, wondering what on earth he could say next. He was up against the Almighty in Susan's eyes – a David and Goliath contest – but this time Susan's God *was* Goliath and the only stones George had to fling were words.

'I just wanted to ask if you would think again about coming. I understand that you believe what Arthur did was wrong, but he was facing a terrible terminal illness and his death, had he not chosen to take matters into his own hands, would most likely have been protracted and painful. Surely he can be forgiven for avoiding that in the only way that was open to him? And isn't there a chance that, however strongly you feel about it now, there may come a day when you regret not going to Arthur's funeral – not taking the chance to say your final goodbye?'

George was fully aware that he was speaking out of turn. He had never met Arthur nor Susan and he was presuming to tell her how she ought to feel about her own brother. But his was the only voice that Arthur had now. He was Arthur's sole advocate.

Susan's voice was choked with emotion when she replied. 'I know you mean well, Mr McGlory, but I was raised a Catholic and so was Arthur. He knew that what he was doing was a mortal sin. He *knew* – but he still did it. Please understand, it's not that I didn't love my brother. I loved him more than I can say ...'

There was a sob, and George felt a complete heel for upsetting this already grieving woman as he waited in silence for her to continue.

'But if I were to go to his funeral, I would be condoning his sin – and I can't. However much it hurts, I just can't. I live my life by my faith, and if I abandon my faith, then my life becomes meaningless.'

George knew then that there was nothing more he could say to persuade her. Susan's Goliath God had won.

'Well, I'm so sorry to have upset you at what I know must be a very difficult time – and I am truly sorry for your loss,' George said, aware that he was speaking in clichés but unable to think of a more original way to express his genuine feelings.

'Thank you for at least listening to me, and I'll make sure you have the details about Arthur's funeral as soon as it's arranged just so that you … know,' he finished, rather lamely.

'And thank you, Mr McGlory, for trying,' Susan replied. 'I don't expect you to understand, but I do think that what you're doing – with those funerals – it's a wonderful thing. God bless you and your Light a Candle Society, Mr McGlory.'

George hung up the phone and sighed, his conscience pricked. He remembered the time Roger had rung him and pleaded with him to go to their dad's funeral. George had been as resolute in his refusal as Susan, but he was beginning to wonder if the justification for his decision had been as questionable as hers was now. Perhaps it was George who regretted missing the chance to say his final goodbye?

Chapter 35

'Congratulations my dear!' Allegra raised her martini glass and gently clinked it against Briony's. 'I knew you could do it.'

'It was all down to Edwin in the end, though,' Briony replied. 'If he hadn't warned me about what was going on it would have been Simon's story and not mine that was published.'

'From what you've told me, that boss of yours is a snake in the grass!' Allegra pronounced, her voice clipped with disdain. 'So how exactly did your colleague persuade him to publish it and credit it to you?'

'I sent my copy to Simon, and he made a few editorial tweaks before he passed it on to Gordon. He reckons Gordon didn't bother to read it properly when I sent it to him the first time – just picked up on the general idea and instructed Simon to follow it up. So when Simon sent it to him, he didn't recognise it as my original story. He just assumed that Simon had written it and gave it a green light. When Simon told him the truth, he had no choice but to publish it under my name or not at all.'

'And however odious a man he is, he clearly recognised a good story when he saw it,' Allegra added. 'What sort of feedback have you had so far?'

Briony grinned. 'Well, the best news is that one of the Sunday nationals has expressed an interest and might run the story later in the month. We've also had lots of hits on the website and Facebook page – mainly people saying what a wonderful thing George and The Light a Candle Society are doing. We've had quite a few people asking if they can attend the funerals too and several offers of specific help. A local vicar has offered to conduct any services she can for free, and a community choir has volunteered to come and sing at any funeral where they'd be wanted if enough of their members are free on the day. We've also had a poet offer to write poems to be read at the funerals.'

'A poet?' Allegra raised her eyebrows and flashed a wicked smile. 'Let's hope that he or she is good, otherwise you could end up with a verse that's the equivalent of a cheesy greetings card –

May flights of angels bear you up to your eternal rest,
You were our sunrise in the east, our sunset in the
  west.
Your smile was bright, your heart was warm, your
  laugh was loud and merry,
We loved you wife, mum, sister, nan, like you loved a
  glass of sherry!'

Briony spluttered into her martini. 'Did you just make that up?'

'Certainly not! I read it in an obituaries column once. It's so dreadful that it has remained burned into my memory ever since. So don't say I didn't warn you – beware the poet!'

'Well, it won't be up to me. It'll be up to George and the other members of The Light a Candle Society.'

Allegra sipped her martini. Her eyes were fixed on Briony and her expression was thoughtful. Briony immediately got the impression she'd said something wrong.

'What?' she asked. 'What is it?'

Allegra put down her glass. 'You're not joining them?'

It hadn't occurred to Briony that she might become a member of The Light a Candle Society. 'I haven't really thought about it – but no, I wasn't planning to.'

'So who will look after the website and the Facebook page?'

Briony shrugged. 'It's not that difficult. I suppose I'll just show George or maybe Roxy how to do it.'

Briony had the distinct impression that her answers were not passing muster with Allegra. But what did she expect? She couldn't become personally involved in every story she wrote about.

'Does George know that? Did you make it clear to him and the others that you were only getting involved so you could write about it?'

There was no rancour in Allegra's voice, but her forthright questions had Briony doubting herself. Was Allegra implying that Briony had somehow taken advantage of George by insinuating herself into The Light a Candle Society simply for the sake of her story, and now that she had written it, she was going to cut and run? She recalled Roxy's sceptical questions when Briony had suggested setting up the website. She had only promised to get it up and running – which she had done.

'I've done everything I said I would,' Briony replied, a little defensively.

Allegra smiled. 'I'm not suggesting for one moment that you should get involved if you don't want to. I just remember how moved you were when you went to Josh's funeral and how much you wanted to help. I got the impression then that it was about more than just a piece for the paper – but perhaps I was wrong. Would you like another drink?'

Briony shook her head. 'Thank you, but I can't. I'm going out.'

Her cheeks reddened a little and Allegra raised her eyebrows. 'Am I allowed to ask with whom?'

Briony grinned, relieved that the tension that had begun to escalate between them had suddenly dissipated. 'I'm going out for a pizza with Zach.'

'Ah – the officer of the law across your landing. Have a lovely time!'

'Congratulations!' Zach raised his bottle of beer to Briony and then took a swig. 'It's a great story – you must be really pleased.'

'I am,' Briony replied, whilst actually thinking, *I was, until Allegra muddied the water.*

'So, what's next for *The Times and Herald*'s intrepid reporter?'

'I'm not sure,' said Briony running her finger down the condensation on the outside of her beer bottle. 'More of the usual dross if Gordon has his way. But the response to the article has been really good so far. One of the Sunday nationals is considering running it, and if they do it will definitely give me a bit more leverage with Mr Bollocks.'

'And what about the bloke who's doing the funerals and his Light a Candle Society? Has it helped them?'

Briony nodded. 'They've had lots of hits on the website and Facebook page, and various people offering their services and volunteering to go to the funerals.'

'Everyone's a winner in that case! You got your story, and they got their publicity. At least you won't have to go to any more of those funerals now.'

'No, I won't *have* to – but I might want to.' Her response came out like a reflex. So maybe it was true. Or maybe it was Allegra putting thoughts in her head.

'Damn Allegra!' Briony muttered under her breath.

'Who?'

Briony looked up at Zach's puzzled face. 'Sorry – nothing. I was just thinking about something Allegra said.'

'The mysterious Allegra Monteverdi! You're quite friendly with her, aren't you?'

'I suppose so. She invites me in for martinis a couple of times a week and I love chatting with her. She's fascinating – but I'm not sure I know much more about her now than I did the first time I met her.'

'What's her flat like?'

'Beautiful! She has souvenirs from all around the world. No touristy tat, though – more objets d'art.'

'She's well travelled, then?'

'Yes. According to Allegra it was for her work.'

'And what was that?'

Briony laughed. 'You sound as though you're gathering evidence!'

'Force of habit. But I bet you're no different – always asking questions, trying to sniff out a story.'

Briony grinned sheepishly. He had a point. 'Allegra's very cagey about what she did for a living. But she told me that she used to live in Mayfair.'

'Bloody hell! Whatever she did must have paid well.'

'She said she couldn't really talk about it, but that she did something in "communications".'

'What perfect irony!' Zach exclaimed. 'Maybe she worked for MI5 – something undercover. Maybe she was a spy!'

Briony was pretty sure Zach was joking, but thinking about it, why not? Briony wouldn't put anything past Allegra. She was beautiful, intelligent and probably exceptional in other ways that Briony had yet to discover. And she was also very secretive. Briony's musings were interrupted by a waiter who arrived at their table with their pizzas.

'Thank God,' said Zach, spreading his napkin on his lap. 'I'm absolutely starving!'

Chapter 36

Happy birthday to me, thought Roxy a little morosely as she opened the four cards she had received. Four cards to mark the four decades that had passed since the day she'd been born. They brought greetings from an old school friend whom she occasionally met for lunch or a night out, her Aunt Iris – her mother's sister – who lived in the Lake District, Tracey, a colleague at the library who worked on the days George didn't, and one from her mum, which one of the care home staff must have posted for her. Roxy was going to see her later, and she was touched that her mum had sent it so she could have it first thing on her birthday morning. George would probably have a card for her too, but she hadn't told him she was taking a day's holiday and Tracey would be covering for her today.

Her relationship with George was still strained. She had hoped he would apologise for the way he had spoken to her. But she could now concede that she had delivered some home truths that had undoubtedly been hard for him to hear, and perhaps not as diplomatically as she might have done. So they had reached an uncomfortable impasse. Roxy had not wanted to spend her birthday at work with George for fear that he would produce a card, a gift and a cake, as he usually did, but the day would just be an awkward and hollow imitation of their previous celebrations. Or worse still, that George would fail to acknowledge her special day altogether.

After an indulgent breakfast of a frothy cappuccino and two pains au chocolat, Roxy set off for the care home. Although the silvery winter sun gave off no warmth, the sky was bright and clear and the air was crisp, making her walk a pleasant one. Roxy's visit with her mum was short, so as not to tire the old lady, but it lifted Roxy's spirits considerably. Her mum slept for hours during the day now, as well as at night, but when she was awake, she was still as sharp as ever and loved to share with Roxy all the gossip about the care home and its residents.

'Mr Liptrop lost his lower denture yesterday,' she told Roxy. 'He had it in his mouth in the morning, but by lunchtime it had gone. He had to make do with tomato soup instead of fish and chips. He wasn't happy. Fish and chips are his favourite. There was such a hoo-ha – they thought he'd swallowed it. But it turned up in his glasses case when he went to the TV lounge to watch a rerun of *Randal and Hopkirk Deceased*.'

'That must have been a relief,' Roxy replied with a grin. 'And at least he could have more than soup for supper.'

'Well, he could have done. But it was macaroni cheese. Mr Liptrop doesn't like macaroni cheese. It's not the taste – it's the texture, he says. Too slimy. Anyway, enough about Mr Liptrop, what about you? Have you got anything nice planned for your birthday?'

'I'm already doing something nice,' Roxy replied, patting her mum's hand. 'I'm visiting you!'

'Yes, but you can do that any day! I mean later on. Have you got a date with one of those men you get online?'

'Mum! You make them sound like male escorts! Anyway, I've given up on dating sites. I never seem to meet anyone I want to see for a second date. In fact, I never seem to meet anyone I really want to see for a first date.'

'You need to get out more, love,' her mum advised. 'That's the only way you're going to meet someone. What about those quiz nights at the pub? Isn't there anyone there you like the look of?'

Yes, thought Roxy. *But he doesn't appear to like the look of me. Well, not like that, anyway.*

'How's George, by the way? I saw the article in *The Times and Herald*. It's a shame they didn't put your name in it, but I've been telling everyone that you're one of The Candles.'

Roxy hesitated for a moment. 'George is fine. In fact, he's got another one of those funerals coming up soon.'

Roxy's mum studied her face and narrowed her eyes. 'Have you two not made up yet?'

Roxy sighed. 'It's awkward. He still hasn't apologised for being rude, but then maybe I pushed him too hard. He was right in a way – it isn't really any of my business.'

'Yes, love – but you were right to try and make him see what a fool he's being. What if anything were to happen to his brother before George has made his peace with him? Life's too short to bear a grudge, and that applies to you and George too. You were only trying to be a good friend – I know that. But make sure you don't lose him because of it.'

Roxy thought about her mum's words as she walked back home through the park. Her mum was right, of course. Roxy would ring George when she got home and invite him for a drink at the pub. Hell, she might even go mad and invite Niall and the others as well. It was short notice, but maybe some of them would come. She was so lost in her own thoughts that she almost fell over the large dog that skidded to a halt in front of her and dropped a ball at her feet.

'Sailor!' she exclaimed as she reached down to scratch his cheek.

He wagged his tail furiously and nudged the ball with his nose.

'Okay! Okay!' She picked it up and flung it across the grass. Sailor scampered after it and Roxy looked around for Captain.

'He doesn't look too fat to me!' she remarked with a mischievous grin as he approached her on the path from the opposite direction.

'I've cut down on his crisps,' he replied, with a wink that belied his gruff voice and deadpan expression.

Sailor arrived back panting and dropped his ball once more. Roxy threw it for him again.

'How's things with that colleague of yours?' Captain asked her. 'Still being a numpty?'

Roxy grinned. 'A bit – but I'm hoping to bury the hatchet tonight. It's my birthday so I'm going to invite him and a couple of other friends to the pub for a drink.'

'Happy birthday.' It was the first time she had ever seen Captain produce a smile that reached his eyes and made them sparkle. But even so, it seemed to be a sad smile – like a brave face on a broken heart.

'Come too!' she said suddenly. 'Bring Sailor. I'd love it if you were both there.' She touched his arm briefly.

He shook his head. 'Thanks. But I can't.' The disappointment must have been clear on her face, for he added, 'I can't risk it. You'd be giving Sailor crisps again.'

Roxy smiled. She understood it was a joke intended to soften the refusal whilst acknowledging the invitation.

'Come on,' Captain said to his dog. 'Time to go.'

Roxy stroked Sailor's ears in farewell as Captain clipped him to his lead, and then the man and his dog went on their way.

When she got home, Roxy fetched the stepladder from the utility room and carried it upstairs. Her mum had asked her to see if she could find an old photo album which she thought was in the loft. They held 'Reminiscence Afternoons' at the care home, where the residents shared stories and photographs from their past, and Roxy's mum wanted to share an album of her annual childhood holidays in Norfolk. Roxy set up the ladder under the loft hatch and made sure its feet were stable. She climbed the steps and opened the hatch door, pushing it upwards until she heard the catch click into the metal clip that held it open. She took another step up, but the heavy door wasn't properly secured and suddenly it swung back down and struck her very hard on the head. For a split second Roxy registered the blinding pain before everything went black. She fell backwards, taking the stepladder with her, and hit her head once more as she landed in a tangle of limbs and ladder on the varnished boards of the landing floor.

Chapter 37

George had been surprised and a little upset when Roxy had failed to turn up at work that morning and Tracey had breezed into the library in her place. It wasn't just her absence that had thrown him, but that she hadn't told him she was taking a day's leave. George had hoped that this would be the day – Roxy's birthday – when they would finally put an end to their disagreement and move on. He had planned to apologise for his behaviour. He had even arranged a surprise get-together that evening at The Duck and Donkey with the other members of The Light a Candle Society so they could toast Roxy's health with a few drinks. Elena had volunteered to make a cake. There was a slight risk, of course, that Roxy might be doing something else with someone else to celebrate her birthday, but he had asked Tracey, who said that Roxy hadn't mentioned anything.

George had been going to tell Roxy all about it when she came into work, but now he would have to go and speak to her at home – if she was in. He had tried calling her, but her mobile just kept going straight to voicemail. He wondered if Roxy was deliberately avoiding speaking to him. At least if he went to her house, it would be harder for her to ignore him. He walked straight there after work and was relieved to see her car parked on the driveway. He rang the doorbell and stood watching and listening for signs of life inside the house. All was still and silent. He rang the bell again, keeping his finger pressed down for longer, and then added a couple of short bursts for good measure. Still nothing. George sighed. Roxy wasn't in, or she was hiding from him. Either way, there wasn't much else he could do. He turned and walked back down the drive. He would try calling her again later.

He had almost reached the corner of the street when he stopped. Later, when he tried to describe what had happened, he could only say that he had felt suddenly cold, as though he had walked from sunshine into shadow, followed by an overwhelming compulsion to return to Roxy's house. He hurried back down the street, already half feeling foolish for retracing his steps. He rang the bell again and then tried peering through the letterbox. His view was directly up the staircase. At the top, he thought he could see an arm hanging limply through the space between the balusters.

'Roxy!' he yelled through the letterbox and then listened. There was no sound.

George's heart was pumping fast now, and he felt hot. He took a deep breath. *Think!* he told himself. He ran round the side of the house and into the garden. He tried the back door, but it was locked. He peered through one of its glass panels and could see the key in the lock on the inside. He snatched up a concrete gnome that Roxy had inherited from her parents and tried to smash the glass in the door, but the safety glass was too tough. George turned his attention to the kitchen windows and noted with relief that they were contemporary with the 1950s house and not double-glazed. The gnome made short work of one of the large windows. George was able to open it wide, and using one of Roxy's metal garden chairs to stand on, he crawled through the window and clambered over the sink onto the kitchen floor. As soon as his feet touched the ground he was running for the stairs. When he saw Roxy's pale face and touched her cold cheek, he knew it was bad. Really bad. With shaking hands, he took his mobile from his pocket and punched in three numbers.

'Is the casualty breathing?' the operator asked him.

'Only just,' he replied.

'The ambulance is on its way. Stay with the casualty and don't move her.'

'Stay with me, Roxy, love,' he whispered, as he registered with dismay the dark pool of blood that formed a halo around the back of her head. He took hold of her hand and squeezed it. 'Help's on the way.'

He went with her in the ambulance to the hospital and sat in the waiting room while they whisked her away for scans and tests. He rang Edwin and asked him to cancel that night's drinks.

'Keep in touch, George,' Edwin had said. 'Let me know how she's doing.'

For two hours George sat and drank chemical flavoured coffee and berated himself for being such a pig-headed idiot. How could he have spoken to Roxy like that? She had only been trying to help. It didn't matter whether he agreed with her or not – the point was that she had been looking out for him as a friend. A friend he clearly didn't deserve.

Just as he got up to buy himself another coffee he didn't want, Niall appeared and sat down in the plastic seat beside him. 'I've been to Roxy's with Edwin, and we've locked the doors and boarded up the window. It's all secure now. How is she?'

George sighed. 'I wish I knew. I've been waiting here since we came in. The last I heard, they were taking her for scans and tests but that was hours ago.'

At that moment, a tall woman wearing a white coat, metal-rimmed glasses and a deep frown walked purposefully into the waiting room and looked around. 'Is anyone here for Roxy Pemberton?'

George and Niall both stood up.

The woman looked at them and nodded. 'If you'd like to come this way,' she said, indicating that they should follow her.

She led them down the corridor to a small side room and invited them to sit down. 'I'm afraid it's not good news.'

Chapter 38

The funeral took place on 14 February – a day when the rest of the world was celebrating love with hearts and flowers. The flowers on the coffin were deep red velveteen roses wreathed with ivy. As the hearse was driven through the gates and snaked its way up the gravel drive, Sid and Elena made their way inside the chapel to join the rest of the congregation. George remained outside with Niall and waited as Edwin directed the pallbearers. George watched the roses tremble slightly as the coffin was hoisted onto six strong shoulders and began its stately procession down the aisle towards the catafalque to the soulful voice of Billie Holiday singing 'I'll Be Seeing You'. He was gratified to see a dozen or so people seated in the pews as he walked to the front of the chapel. He lit the candle next to a family photograph, which was an enlargement of the original so that it would be visible to all the mourners, and placed a vinyl record in its cover on a small stand behind the roses.

'We are here today to remember the life of Arthur John Chambers,' he began. 'Arthur was a local boy and grew up in a village on the outskirts of town. He was part of a close-knit family and had a younger sister, Susan. He and Susan loved playing in the fields at the back of their house, and Arthur always used to say that Susan "wasn't bad for a girl" – even when she became a grown woman.'

There was a ripple of laughter in the pews and George continued. 'Arthur inherited a love of cricket from his dad and played for his village team, even after he moved to town when he began working at a local engineering firm. It was here that he met Marie at the work's Christmas party, and they began dating. They married two years later, and Arthur was a loving husband until he died. Arthur and Marie were both keen to have children and were delighted when just eighteen months after their wedding they become devoted parents to their son, John. Sadly, John was killed in a tragic car accident when he was just twenty-two. Throughout his life, Arthur remained a cricket fan, and once he'd put his bat aside, he followed England's test-match teams with enthusiasm. His other great love was music, and he had an impressive vinyl record collection. We've already heard a sample from Arthur's collection at the beginning of the service, and we'll be hearing some more a little later on. But we're now going to sing one of the hymns that was sung at Arthur's and Marie's wedding.'

Sid had discovered an order of service for their wedding along with cards, telegrams and photographs in an old cardboard suitcase when he had cleared the house. They sang 'Dear Lord and Father of Mankind' and then Sid read a poem by Michael Ashby entitled 'Cricketer's Last Boundary'.

George stood up once again and thanked everyone for coming. He assumed that most of the unfamiliar faces in the chapel belonged to people who had seen the announcement on the website or Facebook page and were either friends of Arthur or had simply decided to support The Light a Candle Society by attending the funeral. But there was, George hoped, one stranger amongst them who would make himself known.

George had managed to find a local Catholic priest who had agreed to come along and give a blessing at the end of the service. He introduced Father Michael, who stood facing Arthur's coffin and held his hand above it as he spoke: 'Be at peace with your own soul, and then heaven and earth will be at peace with you.' Father Michael then turned towards the congregation and said, 'Be kind to one another, tender-hearted, forgiving one another as God in Christ forgave you.'

As the curtains closed around Arthur's coffin, Earl Humphrey and His Footwarmers played 'Please Don't Talk About Me When I'm Gone' – a track from the album that George had found on the turntable in Arthur's house.

George stood by the door of the chapel, thanking people for coming as they made their way out. A couple of older men told George they had been friends of Arthur's and fellow cricket fans, and they had attended matches together, and a younger man in his thirties informed George that he had known Arthur as a regular and long-standing customer in the local record shop he ran. But the one person George was hoping to meet was the last to leave. He was a man in his early seventies smartly dressed in a black suit and very shiny shoes. As he approached George, he held out his hand. 'Mr McGlory – I'm Walter Blacklock, Arthur's brother-in-law.'

George shook the man's hand warmly. 'Call me George,' he said.

'And everyone calls me Wally,' the man replied.

'I'm so pleased you came,' George told him. 'And I can't thank you enough for contacting me and telling me all about Arthur.'

Wally had rung George the day after he had spoken to Susan and offered to help in any way he could.

'Arthur was a thoroughly decent man, and I don't blame him one bit for what he did,' Wally replied. 'He deserved a proper send-off.' He sighed and shook his head sadly. 'My wife, Susan, she loved him so much. But she's devoted to the Church. The older she gets, the tighter she clings to it. I sometimes wonder if it's the fear of her own death that does it – and the promise of salvation if she lives life strictly by the rules. And her priest, Father Ignatius, doesn't help. He's old-school fire and brimstone. I knew I had no hope of persuading her to come today.'

'But you don't share her beliefs?' George asked warily.

'Oh, I'm a Catholic born and bred,' Wally replied. 'And I see a lot of good in the Church. I just believe in a bit more flexibility than Susan – and Father Ignatius. A bit more tolerance. Susan's faith is strictly black and white, whereas mine accommodates a few grey areas – a bit like your Father Michael's does.'

'And does Susan know that you rang me?' George asked, anxious that he might have been the cause of any friction between Wally and his wife.

Wally smiled ruefully. 'She gave me your number.'

'But why on earth would she do that?'

'Because I asked her. And because, I suspect, she was half-hoping that I might do what I have done.'

'But I don't understand. Why would she want you to do something that she believes so strongly is wrong?'

Wally shrugged in reply. 'I don't expect that even she could answer that one. Maybe she's torn between fear and love. Maybe she's hedging her bets. All I know is that I love my wife very much and I hate seeing her in pain. And she is in pain, George. She has been ever since Arthur died, and she has no idea what to do with it. So if me speaking to you has helped her in any way, I'm glad. And as I said before, I don't think Arthur did anything wrong. He certainly doesn't deserve to be judged for what he did. How do any of us know that we wouldn't have done the same in his shoes?'

'Does Susan know that you came today?'

'I didn't tell her where I was going, and she didn't ask. But one day, she might. And one day she might regret that she wasn't here but take comfort from the fact that I was.'

George invited Wally to the wake The Light a Candle Society were having for Arthur in The Duck and Donkey, but he declined. 'It's kind of you, but I'd better get back to Susan. But thank you, George. Thank you for doing this. You're a good man.'

George watched him walk away towards the car park, and then he made his way through to the back of the chapel, where James was preparing to load Arthur's coffin into the furnace.

James handed the roses to Edwin and the Earl Humphrey album to George, and then he took hold of the trolley with both hands. 'Come on, Arthur,' he said softly. 'Time to send you on your way.' He wheeled the coffin over to the furnace, and as he closed the door on the flames he whispered, 'Safe journey and God bless you, Arthur Chambers.'

Edwin took the flowers outside and placed them in the viewing area. 'See you later in the pub,' he called to George as he strolled back to his colleagues, who were waiting for him in the hearse.

George waved at him distractedly. His eyes were on the car park where Walter Blacklock's car was just pulling away. Wally's words had stung him.

'You're a good man.'

George wasn't so sure.

Chapter 39

'How's Roxy?' asked Elena, almost as soon as George sat down with the others in The Duck and Donkey. 'Is she allowed any visitors yet?'

George stared dejectedly into his pint. He knew that everyone would ask him about Roxy whenever they saw him, but he didn't really have any answers.

'She's about the same,' he replied. 'She's still in the critical care unit.'

'And is she allowed any visitors?' Elena persisted.

'I've been to see her a couple of times, but she's mostly unconscious, so I'm not sure there's much point.'

The truth was that George couldn't bear to see Roxy lying unresponsive in a hospital bed. He had sat beside her trying to reach the woman beyond the tubes that dripped fluids in and drained them out, and the clips and wires connected to the machine that beeped and flashed. But Roxy wasn't there, just the body that served her. And no one knew if she would ever find her way back into it. The sight of her was a bitter reminder that he had ruined their friendship – a friendship that was so precious to him – and that he might never now have a chance to make things right.

'But as long as she's allowed visitors, we should go,' Elena stated firmly.

'Elena's right,' Niall agreed. 'Just because she's unconscious doesn't necessarily mean that she's not aware of her surroundings. Does Roxy have any family?'

'Her mum's in a care home, and she has an aunt who lives up in Ambleside, but other than that …' George's words trailed away and he shrugged.

'Then we should definitely go and see her – and talk to her,' Niall replied. 'Isn't that what they say? Talk to patients who are unconscious and play music to them. Isn't it supposed to help bring them back sometimes?'

'Or at least bring them comfort or cheer them up a bit,' Sid suggested. 'I remember when my old dad was dying and he was out of it on drugs in the hospice, I used to go and sit with him and play brass band music. He loved a brass band, did my dad. I swear it used to make him smile, even though he was unconscious, so he must have been able to hear it.'

'But Roxy isn't going to die,' said Elena, seeing the pain on George's face. 'She's going to get better.'

I hope so, thought George. *Dear God, I hope so.*

One of the bar staff appeared at their table with a couple of plates of sandwiches and some small bowls of chips. Lachie was keeping his word about providing refreshments for The Light a Candle Society wakes.

'We should set up a visiting rota,' suggested Edwin, helping himself to a chip. 'That way we could make sure that she gets a visitor most days. I reckon my wife might be up for visiting her too.'

'Well, I can go tomorrow after work,' volunteered Niall.

'And I'll do the following afternoon,' Elena added. 'I'll shut the shop a bit early.'

And so, between them, they arranged visits for Roxy to cover the next week.

'What happened to that reporter woman, Briony?' Sid asked as he picked up a couple of sandwiches. 'Is she not coming any more now she's got her story?'

'I'm not sure,' George replied. 'I need to speak to her about the website and Facebook page and whether she's happy to carry on with them or if she intends to just leave us to it. It was good to see some extra people at the funeral today.'

At that moment Lachie appeared, carrying a biscuit tin and grinning mischievously. He placed the tin down on the table. 'A woman called Mrs Kettle came in today and left these for you, George. She said they were for The Light a Candle Society wake. She's obviously a big fan of yours.' He winked at George. 'She said I was to hand them to you personally and that you were now a local hero and asked had I read about you in the paper.'

For a moment George was at a loss, but then he remembered that Mrs Kettle was in fact Mrs Biscuit. 'Oh God,' he groaned. 'Did she say what flavour they are?'

'She did,' said Lachie, clearly trying to keep a straight face. 'She said they were coconut and cucumber. Oh, and the icing is lemon flavoured.'

Mrs Biscuit had clearly gone the extra mile for The Light a Candle Society. Her biscuits were never usually iced. Everyone looked at George expectantly. He prised the lid off the tin to reveal two dozen coffin-shaped biscuits decorated with the letters R.I.P. in black icing. George wished more than anything that Roxy had been there to see them.

Chapter 40

Spring had rushed in imprudently that year, barely waiting for March to run its course before bursting into bloom. The daffodils, hyacinths and bluebells in Roxy's garden had flowered with scant regard for the probability of a rogue frost in April. And Roxy was there to see them. After six weeks in hospital and two weeks in a rehabilitation clinic recovering from a fractured skull and a small bleed on the brain, Roxy had finally been allowed home. She was still frail, and occasionally a little unsteady on her feet, but that was the result of fatigue rather than any residual balance issues, her specialist had reassured her. A final brain scan had revealed that Roxy had been extremely lucky and had escaped any permanent damage. She wouldn't be able to return to work at the library for several weeks yet, but at least she was back in her own house.

George had picked her up and brought her home that morning. The kitchen window had been fixed, the floor on the upstairs landing had been scrubbed and the ladder returned to the utility room. George had taped a notice to it which read DO NOT USE! in red ink. In the kitchen, there was a banner pinned to the wall which read WELCOME HOME and a cake – a belated birthday cake – baked by Elena. There was also an enormous bouquet of flowers from all the members of The Light a Candle Society. They had each been to see her in hospital, although Roxy's memory of their visits in the first few weeks was rather hazy. She did recall hearing music when Niall had first visited her, but it wasn't anything she had recognised. She must try to remember to ask him what it was.

'Everyone wanted to be here to welcome you home in person,' George told her. 'But we thought it might be a bit much on your first day.'

Roxy smiled. 'It was a lovely idea, but I think I might need a couple of days just to settle back in.'

'I got you some shopping,' George told her. 'Just a few basic bits and pieces. And there's a couple of ready meals in the fridge that just need popping in the microwave. Would you like me to get you anything now?'

Roxy shook her head. 'No thanks. You've been brilliant. I can't thank you enough.'

Ever since Roxy had recovered consciousness, George had been apologising to her for his part in their row. Eventually she had told him that, as he had almost certainly saved her life, they were now officially even. She hadn't asked him if he had confessed his lies to Elizabeth or done anything about Roger. She was pretty sure he hadn't, but that was up to him now.

'Are you sure I can't make you a cup of tea before I go?'

'I'm sure,' Roxy replied. 'Now be off with you! You'll be late.'

George was due at the library that afternoon. Since Roxy had been off, he and Tracey had been working extra shifts to cover for her. Once George had left, Roxy wandered around each room, reacquainting herself with the domestic landscape. She had been gone for eight weeks, but it felt like a lifetime. And for the first time since she had lived there without her mum, her home had felt empty when she had stepped back through the door. It was contrary, she reflected, because once she had regained awareness of her surroundings in the busy hospital, and then later while she was at the clinic, she had longed for some peace and quiet – some solitude. Roxy had always been very comfortable in her own company and was fully aware that being alone and being lonely were two completely different things. But her fall had left her with a vague and unfamiliar sense of vulnerability.

Roxy returned to the kitchen and switched the kettle on. It was understandable, she told herself. A completely natural reaction. In a few days she'd feel differently. She just needed to get back into the swing of things. She had told George that she wanted to go to the pub quiz that week – eager to reclaim some of her old life. She made herself a mug of tea and then sat down to ring her mum. Her mum was so delighted to hear that Roxy would be going to the care home to see her the following day that she became quite tearful. They had spoken regularly as soon as Roxy was able to from the hospital, but for her mum, real reassurance could only be achieved by seeing Roxy in the flesh.

'I've been so worried about you, love. I sometimes thought I'd never see you again!' she told Roxy.

'Well, you'll see me tomorrow! So you don't need to worry any more.'

Roxy had just ended the call when the doorbell rang.

Damn! she thought. She was feeling tired and had intended to have a little snooze on the sofa. She was just wondering if she should ignore it when she heard a dog bark. The sound came from her front garden. She opened the door to find Captain and Sailor standing there. Captain looked a little uneasy, but Sailor was clearly delighted to see her. His tail was wagging furiously, and he nudged her hand repeatedly with his nose.

'Steady on,' Captain told him, pulling the dog back on his leash.

'He's all right,' Roxy replied, scratching Sailor's ears to his obvious delight. 'It's good to see you both.'

'We won't stop,' Captain said quickly. 'We just came to say we're glad you're on the mend. I hope you don't mind, but George told me where you live. I was going to send a card, but then we were passing, and I thought I might as well see if you were in.'

'And I'm very glad you did!' It was the most Roxy had ever heard Captain say all in one go. She knew from George that he had been asking after her at the library, and she was touched that he had taken the trouble to call round, given that he seemed such a solitary soul.

'I was just going to make a cup of tea,' Roxy lied. 'Are you sure you won't come in and have one? I don't think I have any crisps,' she said, grinning at Sailor, 'but I'm pretty sure I have some ginger biscuits.'

She could sense Captain wavering. She didn't want to force him, but she had become fond of this old man and his dog, and although she was tired, she didn't find his company taxing

– rather the opposite. His presence was somehow strangely reassuring.

'If you're sure we're not disturbing you …' Sailor was pulling him through the door before Captain could finish his sentence.

They had their tea in the sitting room, which looked out over the back garden. Captain didn't say much but he seemed happy to listen as Roxy told him about her time in hospital and then moved on to her summer plans for the garden. When there came a break in the conversation, or rather in Roxy's monologue, he suddenly fixed her with his eyes that were almost the same colour as Sailor's and asked her how she was feeling.

Roxy replied honestly. More honestly, perhaps, than she would have done to anyone else. 'Physically, I'm fine. I get tired and my muscles are a bit weak still, but other than that,' she shrugged, 'I'm fine.'

Captain allowed the second, unspoken 'but' to hang unhurried in silence between them until Roxy was ready to continue.

'But it did feel a bit strange coming home,' she admitted. 'The house felt empty, which is odd because it's never felt like that to me before.'

Captain nodded slowly but said nothing. Sailor rested his heavy head on her lap and looked up at her with his piercing blue eyes.

'And I feel a bit – scared,' she admitted reluctantly. 'It sounds ridiculous, I know, and I'm sure I'll get over it in a couple of days once things get back to normal.'

'You were on your own when you fell. You could have died,' Captain replied bluntly but in a gentle voice. 'Why wouldn't you be scared? Fear can be a lesson. Next time you'll be careful, and you'll be fine.'

It sounded so simple, but Captain's words were like a verbal hug – honest, sensible and unsentimental, but comforting nonetheless. Tears pricked Roxy's eyes, but she believed she *would* be fine.

'He's taken a shine to you,' Captain said, nodding towards Sailor, who had quietly climbed up onto the sofa and was snuggled up beside Roxy.

Roxy smiled. 'He's taken a shine to my ginger biscuits!' she replied, and Sailor stared mournfully at the plate on which a couple were still left. 'One more' she told him, breaking one in half and feeding it to him. 'One more and that's your lot!'

'And we'd better be off and leave this lady to rest,' said Captain, pushing himself up a little stiffly from his chair.

'Do you know something?' Roxy said, the thought suddenly occurring to her. 'I don't know what your real name is.'

'Everyone calls me Captain,' he replied. 'I'm happy enough with that.'

Roxy led them through to the hall and opened the front door.

'I can bring him to visit, if you'd like,' Captain said, ruffling the fur on Sailor's neck affectionately. 'He'd be company for you.'

'You're both welcome anytime,' Roxy said truthfully.

'I meant when I have to go out and leave him. Like when I go to the library. I could bring him to you instead sometimes.

But only if you want …' His words trailed away as if he was losing confidence in the idea.

Roxy reached across and touched his arm. 'Really? You'd do that? That would be amazing! I promise I'd take good care of him.'

Captain smiled at her. Another of those rare smiles that reached his eyes and made them shine. 'He'd be the one taking care of you,' he said. 'But no crisps!'

Chapter 41

Case no. 63542-7581

'Keisha! You look amazing!' her best friend Shanice exclaimed as Keisha checked out her appearance in the changing-room mirror.

Keisha turned this way and that trying to get a 360-degree view of her outfit, which consisted of an extremely short snakeskin print slip dress and black patent stiletto knee boots. The girls had bunked off college early that afternoon and were in town shopping for clothes and make-up for a party they were going to the following evening. It was their friend Sophie's eighteenth, and her parents had hired the local rowing club bar. Sophie's dad had his own building company, and Sophie and her brother got pretty much whatever they wanted. Sophie was even getting her own car for her birthday.

'It won't do her any good,' Keisha's mum had said, when Keisha had told her in envious tones about Sophie's birthday present. 'That girl will know the price of everything and the value of nothing!'

Keisha's dad had left them when she was seven, and since then, for the most part, it had been just the two of them. Her mum had had the occasional boyfriend and one had even moved in for a while. But eventually, they had all moved on – and left her mum resolute that she would never again rely on a man for anything. Her mum had two jobs, cleaning at a school and working shifts in their local corner shop, to make ends meet. And since Keisha had left school and started a fashion and design course at college, she had got herself a Saturday job in a hair and beauty salon.

Keisha had been saving for weeks to buy an outfit for the party. She had seen the dress in the shop window and had known at once it was the one she wanted. She stared at her reflection and marvelled at the woman who looked back at her.

'But there's no way your mum will let you out wearing that.' Shanice added, bursting her friend's bubble.

Keisha grinned back at Shanice slyly. 'She doesn't have to. I have a plan! Now, let's pay for these and then I need some new nail polish and some really big gold hoop earrings.'

The girls continued shopping until they were both carrying numerous bags, and then they decided to treat themselves to coffees and fancy doughnuts.

'So what time are you coming to mine tomorrow?' Keisha asked Shanice as she licked sugar from her fingertips. 'I'm finishing work at six, so I'll be home by half past. Mum says you can have tea with us, so if you bring your stuff, we can get ready together.'

'Your mum's so nice letting me have tea at yours.'

Keisha laughed. 'She just wants to make sure we don't go out drinking on an empty stomach.'

'In that case, shall I bring a couple of bottles of WKD to get us in the party mood while we make ourselves fab-u-lous?'

'I won't let you in the house if you don't,' Keisha joked.

'So – who's the dress for?' Shanice asked, arching one eyebrow. 'Aaron or Daley?'

Keisha flicked her hair back from her face and pushed her shiny pink lips into a pout. 'The dress is for me!' she said defiantly.

Shanice shook her head. 'The dress is to impress. But is it Aaron or Daley?'

Keisha screwed up her paper napkin and threw it at Shanice, earning a disapproving glance from a middle-aged woman sitting at the next table. 'That's for me to know and you to find out!'

The next evening, Keisha's mum fed the girls chicken fajitas before they retired upstairs to Keisha's bedroom to make themselves gorgeous. They swigged WKD Blue from bottles to the sound of 50 Cent's 'In Da Club' as they primped and preened their hair and faces, spritzed themselves with perfume and squeezed into their outfits. Shanice had chosen low-slung silky combat trousers, chunky silver trainers and a tiny crop top, an outfit which compared with Keisha's eye-popping ensemble looked positively conservative.

'You look about twenty-five!' Shanice's comment was intended – and taken – as a compliment. 'But there's no way you're gonna get that past your mum.'

'I'm eighteen! She can't stop me!'

Shanice's face displayed the absolute disbelief that they both knew to be fully justified.

Keisha drained the last of the blue liquid from her bottle and laughed. 'I told you – I have a plan!'

She took a black dress from her wardrobe and held it up to show Shanice. It was short, but not indecently short, and loose fitting. Keisha pulled it from its hanger and slipped it over her head, completely covering the snakeskin slip beneath. She shrugged on her jacket and, after a final self-congratulatory glance in the mirror, she picked up her bag and grabbed her friend's arm.

'Come on, gorgeous girl,' she said. 'It's time to get the party started!'

Keisha couldn't understand how they could have got in. The door was locked and bolted, and she had pushed a towel against the bottom to make sure they couldn't crawl underneath through the tiny crack. Because you had to be really careful. They could get through the tiniest of cracks and crevices. She checked the windows to see if they were all still shut. She held the back of her hand to all the edges, feeling for the slightest breath of air in case they had blown into the flat that way, but the double-glazing was draught proof. She had taped up the overflows on the sink and the bath, but perhaps they had hidden in the water and come in through the taps. That's why it wasn't safe to wash or have a bath or brush your teeth. She used water to make tea and coffee, but she boiled it in the kettle, and she had thought that the boiling would kill them, but perhaps it didn't. She could feel them inside her head now, scratching and pricking and whispering and hissing. Perhaps it was the milk and not the water. It was long-life milk, but they could live for ever. Perhaps the cows had breathed them in or perhaps they had been in the grass that the cows had eaten and then they had hidden themselves in the milk. She wouldn't drink any more milk just in case.

Keisha hit her head hard with the palm of her hand. And again. And again. If only she could make them be quiet so she could think. She used to listen to the radio – not the speaking, that was too dangerous, but the music. She used to like music. She used to like to dance. But now she knew they could hide in the music too, and when the music went into your ears, they went with it and started living in your head and telling you to do things. She went into the bathroom to look into the mirror. The face she saw was grey and drawn, with frightened eyes shrunk back into blackened sockets. She looked closely at her skin to see if she could see them crawling underneath it. If she could see them, perhaps she could cut them out. But they were too clever to show themselves. The door of the bathroom cabinet hung open, revealing the coloured boxes that contained the pills everyone said she should take. Medication. Dr Ali said she should definitely take her medication. Definitely. But could she trust him? He was so definite that she worried he could be on their side. They could be in the medication, so she didn't take it any more.

She was so tired today. Her arms and legs wouldn't work properly. She looked at them and saw they were slowly disappearing. She was disappearing. They had got inside her somehow and they were making her disappear. She lay down on the floor and curled herself up – like a hedgehog, she thought. Maybe her spikes would protect her.

Chapter 42

'How's life in the offices of *The Times and Herald*?' Allegra enquired as she mixed martinis for herself and Briony.

Briony sighed. 'Much the same. The story about the funerals got a great response but it didn't lead to anything else.'

Allegra handed her a drink. 'It hasn't led to anything else yet, but there's still time.'

'I don't see how. None of the nationals picked it up – and it's old news now.'

'Don't be ridiculous. Of course it isn't. It's ongoing. Behind every one of those funerals is a story.'

'Yes. But Gordon's not going to let me write a story each time there's a public health funeral.'

It was Allegra's turn to sigh. 'You really are being incredibly unimaginative about this.'

Briony took a gulp of her martini. She was used to Allegra's candour but sometimes it was tough to take. 'Well, what do you suggest?' she replied a little testily.

Allegra smiled. 'Don't take offence, my dear. I'm only trying to help. And I do find that the older I get, the less time I have for niceties. Indeed, the less time I have for anything – because

I have less time left! Are you still looking after the Facebook page and website?'

'Yes. George has been so busy with Roxy since she had that nasty fall that I haven't had a chance to show him what to do with them. But she's home and much better, so now maybe I can.'

'I don't think you should. You could use them to get your writing noticed. Tell the stories of each and every one of those people who die alone. You said that each person would have a memorial page. Well, how much better would it be if that page told a real, human story rather than listing a few sterile facts?'

'I'm not sure. Some of their stories aren't exactly very … palatable.'

Allegra tossed her head impatiently. 'Palatable!' she exclaimed. 'In case you hadn't noticed, life isn't always very palatable. And neither is death, for that matter. But if you can find a way of telling these stories with compassion as well as honesty, then not only will they be fitting memorials, but they might also help to raise awareness about the issues that some of these people faced.'

Briony nodded thoughtfully. She was beginning to see potential in what Allegra was suggesting, but she knew that she would have to convince George and the others first.

'I don't want The Light a Candle Society to think that I'm just using them and what they do to further my own career,' she said, thinking aloud.

'Well then, don't,' Allegra replied. 'Join The Light a Candle Society and prove to them that what you'll be doing will help

– not only to find friends and relatives of the deceased, but also to bring their stories to a wider audience. You said the Facebook page and website are easy enough to maintain – well, offer to maintain them. And then use them to spread the word. Perhaps if more people knew how easy it is to fall through the cracks and end up all alone it might happen less often. People might look out for their neighbours a bit more or think twice about losing touch with their friends and families.'

She spoke quite passionately and Briony couldn't help but wonder if the subject had some personal significance for Allegra. After all, she lived alone and had never spoken about any family to Briony or ever had any friends to visit, so far as Briony was aware.

'I'll need to speak to George, but when you put it like that it sounds, well, really worthwhile. It sounds like something I'd actually be proud to put my name to.'

Allegra smiled her wicked smile. 'And so much better than mangled mangel-wurzels. It's journalism with heart!' she declared, raising her glass in a toast, but then discovering it was empty. She got up and fixed them both another drink.

'Now tell me,' she said as she handed a glass to Briony and then sat back down holding her martini, 'how's it going with your police officer – Zach, isn't it?'

Briony grinned. 'Okay, thank you. He seems really nice.'

Briony had been out with Zach a couple of times now and she enjoyed his company. He was easy-going, funny and they always seemed to have plenty to chat about. She couldn't deny that she found him attractive too, but as yet a goodnight kiss was as far as they had ventured beyond the friend zone.

'"Really nice"!' Allegra expostulated. 'Goodness, I was hoping for something a little spicier than that.'

Briony shook her head. 'Honestly, Allegra, you're incorrigible! We've only been out a couple of times, and I'm not even sure if they count as dates or if we're just seeing each other as friends – at the moment.'

Allegra raised her eyebrows. 'Friends with benefits?'

Briony spluttered into her martini.

'Now, now,' Allegra chided, clearly enjoying the effect her words had had on Briony, 'don't be coy! Are you attracted to him? I must say, he is rather pleasing to the eye – although, of course that's not the sort of comment one is allowed to make these days.'

'All right – yes, I am,' replied Briony, fully aware that Allegra would tolerate no evasion nor prevarication.

'Then seize the day, my dear – or rather, seize the man. Are you seeing him this evening?'

Briony nodded.

Allegra said nothing, but then she didn't need to. Her amused expression said it all.

Chapter 43

'I don't think we've covered ourselves in glory tonight,' said George, a little despondently, as Lachie collected up the answer sheets for the pub quiz.

'We're getting old, George. That's the problem,' replied Edwin with a grin. 'Those questions about online gaming and K-pop ... Let's face it – we're out of touch.'

'I thought K-pop was a breakfast cereal,' said Niall.

'And you've got no excuse!' replied George. 'You're a good twenty years younger than me – and you've got a teenage daughter.'

'Yes, but I've never heard her mention K-pop.'

'What kind of music does she like?' asked Roxy.

Niall shook his head. 'I have no idea where she gets it from, but her favourite bands at the moment are Sisters of Mercy and Bauhaus.'

'But I remember them back in the eighties,' said George. 'They were all doom and gloom and black eyeliner.'

'Yep, and that's a perfect description of Caragh. She looks like a younger version of Morticia Addams most of the time. She dyed her hair jet black with blue tips during the Christmas holidays and her mother was furious. Her head teacher was none too pleased either.'

Roxy smiled. 'She sounds like me when I was a teenager.'

'And if she's a mini Morticia she'd fit in perfectly with us lot!' Edwin added. 'Come on, George, let's go and get a round in to console ourselves before Lachie announces the results.'

While George and Edwin were at the bar, Roxy remembered what she had been meaning to ask Niall. 'Did you play music to me when you came to visit me at the hospital?'

Niall smiled with genuine pleasure. 'You remember? So you did hear it! George wasn't sure if you would know that anyone was visiting at first, because you were unconscious for most of the time. But me and Elena thought you might be able to hear what was going on around you, so we decided to come in and talk to you anyway. And I played you some music from my phone. I got new earbuds,' he added anxiously. 'I didn't use my own.'

'That was really kind. I wasn't sure if I had imagined it, but I do remember that the music was beautiful. What was it? Not Sisters of Mercy, I know that much.'

Niall shook his head. 'Caragh and I definitely don't share the same taste in music. It was the prelude from Act 1 of *La traviata* by Verdi. It's one of my favourites.'

'I'm more of a musical theatre woman myself. I've never been to the opera, but it sounded …' Roxy searched for a word that would do the music justice.

'Sublime?' Niall supplied.

Roxy nodded.

'I've got a DVD of the entire opera if you'd like to borrow it.'

'But it's all in Italian, isn't it? I wouldn't be able to understand it,' Roxy replied.

'Oh, I think you would. That's the thing about opera – the music itself tells the story. The music tells you exactly how each character is feeling.'

George and Edwin arrived back at the table with the drinks.

'What have we missed?' asked Edwin.

'We've been talking about opera,' said Roxy.

'Blimey! That's a bit of a leap from Sisters of Mercy.'

'Yes – but often just as tragic,' joked Niall. 'And actually, talking about tragic,' he continued, his tone serious now, 'I've got another funeral for The Light a Candle Society, but we don't have to talk about it tonight. I don't want to depress everyone.'

'I'm depressed already,' said Edwin, 'considering our dismal performance tonight, so I don't mind if Roxy and George don't. I assume you're talking about Keisha Campbell?'

Niall nodded. 'I know all these public health funerals are sad, but this one is particularly heartbreaking.'

'Well, in that case,' said Roxy, 'it's even more important that we do what we can to help.'

Niall took a sip from his pint before continuing. He looked so pained that Roxy wanted to give him a hug. But she was too self-conscious and the best she could manage was to squeeze his arm.

'Keisha was found in her flat,' Niall began, 'and according to the coroner's report she'd been dead for a couple of months. Keisha suffered with schizophrenia for most of her adult life, and this meant she'd never been able to hold down a job, and she increasingly withdrew from the outside world. She had lived with her mum, but when her mum died the council moved Keisha into her own flat. It seems that in the time leading up to her death, she'd stopped taking her medication for some reason, and as a result, her mental health had gone downhill rapidly. I went to her flat after her body had been recovered to try and find any relevant paperwork, personal belongings – anything, really, that could help me do my job. But the place was in a terrible state. There was virtually no food in the flat and everywhere was filthy. Keisha died from heart failure, but she had pretty much starved herself to death.'

'Oh God, that's awful! But how come no one stepped in before things got that bad? Did none of her neighbours notice that she wasn't around? Didn't she have a social worker or something? Didn't her GP practice register that she wasn't taking her medication?' Roxy was equally horrified and incredulous that a woman could die in a block of flats and no one notice.

'I did knock on a few doors and chat to some of Keisha's neighbours, but apparently she rarely went out, so it wasn't that unusual that she hadn't been seen for a while. According to one elderly man that I spoke to, Keisha could be pretty scary – presumably when she wasn't taking her medication – and could be both verbally and physically aggressive, which probably meant that people avoided her too.'

'But what about her rent and her bills?' asked George. 'Did no one notice they weren't being paid?'

'That's part of the problem – they were being paid. Keisha's benefits went straight into her bank account, and the bills and rent were paid automatically by direct debit.'

'So how *was* she found?' Roxy asked.

'The housing association that manages the flats carries out annual maintenance inspections. After trying – and failing – to get access to Keisha's flat on several occasions, the police were called. And that reminds me, George, have you heard from Briony?'

Roxy shifted in her seat at the mention of the reporter's name. George shook his head.

'Well, I think she's going to get in touch. She rang me to say she'd heard that I might be dealing with another public health funeral, and she offered to help try and find any friends and relatives using the Facebook page and various other online searches.'

'How did she know about Keisha?' asked Roxy.

'It seems she has a friend in the police who was one of the officers called to the flat. In fact, I got the impression he might be a little more than a friend,' said Niall with a wry smile.

'So did you take her up on her offer?' George asked.

'Provisionally, yes. But I said she'd need to clear it with you first. She said she wants to join the society and offered to look after the online stuff on a permanent basis. I think she could be a great help, but I didn't want to say anything too definite without everyone else's agreement.'

'Well, I've got no problem with that. What about you, Roxy?'

Roxy was slightly more inclined to be tolerant towards Briony now that she had acquired a 'friend'. 'It's fine by me,' she replied.

'Edwin?'

'It's a yes from me.'

'Great. I'm sure that Sid and Elena will be fine with it too, but I'll check with them in the morning.'

'Look out,' said Edwin. 'It's the moment of truth – Lachie's got the results.'

The landlord of The Duck and Donkey rang the bar bell for quiet.

'I don't care if we haven't won,' whispered Roxy. 'So long as we've beaten Cobweb Dave's lot. Because if we haven't, we'll never hear the last of it!'

Chapter 44

'It's lovely to have you back!' Mrs Biscuit told Roxy, who had returned to work at the library for a couple of half days a week while she was still recovering. 'Did you know that I'm now the official biscuit maker for The Light a Candle Society? It's a pity you didn't see the ones I made for the last funeral. They were lovely, weren't they, George?'

'They were most original,' replied George. 'Everyone said so.'

Mrs Biscuit beamed with pride. 'My Norman said he'd never seen anything like them before!'

None of us had, thought George.

'We've got another funeral coming up next week,' Roxy told her. 'So perhaps you'd like to make some biscuits for that wake too?'

Mrs Biscuit face lit up. 'Of course I will! It's my job now, isn't it? I'll drop them off at the pub again if you like.'

'That would be very kind,' Roxy replied.

Mrs Biscuit went off to choose her books and George shook his head despairingly at Roxy. 'You shouldn't encourage her!' he said. 'You didn't see – or taste – the last lot she made.'

'No, but I wish I had. They sounded magnificent! And I can't wait to see what she comes up with this time.'

'But Keisha's funeral isn't funny. It just feels a bit disrespectful to have Mrs Biscuit making weird biscuits in her memory as some sort of joke.'

Roxy sighed. When Audrey had been alive, she had always managed to keep George in order and talk some sense into him when he needed it. He was a lovely man, but he could be a bit old-fashioned – despite his taste in shirts – and he had a tendency towards narrow-mindedness when the mood took him.

'Of course Keisha's funeral isn't funny. Her death was tragic,' Roxy replied. 'But we're supposed to be celebrating her life, not her death. According to Niall, Briony has found a college friend of Keisha's who said she was a lively, slightly wild teenager who loved having a good time and had a wicked sense of humour. It doesn't sound as though she was the type of girl who would take offence at Mrs Biscuit's memorial baking.'

Roxy waited for a moment to allow her words to sink in, because she wasn't finished yet. She'd spent a lot of time in the past few weeks thinking about her life and the people who were in it. And the people whom she'd like to be in it. She'd decided to be more honest about things that mattered to her instead of keeping quiet or agreeing with other people to keep the peace. Life was too short to be a nodding dog in the back of someone else's car.

'And Mrs Biscuit doesn't make her biscuits as a joke. She makes them because she's kind and she wants to help. Yes, she can be a proper busybody, but she enjoys being involved and making people happy. And isn't that something we should value and encourage?'

George was looking suitably chastened, but Roxy wasn't trying to make him feel guilty.

'I don't think you realise, George, that The Light a Candle Society isn't just about the ones who die. It's about the ones who are still alive too. You've given us the chance to help the people that no one else notices or cares about, and that's a precious opportunity. Maybe they have no one left, or maybe they've driven everyone away. But whoever these people are who end up alone, you've made sure they don't stay that way because The Light a Candle Society takes them in and sends them on their way with love and respect – and, yes, sometimes humour – because why not? And you've made me – and I'm sure Niall, Edwin, Elena and Sid – feel good about ourselves in the process. So why shouldn't we share that feeling with Mrs Biscuit, and anyone else who comes along and wants to help?'

'Even Briony?' George asked with a grin.

'Even Briony,' Roxy agreed.

'Why don't you like her?'

'Who said I don't like her?'

George raised his eyebrows questioningly.

'Okay, well, I didn't exactly warm to her. At least not at first.'

'But why not?'

Roxy sighed. Was she going to be completely honest about this too? 'Because to begin with, I thought the only thing she was interested in was getting her story, and once she got it she'd leave us high and dry.'

'But she hasn't.'

'Hmm. She did for a bit, from what I can gather. She's only just come back and volunteered to do the online stuff, don't forget.'

'And that was the only reason?'

Roxy could feel her cheeks flushing.

'I thought it might have had something to do with Niall,' George continued.

Roxy laughed. 'Don't be daft! What's Niall got to do with anything?' Maybe she wasn't ready to be *that* honest just yet. 'Anyway,' she said, changing the subject, 'isn't it time you made the coffee?'

George held her gaze for just a moment before he got up and headed off towards the staffroom.

It was quiet for a Friday, and Roxy sat working undisturbed at the desk until the sound of the door opening made her look up and she saw the familiar figure of Captain making his way over to the desk. Roxy thought that he looked tired. His walk was slower than usual, and each step seemed to require a greater effort, as though his battery was running out.

'You're back then?' he said to Roxy.

'Just part-time for now – three mornings a week until I'm completely fighting fit.'

Captain nodded. 'I was going to bring Sailor round this afternoon if you don't mind.'

'Of course I don't! I've told you before – you're both welcome any time.'

Captain had bought Sailor round to see her several times since she had been out of hospital and Roxy was always delighted to see them.

Captain nodded. 'About two o'clock all right?'

'Perfect. I'll make sure the kettle's on.'

Captain nodded again and then turned and went back out the way he came. Roxy watched him go with a heavy heart. Something wasn't right.

The man and his dog were on Roxy's doorstep at two sharp that afternoon.

Captain looked a little better than he had that morning – more relaxed – and Sailor was his usual exuberant self. Roxy had stopped on the way home to buy gooseberry tartlets from the bakery, which she served with the tea.

Captain bit into his tartlet and smiled approvingly. 'I've always liked gooseberries,' he said in his quiet, low voice.

'Me too,' Roxy agreed. 'People tend to add too much sugar, but these are just right. I love a tart tart,' she said with a grin.

Sailor was looking at her longingly and she fed him a tiny piece of pie crust. Sailor was entirely unimpressed. Unusually, Captain said nothing.

'Don't worry,' Roxy said to the dog. 'I've got you some proper dog biscuits. And don't turn your nose up just because they're not gingernuts. They're organic salmon and rice – very healthy.'

Roxy fetched the box from the kitchen and offered Sailor a sample. He sniffed it uncertainly at first but then wolfed it down.

'I take it you approve?' she said, ruffling the fur behind his ears.

Captain had been watching this interaction intently. 'I want to ask you something,' he said suddenly.

Roxy looked up, startled. 'What's the matter? Is anything wrong?'

Captain smiled – a slow, sad smile that made Roxy want to weep.

'There's nothing wrong,' he said. 'But I'm getting old. And I want to ask you something – just in case anything was to happen. Not now, but if it does sometime.'

'Ask me,' said Roxy, as she sat stroking Sailor's ears. 'Just ask me,' she repeated firmly.

'Would you take my boy and look after him?' Captain said, nodding towards Sailor. 'Not now, but if …' The old man looked away.

Roxy was speechless. This man whom she knew so little about, but had grown so fond of, was asking if he could entrust her with what was clearly the most precious thing in his life. But not a thing, of course – a living creature whom she already loved as though he were her own. She had tried not to love him, because he wasn't hers, but she hadn't been able to help it.

'Yes,' she said simply.

She got up, went over to Captain and took his hand in hers, and then she looked straight into his eyes and repeated her answer so that there could be no doubt. 'Yes. I swear that if anything happens to you, I will take Sailor and look after him and give him the best life. And I will love him like you love him. Perhaps I already do.'

A single tear rolled down Captain's cheek and he wiped it away with the back of his hand.

'And no crisps?' he asked.

'Only on high days and holidays,' Roxy promised solemnly.

Chapter 45

Elena had chosen a selection of spring flowers for Keisha's funeral. A magnificent spray of tulips, daffodils, hyacinths and narcissi crowned the coffin with glowing colours and trailed fresh, sweet perfume in its wake as Keisha was carried into the chapel. Briony had put George in touch with a woman called Shanice, who had once been a close friend of Keisha's, and at her suggestion the service began with 'Amazing Grace' sung by a gospel choir from the church Keisha's mother had attended. As George followed the coffin inside side by side with Shanice, he was pleased to see that several pews were fully occupied. Roxy was there with Niall, Elena and Sid, and Briony had turned up with her police officer friend who had forced entry into Keisha's flat and discovered her body. Mrs Biscuit was there with a man whom George assumed to be her husband, Norman, and in another pew were two of Keisha's old friends from their college days, whom Shanice had managed to contact through Facebook.

A candle flickered in front of the photograph that stood beside the coffin. The Keisha in the photograph was a vibrant young woman who looked ready to take on the world. Her energy seemed to radiate from the image and her smile was captivating. When the choir had finished singing and taken their seats, George got up and faced the congregation.

'We are here today to celebrate the life of Keisha Campbell, the much-loved daughter of Denise, and a much-missed friend,' he said. 'I'd like to welcome everyone and thank you all for coming – those of you who knew Keisha and those of you who didn't, but wanted to join us in remembering her and all the love and joy she brought to those who were close to her. We're now going to hear something about that from Keisha's friend Shanice.'

George smiled encouragingly at the smartly dressed woman in her forties who had accompanied him behind the coffin and now was sitting beside Niall. She got up and stood at the front of the chapel, where she cleared her throat nervously and looked down at the piece of paper she was clutching in her hands.

'I met Keisha at school,' she began. 'I noticed her in the canteen on my first day because she was messing about and laughing.' Shanice smiled. 'Her laugh was so loud, so happy that you couldn't help but laugh with her. I was quite shy back then, but she took me under her wing and pretty soon we were inseparable. At college we were on the same fashion and design course. Keisha loved fashion and she was easily the best student in our year. I only really chose that course because I wanted to be with her. Keisha was a party girl, and we were always out every weekend – and during the week too, if Keisha could sneak out without her mum knowing, which she was pretty good at. But she was a good daughter too, and she and her mum were very close.'

Shanice paused for a moment and studied her piece of paper again.

'Keisha did really well in her final exams – unlike me,' Shanice added with a rueful smile, and there was a sympathetic laugh from the congregation. 'She was offered a job in London after our exams, but that summer was when she started to get ill. I remember how scary it was seeing my best friend become someone completely different. But it must have been so much scarier for her. Keisha was eventually diagnosed with schizophrenia and even though she began taking medication and getting help, she was never the same after that. She didn't want to go out, and she didn't want to see anyone. She pushed me and all her other friends away, and eventually we lost touch. The last time I saw Keisha was at her mum's funeral and I hardly recognised her. She acted like she didn't know me – and perhaps she didn't. When Keisha passed away, she had no one – not even me. And I used to be her best friend. When I found out what had happened and how Keisha had spent her final weeks, I felt terrible that I hadn't been there for her, but we hadn't had any contact for years. Her disease took Keisha from me a long time ago, and there was nothing I could have done to prevent that. But there is something that I can do for her today. I can tell her story and make sure that people remember Keisha as she truly was before her illness stole that person away.'

Shanice took a deep breath before continuing and when she did, there was a note of defiance in her voice. 'The Keisha

I knew loved very short dresses and very long nights out. Her favourite drink was WKD Blue, her favourite food was chicken fajitas and chips, her favourite band was Black Eyed Peas, and her favourite perfume was Loulou. She loved laughing, dancing, playing practical jokes and elephants. She was the kind of person who could light up a room just by walking into it, and I was so blessed to have her as my brilliant, funny, kind and always loyal best friend.'

Shanice gazed at the photograph for a moment, and then she folded her piece of paper and returned to her seat.

'And now we're going to sing "The Lord of the Dance",' announced George. 'This was, so Shanice tells me, the only hymn Keisha would ever sing during school assemblies because it had dancing in it.'

The gospel choir started them off, and gradually the congregation found their singing voices.

As he sang, George thought about the young woman Keisha had been and how Shanice's words had brought her to life so vividly. He was glad that was how they would all remember her now, and just a little bit proud that he and The Light a Candle Society had made it happen. After the hymn, Roxy read The Lord's Prayer and they listened to Celine Dion singing 'My Heart Will Go On'. This again had been Shanice's choice because *Titanic* had been the first film she had seen at the cinema with Keisha, and afterwards Keisha had kept singing the theme song loudly and often at inappropriate moments to make Shanice laugh. The service ended with a short blessing sung by the gospel choir, followed by the Black Eyed Peas singing 'Where Is the Love?'

Outside the chapel, Mrs Biscuit came over to George and Roxy with her husband.

'What a lovely service!' she exclaimed. 'And didn't her friend make a lovely speech? I wanted to come and show my support for what you're doing. I think it's marvellous. And I thought I might as well bring my Norman along to bump up the numbers a bit, in case you were short of bottoms on seats, so to speak. This is Norman, my husband,' she added rather unnecessarily.

Norman grinned and shook hands with George and Roxy. 'Pleased to meet you. Good to see that my Glenda hasn't poisoned you with her biscuits yet!' he joked.

His wife nudged him with her elbow. 'Norman! Don't be so rude. I'll have you know my biscuits are very popular at the library, aren't they, dear?' she said, looking at Roxy for support.

'They certainly are,' Roxy confirmed. 'We always look forward to your new recipes.'

'See – what did I tell you? And fancy talking about poisoning at a funeral,' Mrs Biscuit scolded, lowering her voice. 'You shouldn't disrespect the dead!'

'I wasn't,' replied Norman placidly. 'The deceased won't have to eat them,' he added softly, winking at Roxy.

'I've left the biscuits for the wake at the pub like I promised,' Mrs Biscuit told George, ignoring her husband's last comment.

'That's very kind of you. But aren't you joining us?' George asked.

'Not this time. Norman's taking me to the garden centre to buy some potting compost,' she replied, taking her husband's arm and steering him in the direction of the car park.

Shanice, who had been talking to her old college friends, made her way over to George just as he was about to join Niall and the others. 'Thank you, Mr McGlory. And please thank your friends on my behalf for giving Keisha the funeral she deserved, and also for finding me so that I could be a part of it.'

'Call me George. And why don't you thank them yourself?' George suggested. 'We're having a small wake for Keisha at The Duck and Donkey and you're very welcome to join us. You could tell us some more about Keisha.'

Shanice's eyes lit up. 'Are you sure?'

'Of course! You're the only one of us who knew her.'

'I'd love to. But first, I need to give you something.' Shanice opened her bag and began searching inside it. 'You said you have a cabinet where you put things in memory of the people whose funerals you arrange?'

'That's right.'

'Well, I wondered if you could put these in there for Keisha,' Shanice said, handing George a small soft toy elephant and a blue bottle of perfume. 'It's Loulou,' she told him, 'her favourite.'

George cradled the objects carefully in his hands. 'It will be my pleasure' he replied.

It was a Friday afternoon and around 4 pm by the time they reconvened at The Duck and Donkey, so even Niall was able to join them instead of returning to the office.

'Brenda always sneaks off early on a Friday anyway,' he told them. 'So she won't notice that I'm not there.'

Roxy was glad, and even more pleased when he chose to sit next to her.

'I've brought you something,' he said, taking a CD from his pocket. 'It's *La traviata* – the music I played to you when you were in hospital.'

Roxy flushed with pleasure. 'That's great,' she said. 'Now I can listen to the whole thing. Thank you – that's really kind.'

'And the sleeve notes have a summary of the story, which will give you an idea of what's going on. If you like it, maybe we could go and see a live performance some time,' Niall added, trying to sound casual.

George observed this interaction with interest. Perhaps he had been wrong about Niall, he reflected. He certainly hadn't been wrong about Roxy, judging from the smile on her face. He was pleased. Roxy deserved to have someone special in her life. It was something George missed very much. Until recently, he couldn't have imagined he would ever want to be with anyone else after Audrey, but now he wasn't so sure. He could live for years yet, and he didn't want to spend those years cooking and eating meals for one and watching TV alone. Always coming home to an empty house.

Roxy was chatting amicably to Briony now, who introduced her companion to everyone as Zach. George hoped that his presence wouldn't precipitate any discussion about the discovery of Keisha's body. Shanice had been appraised of the basic facts but spared the devastating details, and George wanted to keep things that way.

But Zach seemed more interested in The Light a Candle Society and even offered to help in any way he could. 'I'm not sure if there's much I can do that's useful, but if you think of anything, just let me know.'

Briony had written stories for all the memorial pages on the website and was keen to hear what the others thought before she posted them publicly.

'I think you've done a very good job,' said Elena. 'You've brought them back to life by telling their stories. I know that sounds strange because they're all dead, but you've made them into real people whose lives mattered and will now always be remembered – even by strangers, if they read the memorial pages.'

'If you're happy to let me have your email address, I'll draft something for Keisha's page, and you can have a look and make sure you're happy with it before I post it on the website,' Briony told Shanice.

As they ate sandwiches and chips and toasted Keisha's memory, Shanice regaled them with tales of their exploits, including the time Keisha had put superglue in the keyhole of the locker of a boy who had cheated on her with his ex, and the day they had set off the fire alarm at college by smoking a spliff in the ladies' toilets.

Lachie presented them with the tin Mrs Biscuit had left, and there was an expectant silence at their table as George prised off the lid. The tombstone-shaped cookies inside were iced with rainbows to represent Keisha's final journey over the rainbow bridge, Lachie told them, carefully delivering Mrs Biscuit's explanation with an admirably straight face.

'Did Mrs Biscuit say what flavour they are?' asked Roxy, grinning.

Lachie shook his head. Roxy took one and bit it. She chewed thoughtfully while the others watched. 'The biscuit tastes like coffee and walnut,' she declared.

'And what flavour's the icing?' George enquired, hoping that for once the combination of flavours would prove palatable.

'Cough medicine,' Roxy replied.

Before she left, Shanice thanked them all for what she described as Keisha's beautiful funeral. 'I really appreciate it,' she told them. 'The flowers, the music – it was all beautiful.'

'We couldn't have done it without you,' George replied.

'Yes, but without The Light a Candle Society, I wouldn't have known anything about it,' Shanice replied. 'And I was wondering – because today meant so much – if you'd let me help you give that comfort to others. Even if it's just by turning up to the funerals. Would you let me join you?'

George looked around the faces at the table and registered the smiles of assent. 'We'd be delighted to have you,' he replied.

Chapter 46

George was glad to step out of the searing sunshine and into the cool, fragrant interior of Elena's shop. After a prolonged and indifferent spring, summer had arrived in a rush and at full throttle as though to make up for lost time. George's garden was ablaze with homegrown blooms, and although he had a large bunch of sweet peas in the car, he didn't want to abandon Elena, so he had come to buy some roses to complete his bouquet. He enjoyed his visits to the shop – perhaps more than he cared to admit. Elena put a spring in his step and a smile on his face.

'How are you today, George?' she asked.

'Hot!' he replied. 'But it's lovely and cool in here.'

'Not cool enough,' replied Elena, fanning herself with her hand. 'But I'm not complaining,' she added. 'I'm just looking forward to going home and sitting in the shade with a nice glass of chilled wine.'

'Sounds wonderful! I'm off to see Audrey, but when I get back, I might just follow your example and have a cold beer in my deckchair under the apple tree.'

'I think you should. You know, George, the more funerals

we do, the more I realise that we have to make the most of every day. As Edwin is always saying, you're a long time dead. Now, what can I get for Audrey today?'

'I'll take six of those cream roses, please, and six of the pale pink ones too.'

At the cemetery, the heat was relentless. The sun reflected off stone and marble everywhere and the light was dazzling. George arranged the fresh flowers in front of Audrey's headstone and sat down on the warm grass beside it to have a chat.

'The sweet peas are from the garden, love – they've done really well this year, and they smell beautiful. The roses are from Elena's. I don't like to desert her just because I've got a gardenful of my own flowers, especially after all she's done for the funerals. You'd like her, Audrey. She's a lovely woman.'

George closed his eyes for a moment and breathed deeply. The scent of the sweet peas and roses was a heady essence of pure summer. The distant hum of traffic was punctuated by bright notes of birdsong and the steady drone of a nearby bee.

'Elizabeth and the kids are coming to stay in a couple of weeks. Not that they're kids any more. Angus is off to uni this year, and Amelie is on boyfriend number three already!'

George hadn't seen them since his aborted birthday lunch, and though he had spoken to Elizabeth many times since then, he still hadn't told her what had really happened, and she hadn't once mentioned Roger to him. He was beginning to worry that her visit might include another ambush, but he wasn't sure what he could do to predict or prevent it.

'*You're going to have to speak to her,*' he could hear Audrey saying. '*You can't keep avoiding it forever. You need to deal with it once and for all.*'

'I know, I know,' George spoke out loud. 'But I don't know how to.'

'*Oh yes you do!*' Audrey countered inside his head. '*You know exactly how to – you just don't want to! It's time you told the truth.*'

George sighed. She was right, of course. But that didn't necessarily mean he was going to do it. Especially if he could find a way of getting out of it. It was a chapter in his past he had kept closed for so long that reopening it was almost unthinkable. He pushed himself up onto his feet and cursed as his knees protested. He really needed to join a yoga class or something, he thought. He gathered up the dead flowers he had replaced on Audrey's grave and headed off towards the bins, where he spotted a familiar figure puffing away.

'You've caught me again!' Edwin laughed. 'But we're done for the day, so I thought I'd treat myself. Just got to take the hearse home and put her to bed. It's been a busy day, and the last funeral was pretty tough.'

'Whose was it?'

'A woman in her late forties. Left behind a husband and two teenage daughters – all completely devastated. She had a big family, and hordes of friends too. The chapel was packed.'

'What did she die of?' asked George.

'She was an alcoholic,' Edwin replied simply. 'To the outside world it must have seemed like she had everything – a lovely family, big house, plenty of money – but it wasn't enough. So perhaps she kept looking for whatever was missing at the bottom of a glass.'

George's expression hardened. 'How could she do that to her family?' he asked, his tone unmistakeably judgemental. 'Especially her girls!'

Edwin shook his head sadly. 'It's an illness, George. An addiction. There comes a point when it's no longer a choice, it's a compulsion. Alcoholics need alcohol to survive but the cruel irony is that it usually kills them in the end.'

'But surely they must be able to see what it does to their families? How much it hurts them?' George thought about all the times he had seen his mum cry and the way they had dreaded his dad coming home from the pub.

'It doesn't work like that, George. The drink takes over. It's both tyrant and parasite – a lethal mongrel.'

'How do you know so much about it?'

'I lost a good friend to drink just over fifteen years ago. He had a wife and a son who was only fifteen when his dad died. I tried everything I could think of to help him. Took him to AA meetings, where he'd hide in the toilets until I'd gone and then go down the pub. Even when he was hospitalised, he'd sneak out and buy booze from the shop over the road and smuggle it back onto the ward in a squash bottle. But I found out the hard way that you can't help someone unless they admit they need help – unless they want it. And, yes, there were times when I hated the person he had become. The man who wet himself in public and didn't care, and yelled abuse at strangers in the street. And I was so angry about what he was doing to himself and to the people that loved him. But eventually I realised there was no point blaming him.'

Edwin took a final, deep drag on his cigarette and stubbed it out. 'I know that the hardworking, decent, sensitive and funny man he was when I first met him would never have deliberately hurt his family in a million years. He would never have chosen to humiliate them and himself in the way that he did. There were times, when he was sober, that he was horrified by what he'd done and how he'd behaved, and he'd beg for forgiveness and promise never to do it again. But the drink always won. Such a waste.'

'What happened to his family?'

Edwin smiled. 'They struggled for a bit, but his wife, Maggie, is made of stern stuff. She's got a new man now and even volunteers for AA. I think it helped her to understand a bit about what Andy went through. She was able to make her peace with it and move on.'

'And what about the son?'

'He's happily married with two kids of his own. I'm godfather to the eldest, and a right little terror he is!' Edwin checked his watch. 'Well, I best be off. Esmee and me are going to the pictures tonight. Date night, she calls it!' He winked at George and grinned. 'See you on Thursday for the quiz?'

George nodded. 'Have a good time tonight.'

He watched Edwin walk away. He was unreasonably irritated with him and his empathy and understanding. Edwin might have *known* an alcoholic, but he hadn't lived with one. He hadn't been a frightened little boy trying to protect his mum and his brother from the monster genie that came out of the bottles of booze instead of the dad who was supposed to bring his mum flowers and play football with his boys and help them with their homework. No, thought George, Edwin didn't know what it was really like, because if he did, he would understand that you could never forgive someone like that. But … It was perhaps the 'but' that had disturbed George the most.

'But eventually I realised there was no point blaming him,' Edwin had said.

Had George got it wrong for all these years?

He made his way through the cemetery to where the memorial cabinet stood close to the ornamental pond. The sound of gentle splashing from the fountain was instantly soothing, and the air seemed slightly cooler here. The cabinet was filling up now, and George took a cloth from his pocket and polished the glass panes until they gleamed, and then he sat down by the pond and watched the light dance and sparkle on the water. He took a deep breath and rolled his shoulders back, trying to dispel the tension that had gripped both his body and his mind. The woman's funeral and Edwin's words had unsettled and angered him. The anger, he knew, was a repository for the muddle of emotions that he was unable or unwilling to address. Guilt, loss, hurt and confusion were all much easier to cope with when distilled into anger. To question his dad's culpability would be to question the truths upon which George had built his life since childhood. George picked up a pebble that lay at his feet, flung it into the water and watched as the ripples bloomed across the pond's surface. He felt so tired – and very alone. He thought about his deckchair under the apple tree and the cold beer in the fridge. Time to go home.

Chapter 47

'Chin chin!' Allegra raised her glass to Briony, leaned back in her deckchair and took a sip.

They were sitting in Allegra's garden and, in honour of the spectacularly good weather, Allegra had forsaken their customary martinis for something which she said was synonymous with the perfect English summer – Pimm's. Allegra was looking very glamorous in enormous sunglasses, a wide-brimmed sunhat and a flimsy silk kimono. Briony was tanned and freckled in shorts and a vest top. It was late afternoon and Briony had not long been home from work, but it was still hot enough to fry eggs on the paving slabs of the path according to Allegra, who was wafting a Chinese paper fan in front of her face. Not that she was complaining.

'It's heaven!' she declared. 'It's such a treat to sit outside and feel the sun warm my bones.' She stretched her legs out in front of her, displaying her elegant bare feet with toenails perfectly painted scarlet. 'How's your young man?'

Briony smiled. She and Zach had been dating for several weeks now, having finally and decisively left the friend zone behind with sleepovers on both sides of their landing.

'He's fine, thank you. But he's working night shifts this week, so I haven't seen much of him.'

'Good,' replied Allegra. 'I mean, not good because you haven't seen much of him, but good that you're not busy because I want to talk to you. What are you planning to do next with your career?'

Briony sat up in her deckchair and frowned at Allegra. 'What do you mean?'

'Well, you wrote the story about The Light a Candle Society, and it was well received. It almost made it into one of the nationals, which proves it had merit, so what are you doing to follow it up?'

To be honest, Briony hadn't thought about her job much lately. Gordon had sent her out on some more interesting assignments, and her blossoming relationship with Zach had distracted her from any lingering dissatisfaction she felt at work.

'I'm not really sure,' she confessed. 'Gordon hasn't been so bad recently and I'm getting more experience now so …' She shrugged as her words trailed away.

Allegra shook her head. 'That story was supposed to be a springboard. It was supposed to jump-start a new phase in your career. What happened to your passion for journalism? I remember you telling me that you wanted to write about things people cared about, stories people actually wanted to read.'

Allegra was right, thought Briony. She had become distracted. But that was okay, wasn't it? She was beginning to think that perhaps she wasn't the driven career woman she had always thought she was after all. But now that Allegra had raised the issue, she felt guilty and vaguely unsettled, as though she had been caught skiving.

Allegra sat up in her deckchair and removed her sunglasses. 'Look, my dear. I'm happy for you that your relationship with Zach is going well – I really am. But a man isn't the answer to everything. You are a bright young woman with a promising career ahead of you. Don't let opportunities pass you by because you're looking in another direction. The best gifts you can ever give yourself are financial and emotional independence. That doesn't mean you can't have a man as well – it just means that you don't have to rely on him for a decent life. It's lovely to have someone to look after you, but so much better when you know that, if you have to, you're perfectly capable of looking after yourself.'

'Like you, you mean?' Briony replied, a little tetchily. She felt as though she was being lectured.

Allegra sipped her drink, unruffled by Briony's tone. 'Yes, like me. It wasn't what I would have chosen – nor what I expected. But it turned out to be my fate, nonetheless, and I believe I have managed admirably.'

Briony wondered if she were being afforded a rare glimpse through a barely open doorway into a secret place – Allegra's past. She couldn't decide whether she should try to push the door or wait for it to swing open of its own accord.

'I've been reading the memorial pages you've been writing for the website.'

The change of subject appeared to have slammed the door shut.

'They're very good,' Allegra continued. 'You write with sensitivity and compassion, without compromising the integrity of your subject. It's a tricky assignment to pull off, but you've managed it beautifully. You have a real talent.'

Briony was genuinely flattered. Allegra's good opinion was important to her – sometimes annoyingly so.

'Thank you,' she replied. 'I actually enjoy writing them. Perhaps because they really matter. Because each story is a life.'

'And that's what I wanted to talk to you about,' Allegra said, smiling her inscrutable smile. 'But first I think we need another drink.'

Chapter 48

Case no. ?????-????

The woman stretched her long, bare limbs lazily beneath the silk sheets of the king-size bed and yawned. The sounds of the city waking up to the business of a new day drifted in through the open doors of the balcony. But in this sumptuous suite on the fifth floor high above the avenue Montaigne, the hum of traffic and the ringing of church bells were decorously distant, so as not to disturb the hotel's most esteemed guests. She opened her eyes and saw a dark figure silhouetted against the bright morning light spilling in from the balcony.

'Good morning, lazy bones! You're finally awake.'

The man was in his early fifties – not exactly handsome, but with strong features and warm brown eyes. He was already dressed in an immaculately tailored suit and Hermès silk tie. He strolled across to the bed, leaned over and planted a lingering kiss on her lips.

'I have to go,' he told her. 'I have a meeting and then I'm flying to Geneva this afternoon. I'll see you back in London sometime next week. I'll call you.'

He took a fat envelope from his jacket pocket and placed it on the bedside table closest to her, and then he hesitated for a moment and smiled. It was his smile that had been her undoing, however hard she had tried to resist and however adamantly she refused to acknowledge it. The smile that had made her – cool, calculating professional that she was – fall in love with him. But that had been her secret cross to bear for years now, and she had never allowed herself even to consider the possibility that he might love her back.

'It's our anniversary,' he said. 'Ten years.'

She sat up and smiled back at him. 'Is it? I hadn't realised,' she lied.

It was ten years to the day since they had first met. She could remember there had been puddles on the pavement that rainy Tuesday evening in London, and they had drunk cocktails at The Savoy: him – a whisky sour; her – a dry martini.

'You have no idea how much you mean to me,' he said. 'But perhaps this might convince you.' He handed her a small dark blue leather-bound box – the type that normally contained expensive jewellery.

'I've ordered you some breakfast. You'd better put something on before room service arrives,' he teased, pulling back the sheet a little to reveal her nakedness.

'I thought you had a meeting to go to,' she reminded him, reclaiming the bedcover.

He checked his watch and kissed her again before picking up his bag and heading for the door.

'Thank you,' she said, holding up the box. 'Happy anniversary.'

Once he'd gone, she got out of bed, pulled on a silk dressing gown and took the box out onto the balcony. It was still early – a little after seven – but it was already hot. The view across Paris was spectacular, the skyline dominated by the iconic ironwork of the Eiffel Tower. She put the box down on the table in front of her and stroked the smooth lid with her fingers. Was it jewellery? Could it be a ring? She shook her head and told herself not to be so ridiculous. He was already married and, besides, the box was too big. There was a knock at the door and at her 'Entrez!' a waiter pushed a trolley into the room. She thanked and tipped him and took the breakfast tray back out onto the balcony. She poured herself a cup of coffee and added steaming frothy milk. It wasn't until she'd drunk the coffee that she picked up the box and opened it. Inside was a set of keys attached to a solid silver tag. Engraved on the tag was an address in Mayfair.

'I'm offering you the chance to write my life story – an entire biography rather than a newspaper article,' Allegra told Briony. 'Forgive me, dear, but I'm not sure your elbows are sharp enough for the cut and thrust of journalism. I think perhaps you might be better suited to writing books. But I'd prefer that you didn't submit it for publication until after I'm dead, and there must be no names mentioned – it's not a "kiss and tell". Close your mouth, dear. You'll swallow a fly.'

Briony's jaw had indeed dropped open in surprise at Allegra's revelations.

'Of course, you might not think it's worth writing,' Allegra continued. 'But I have had a pretty interesting time of it.'

Briony was still trying to process what little information Allegra had shared so far. 'Zach thought you might have worked for MI5,' she said. 'You did once tell me that you worked in communications.'

Allegra laughed. 'Well, I suppose I did spend a lot of time undercover – and, indeed, under the covers. But communication was a very important part of my job. My gentlemen wanted someone to take out to dinner, the theatre and the opera – not just to bed. They wanted culture, conversation and companionship as well as coitus. And sometimes they didn't want sex at all, just someone to be with. These men were extremely wealthy, some of them famous, and very powerful in their own worlds. They were leaders who were expected to have all the answers and always be strong and capable – almost infallible, I suppose. But I was their brief escape from all that pressure, and with me they could be anyone they wanted. And as they grew to trust me, the thing that most of them wanted was to be human and sometimes vulnerable.'

'But how did it all start?' Briony asked, still completely incredulous. 'How did you become a …' She stopped suddenly, searching for an alternative to prostitute.

'Courtesan?' Allegra interceded. 'That was my preferred job title.'

Briony nodded and drained the last of the Pimm's from her glass.

'Many years ago, I was Alison Greenhill. I was born into a nice, respectable middle-class family who lived in a nice, respectable suburb. My father was a solicitor, and my mother was his secretary until they married, then she became a mother and a housewife. My brother, Matthew, was born first, and then three years later I came along. I suppose I rather idolised Matthew. He was handsome and kind, but full of wild ideas. He had this dream of travelling across Europe on a motorbike, picking up casual work as and when he could find it and maybe even joining a commune of some sort. Well, it was the sixties! My father was horrified and persuaded him to join the firm where he worked as a clerk. I expect he thought that if he could get Matthew settled in a job and earning his own money then he would give up his "madcap scheme", as my father called his proposed European trip, and knuckle down to "real life".'

Allegra paused for a moment and a blackbird filled the silence with an incongruously cheery song.

'Matthew confided in me that he had only agreed to appease our father. He planned to stick it out for six months or so, just so he could say he had tried, and then he would be off. But the closest he came to fulfilling his dream was the motorbike that he used to get to and from the office. He was coming home one evening in November and the bike slid on black ice and crashed into a lamp post. Matthew was killed instantly.'

Briony gasped. 'Oh, Allegra, I'm so sorry. That's awful.'

'It was. Appalling. And it made me determined not to settle for a quiet, respectable life, but to follow my dreams – even though I had no idea what they were back then. So I decided to borrow Matthew's dream to travel, in the meantime, and when I finished school, I ran away to London. I had a friend who was about to start at art college, and she said there was a room for me in the flat she was sharing with some other students. Of course, I had to get a job to pay my way, and I ended up applying for the position of personal assistant to a woman called Isabella Ogilvie. I had worked for her for several months before I realised what she did for a living, and that's when my apprenticeship began. Isabella educated me in every aspect of her work. She was in her early fifties – although she looked much younger – and was beginning to think about retirement. I never knew if she was looking for a successor when she interviewed me, or if the idea came after I began working for her. Either way, Alison Greenhill gradually metamorphosed into Allegra Monteverdi and never looked back.'

'But what about your parents?' Briony asked.

'They were upset at first. But I always kept in contact, and eventually they became proud of their daughter who made such a success of her life and travelled the world. They were disappointed that I never married and provided them with any grandchildren, of course, but then those things were never going to be compatible with my chosen profession.'

'But did you ever tell them what your profession was?'

Allegra laughed out loud. 'Of course not! I told them I worked for a travel agency that specialised in foreign holidays. I sent them postcards from all the places I visited.'

'Are they the postcards in your albums?' Briony asked.

Allegra shook her head. 'The albums are my diary. I sent them to myself so that I would remember all my adventures. There were never any photographs, you see. It was too risky. Most of my gentlemen were married, so discretion was essential. And even those who weren't married wanted to keep our liaisons as secret as possible, which is why so many of them took place abroad. But if you want to write my story you can certainly read all my postcards.'

'Of course I want to write your story!' Briony replied. 'But why don't you want it published until after you die?'

'Fix us some more drinks and I'll tell you,' Allegra replied.

While Briony went inside to refill their glasses, Allegra closed her eyes and allowed herself to picture that morning in Paris. That hotel room, that kiss, the blue box, the view from the balcony. The one man whom she had loved. He had never said he loved her, but when he died, he had left her the flat in Mayfair.

'So tell me – why the need for posthumous publication?' asked Briony, handing her a full glass.

Allegra considered her words for a moment before replying. 'I have never been ashamed of what I've done. Everything that happened was between consenting adults. I like to think that the service I provided was dignified, compassionate and discreet. And I always worked on my own terms. Yes, I worked for men, but I never relied on any of them for anything else. There were strict boundaries that were never crossed. I was never beholden to anyone. But I am aware that many people would not see it that way and would be quick to judge, which is one of the reasons why I didn't risk making friends in the past.'

'Until now,' Briony added. 'I'm your friend. So what changed?'

Allegra smiled. 'I'm getting old. And sometimes it's lonely. That story you wrote about The Light a Candle Society made me think. My funeral will be one of *those* funerals. I've had an amazing life, and I don't regret it. But perhaps it's not quite over yet, and it might be nice to share what's left with a friend or two.'

Briony reached across and touched Allegra's arm. 'Well, I'm so pleased that you decided to give me a go as a potential friend. I hope I'm up to scratch! And as for people judging your past – I'm not so sure they would these days. But I could write your story first and then you can decide. How does that sound?'

Allegra raised her glass in a toast. 'It's a deal!'

'And don't worry,' Briony added with a wicked grin, 'I'll make sure that when the time comes The Light a Candle Society give you a funeral fit for a queen!'

Chapter 49

'How was your weekend?' Roxy asked as George joined her in the staff room and immediately switched on the kettle.

'Lovely, but to be honest, I'm quite glad it's over.'

Roxy dropped teabags into two mugs. 'Have Elizabeth and the kids gone back?'

'Yes. I dropped them at the station on my way here, which is why I'm a bit late.'

Roxy grinned. 'Don't worry – I won't tell on you! So did you have a fun week?'

George had taken some time off to spend with Elizabeth, Angus and Amelie, and whilst he'd enjoyed having them to stay, he'd also found it quite tiring.

'The house seemed so noisy,' he replied. 'And I'd forgotten how long teenage girls spend in the bathroom!'

'How old is Amelie now?' Roxy asked.

'Sixteen going on twenty-four! And when she wasn't in the bathroom, she was on her mobile messaging her boyfriend.'

'I hated being sixteen,' said Roxy with feeling. 'I had terrible spots and boobs like fried eggs!'

'Too much information,' replied George.

He made the tea, and they carried their mugs through to the library and then Roxy unlocked the main doors.

'How was *your* weekend?' George asked when she returned to their desk.

'It was great. Niall finally got tickets for *La traviata* at The Royal Opera House, and we went on Saturday. I was a bit worried that I might disgrace myself – it sounds so posh going to the opera! I spent a fair bit of time in the bathroom too before we went, trying to make myself look presentable. I even bought a new dress!'

'I'm sure you looked lovely. But more importantly, did you enjoy it?'

'I loved it! It was magical. And afterwards, Niall took me out to dinner in Covent Garden.'

'So is it serious between you two now?' George asked.

But before Roxy could answer, The Shipping Forecast presented himself at the desk and asked if they had a particular biography of Gertrude Jekyll. This was an unexpected departure from his usual reading matter, and Roxy got up at once to see if she could help.

'I'll show you where we keep the biographies, Mr Cromarty,' she said, 'and we'll see if we can find it.'

Left on his own, George considered their respective weekends and was glad that Roxy had enjoyed hers so much. It seemed he *had* been wrong about Niall, and he hoped that Niall's relationship with Roxy might develop into something permanent. George had successfully navigated his week with Elizabeth without any serious antagonism. He hadn't mentioned anything about The Light a Candle Society, and she hadn't mentioned anything about her grandfather or Roger. But he knew it was an uneasy truce and one that neither of them would be able to sustain indefinitely. He had been sad not to be able to share what he and his friends had been doing for the public health funerals, and he couldn't help but feel it was ridiculous to be tiptoeing around his own daughter at his time of life.

'Well,' said Roxy, returning to the desk, 'that's a turn up for the books – literally! Fancy The Shipping Forecast branching out into gardening? Still, I suppose it's never too late to try something new. And speaking of something new, Niall mentioned another funeral he wants us to help with. The circumstances are quite unusual – not like anything we've done before.'

'I'm intrigued,' George replied. 'Tell me more.'

'It's a gentleman who donated his body to medical science. The medical school have finished with his body now, and the man stipulated that whatever remained of his remains should be cremated in his hometown and scattered in the cemetery. His family held a memorial service for him when he died and don't want to do anything else. Niall said that when he spoke to the man's brother, he got the impression that the family had said their goodbyes and didn't want to reopen old wounds. It seems that not everyone close to him approved of his generous donation.'

George nodded thoughtfully. 'It's strange, isn't it, how people react? I always think of the body as being nothing more than an empty container once the person who inhabited it has left. I sat with Audrey's body for almost an hour after she had died, and it definitely wasn't Audrey any more. But I had to make sure, you see. I had to be certain that she had truly gone – and of course she had. But even so, I would have hated to think of her body being treated disrespectfully in any way. Edwin once told me that his father always said that the way we treat our dead is a measure of our own humanity – and it's true.'

'But you don't think the medical school would treat any body that they were gifted badly, do you? Surely, they'd be really thankful?'

'I hope so,' George replied.

'Well, anyway,' continued Roxy, 'if we don't do something for this gentleman, there will be no proper service prior to his cremation, which I think would be terrible – and ungrateful – considering the legacy that he left. According to Niall, the medical school are happy to pay for a basic service and send someone along to attend, but it would be up to us to do the rest.'

'Then we must make sure that we honour this gentleman in our usual way,' George agreed.

That afternoon, George walked home through the park. It was an idyllic scene – a summer symphony of birdsong, children playing and a mower carving neat bands through the grass. People were stretched out on their backs soaking up the sun, reading in the shade or chatting with their companions. Contentment hung in the air like the scent of freshly baked bread. But George felt completely at odds with this communal serenity. Since the alcoholic woman's funeral and his subsequent conversation with Edwin, George's long-held perspective on his childhood had been shifting in and out of focus, and the clarity with which he had always been able to justify his opinions and actions to himself was gradually dissolving.

He had no qualms about the accuracy of his memory. He knew what had happened because he had been there. But he was finally beginning to understand that these events had not taken place in a vacuum, and it was their context that was causing him to question his version of the truth. He was a stubborn man by nature, but not stupid. And some of the funerals that The Light a Candle Society had been organising had caused him to reflect on the importance of fixing things before they became indelible regrets – a tragic obituary of 'what if's and 'if only's, a tangle of loose ends that could have been sorted and smoothed instead of becoming a poisonous legacy of doubt and dissatisfaction.

In the cool quiet of his kitchen, George's heart was pounding as he took out his mobile and dialled. As soon as his call was answered he began to speak before his courage failed him.

'There's something I really need to talk about,' he began. 'The last time I ever saw my dad he came home so drunk that he could barely stand. I was supposed to be in bed, but I crept downstairs when I heard him stagger through the back door. I was only eleven, but whenever Dad came home drunk, I always felt that I needed to protect Mum. She was waiting for him in the kitchen and his tea was still on the table from hours ago, stone cold. It was pork chops with mashed potatoes and peas in a puddle of congealed gravy. I remember as we had sat there – me and Mum and Roger – eating our tea, Mum had kept checking the clock. Dad looked at the plate when he came in and laughed.

'"I'm not eating that muck," he said. "It's cold."

'I was shivering in just my pyjamas, standing in the hallway. They couldn't see me and part of me wanted to run back upstairs and hide under the covers of my bed, but I was frozen to the spot.

'"It wasn't five hours ago when I served it up. So, you can take it or leave it."

'Mum seemed very calm and spoke quietly, but I could tell she was really angry.

'Dad stood there for a moment, swaying, and what he did next seemed to be in slow motion. He unzipped his trousers and urinated over the plate of food, the steaming yellow liquid splashing onto the tablecloth. I didn't see what happened after that, because I ran back upstairs. I know I should have said something. I should have gone in and yelled at him. Hit him. Told him how disgusting he was. But I didn't. I went back to bed. I'm not sure now if I was scared or just completely dumbstruck. But every time I think of it I feel guilty that I did nothing. I was a coward, and I was weak. I didn't hear any shouting, but I did hear the door slam, and Mum came upstairs into our room and wedged a chair under the door handle. I pretended to be asleep, and the next morning when we got up, Mum was in the kitchen making our breakfast as usual and she told us that Dad was in bed. When we came home from school he was gone, and I never saw him again.'

Chapter 50

When Roxy went to the fridge to get the radishes for the salad, Sailor immediately dropped into his 'good boy' sit and gazed up at her adoringly with his icy blue eyes.

'Just one,' Roxy said, handing him a cocktail sausage before closing the fridge door. 'And don't tell your dad!'

She glanced out of the window into the back garden where Captain was dozing in a deckchair. Over the spring and summer months, Captain and Sailor had become regular visitors to Roxy's house, and she had gradually learned a little more about this taciturn man and his life before she had known him. Roxy was careful never to fish for information, but merely to respond with interest when he offered any clue about his past. She had learned that he had been born and lived on the Pembrokeshire coast until he had moved inland around thirty-five years ago, when he had begun working as an HGV driver. He had never married and had no siblings – and no friends that he mentioned other than Sailor, who had come from an animal sanctuary in Norfolk as a six-month-old bundle of fluff.

'I picked him up on one of my last runs in a truck,' Captain had told her.

Roxy beat eggs, milk and cheese together and mixed in finely chopped onions and a little fresh parsley. She poured the mixture into a pastry case and slid it into the oven and then made a salad with the radishes, and lettuce, tomatoes and spring onions from the garden. There was plenty of time for a quiet beer with Captain before Niall would be there to join them for a late lunch. Roxy took two bottles from the fridge and quickly closed the door before Sailor had a chance to plead for another sausage. She handed Captain a beer and sat down in the other deckchair.

'Cheers!' she said, clinking her bottle against his.

'Cheers!' he replied, his eyes fixed on the apron she was still wearing, which she bought as a souvenir from a holiday some years ago in Cromer. It bore the Royal National Lifeboat Institution flag.

'Is there anything wrong?' Roxy asked, seeing the almost pained expression on his face.

He shook his head. 'I was just thinking,' he said, nodding towards her apron, 'they do a tough job.'

They sat in companionable silence for a while sipping their beers. They didn't hear the doorbell when it rang, but Sailor did, alerting them with a bark.

'That'll be Niall,' said Roxy, getting up.

For once, Sailor didn't follow her. Instead, he sat beside Captain and rested his head in his old friend's lap. Captain stroked the dog's soft fur as he leaned back in the deckchair and closed his eyes.

Chapter 51

Case no. 63542-7583

Dylan Jones had volunteered as a crew member for the RNLI as soon as he was old enough – as his father and grandfather had done before him. The sea was in his blood, so his dad had always said. Even his name meant 'son of the sea'. After twenty-five years' service, the sound of his pager still sent adrenalin surging through his body.

It had been one of those golden days that September so often gifted at the end of a lacklustre summer, and although the beaches had been busy, there had been no shouts to rescue any wayward swimmers or stranded kayakers. But weather conditions along the rugged coastline in this part of Pembrokeshire were notoriously fickle and sometimes brutal, and as early evening drew on, the sky turned a menacing grey and an offshore wind began to whip foaming peaks across the breakers. Dylan was on his way home from work. He was driving out of St Davids towards Solva, where he lived in a terraced cottage that looked out over the harbour. He had spent the day servicing a couple of tractors at a farm just outside Croesgoch and was looking forward to shedding his grimy overalls and having a long hot shower. He was singing along to a David Bowie track on the radio when his pager summoned him to be a real-life hero. Dylan pulled over and swung his truck around in a U-turn, pushing his foot down on the accelerator as soon as he was heading back in the direction of St Davids. It began to rain – a fierce, lashing torrent that rattled down on the roof and challenged the wipers to keep up with its bombardment of the windscreen. By the time Dylan reached the lifeboat station, several crew members were already there and more information about the nature of the rescue was coming in. He could tell by the look on Gethin's face that it was serious.

'Two girls have been reported missing by their mother,' he said. 'They're local girls from Solva – Bethan and Erin Thomas, aged ten and twelve respectively.'

Dylan knew the family – not well, but well enough that he would recognise the girls if he saw them.

'They went down to the beach at Solva this afternoon and were supposed to be back home for their tea at five,' Gethin continued. 'When they didn't turn up, their parents went looking, but there was no sign of them. A pair of kayakers think they may have seen them climbing over the rocks near the beach at around four o'clock, but there haven't been any further sightings. Now the weather's turned and the tide's coming in fast. We need to get out there and find them. A land search is underway, but we have to consider the possibility that they've been cut off by the tide and could be stranded somewhere.'

Dylan ran through the possible scenarios in his head as they pulled on their kit and got ready to launch the D-class lifeboat.

None of them were good. It was getting dark and visibility would be poor. It was a spring tide and rising fast so conditions would be rough. If the girls were stranded on the rocks, finding them would be a serious challenge – and that was provided they could hang on until the boat got to them. Within minutes, Dylan, Gethin and Robert – the three most experienced crew members – were powering through the choppy sea. Water slapped angrily against the sides of the lifeboat as it bounced across the towering waves. Gethin battled to keep them on course while Dylan and Robert scoured the shoreline for any sign of the girls. The Pembrokeshire coast was renowned for its rugged beauty, but though undoubtedly picturesque, the vertiginous cliffs, jagged rocks and caves could prove hazardous and sometimes deadly when the elements turned hostile.

After almost an hour at sea, their searchlight caught a scrap of something pale moving on a rocky outcrop just above the entrance to a cave. Gethin tried to manoeuvre the boat towards the shore, but the closer they got the more hazardous the combination of shallow water and half-hidden rocks became. They shouted to the girls, who were huddled together with their arms around one another, but they barely had the strength to reply. Their shorts and T-shirts were sodden, and their faces deathly white with cold and fear. The smaller girl was shivering uncontrollably.

'It's okay!' Dylan yelled. 'Bethan, Erin, you're safe now! Don't move – just stay where you are, and we'll come and get you.'

'I can't get any closer,' Gethin shouted above the noise of the wind and waves. 'There's too many rocks.'

'I'll go,' Dylan said. 'We can't wait. They won't last much longer. We have to get them now.'

As he spoke, a huge wave crashed over the rocks where the girls were crouched and they slid down, dragged by the backwash, until they were almost in the water.

'Hold on!' Dylan yelled. 'I'm coming.'

He slipped over the side of the boat into the swirling water that smashed into him, battering his body and knocking the breath from his lungs. Robert tugged on his line to steady him, and Dylan began to fight his way through the dark sea towards the girls. It was only a distance of about fifty metres, but it seemed so much further, and as he picked his way through the rocks and foam, he focused on the terrified faces of the two little girls frozen in the beam of the searchlight. He was almost close enough to touch them, and could see the desperation in their blue eyes, when another brutal wave swept him off his feet and back into the water. For a moment he was pulled beneath the surface, but buoyed by his lifejacket he bobbed up again, choking the sea from his mouth and nose and blinking the stinging salt from his eyes.

'Are you okay?' Robert yelled.

Dylan gave him a swift thumbs up before heading back towards the girls. This time he made it and briefly gathered them both into a reassuring hug. But he knew he could only risk taking them back to the boat one at a time. The younger girl was barely conscious, but Erin was more alert and able to talk.

'Erin, I have to leave you for just a moment while I get Bethan to the boat,' Dylan told her. 'Just hold on and I'll come straight back for you, I promise. Okay?'

Erin nodded and even managed a ghost of a smile. Dylan wrapped one arm around Bethan, lifted her up and pulled her tightly against his body. He slipped into the water and, with Robert guiding them, they were back at the boat in minutes. Robert hauled Bethan on board and Dylan turned to make his way back to Erin. The sight of her still clinging on and waiting for him banished his exhaustion as he battled through the water.

'Come on, Erin,' he said as he scrabbled up the rocks. 'Let's get you home.'

'Thank you,' she whispered as he reached out his hand to take hers. But their fingertips barely brushed before another wave swept over them and sent them crashing into the sea.

Captain dozed contentedly as the sun warmed his face and a thrush warbled his finest trills and arpeggios from the top of the tree at the end of the garden. The tree's branches were heavy with ripe plums, and wasps buzzed around the split, sticky flesh of the windfall fruit that lay in the grass below. Sailor nuzzled the old man's hands and then settled down at his feet with a satisfied sigh. Captain felt lighter than he had in years. It was almost as though he was floating above himself – finally untethered from a dark and unnamed shame that had shadowed him for so long. In Roxy, he had found a friend who accepted him as he was, without inquisition or judgement. And more importantly, he had found a loving home for his precious Sailor should the need arise. He was closer now to happy than he could ever have expected.

Although his eyes were closed, he could sense a brightness approaching him. He peered through his eyelashes and saw a figure, backlit by the sun, walking towards him. As she grew closer, he could see her face. She looked familiar. She smiled, reached out and took his hand in her own. It was Erin.

―

Roxy and Niall stood chatting in the kitchen while Roxy made a dressing for the salad.

'Caragh's in trouble again,' Niall reported with a sigh.

Roxy grinned. 'What's she done this time?'

'She's had her nose pierced. She knows she's not allowed to wear a nose ring to school. Her mum went ballistic – and for once I can't say I blame her!'

'I used to have a nose ring – and a stud.'

Niall looked at her and narrowed his eyes. 'Yes – you did when I first met you. Why did you take them out?'

Roxy shrugged. 'I supposed I just got fed up with them. I wanted a different look.'

Niall pulled her towards him and kissed her. 'Well, I think you've always looked lovely! But Caragh's only fifteen, and I'm pretty sure she only does these things to wind her mother up.'

'Of course she does. She's a teenager – it's her job!'

'She's coming to stay in a couple of weeks, and I wondered if you'd like to meet her. We could maybe all go up to London for the day?'

'I'd love to. But do you think Caragh would want to? She might just want to have you to herself.'

Niall snorted with laughter. 'You must be kidding! She once told me that I'm as boring as shredded wheat cereal with no milk or sugar. Besides, she's dying to meet you. She's always asking about you. I don't think she can quite believe that I've managed to persuade any woman at all to go out with me!'

'Well, that's settled,' Roxy agreed. 'We'll have a grand day out in London.'

She checked the quiche, took it out of the oven and set it on the side to cool a little. 'Shall we eat outside – make the most of the sunshine? Can you get the plates out while I go and check that Captain's awake?'

Roxy stepped outside into the garden and found Captain still in the deckchair with his eyes closed and Sailor asleep at his feet.

'Captain,' she said softly, 'are you ready for something to eat?'

Sailor raised his head and looked at her steadily. His tail was still.

'Captain,' she said again. She took his hand and squeezed it. For a fleeting moment his fingers closed around hers – and then he was gone.

Chapter 52

Roxy had debated whether or not to bring to Sailor with her in case it might upset him. But then she had reasoned that he had witnessed Captain's death and so hopefully he wouldn't expect to find him at their former home. She had read that animals understand death if they see it for themselves and that the sudden disappearance of a loved one is far more traumatic for them. Sailor had sat faithfully by his master's side until the doctor had been and Edwin and his colleague had come to take Captain's body away. Captain had brought a sweater with him that day, in case it had turned chilly later on, and he had thrown it over the back of the deckchair he had been sitting in. That night, Sailor slept on Roxy's sofa snuggled up next to the sweater, and Roxy had sat beside him stroking his ears while silent tears ran down her cheeks.

Captain had given Roxy a key to his house several weeks before he died. It was almost as though he had been putting things in order in preparation for this eventuality. Roxy had never been to Captain's home before – he and Sailor had always come to her. It was a small terraced house just a fifteen-minute walk from where Roxy lived. The blue-painted front door had a brass knocker in the shape of an anchor. Niall and Sailor stood waiting while Roxy searched for the key in her bag, and as she did so, the door of the neighbouring house opened and a middle-aged woman peered out.

'Is everything all right?' she asked. 'Only I haven't seen him next door for a few days now and that's not like him. He never usually goes away.'

She spotted Sailor and smiled a little uncertainly. 'Oh – I see you've got his dog. Is he poorly? In hospital?'

Roxy paused, key in hand, wondering how to break the news. The woman obviously hadn't known Captain very well because she wasn't calling him by name.

Sensing Roxy's uncertainty, Niall stepped in adopting his professional persona. 'I'm afraid the gentleman who lived here has died. I'm from the council and it's my job to try and establish the identity of any next of kin. Roxy was his friend and she's here to help me. And perhaps you can too,' he added with an encouraging smile. 'Did your neighbour have any family that you know of?'

The woman shook her head. 'He was nice enough,' she replied, 'but very quiet. Kept himself to himself. He'd always nod or tip his cap when I saw him, but he very rarely spoke. It's a dreadful thing to admit, but I didn't even know his name, and I've been living next door to him for nearly ten years. In fact, I don't really know anything about him at all.' She paused for a moment and pursed her lips. 'I actually feel a bit disappointed in myself now,' she added. 'Perhaps I should have made more effort. He never seemed as though he wanted to talk much, but perhaps he was lonely.'

'Well, he had Sailor,' Roxy replied, and at the sound of his name the dog wagged his tail enthusiastically. 'And I think he was quite a private person. I only got to know him fairly recently.'

'Did he ever have any visitors?' Niall asked.

The woman frowned. 'Do you know, apart from the occasional delivery and the postman, I can't remember anyone ever coming to see him.'

The three of them stood in silence for a moment, as though allowing that sobering fact to sink in, until Sailor barked and scratched at the front door with his paw.

'Well, thank you very much Mrs …?'

'Newgale. Gillian Newgale.' She hesitated for a moment. 'What will happen about the funeral? Who'll be arranging it?'

'We will,' replied Roxy and Niall in unison.

'Do you think it would be all right if I came?' Mrs Newgale asked. 'I know it seems a bit late – a bit like shutting the stable door after the horse has bolted – but I would like to pay my respects. And I expect my husband would too.'

'Of course it would be all right,' Roxy reassured her. 'I'll let you know the details once we've sorted things out.'

Once they were inside the house, Sailor went from room to room, upstairs and down. He moved calmly, not appearing to be searching for anything, but simply inspecting the spaces. The house was neat and clean and sparsely furnished, but with comfort and practicality in mind.

'We're looking for paperwork,' Niall told Roxy. 'Anything that might tell us if Captain had any family still living. A will would be great, but letters, an address book, Christmas and birthday cards, photographs – that sort of thing.'

They had discovered Captain's real name from the wallet he had been carrying, but there had been nothing else in it to provide any further clues. In the end, Roxy and Niall didn't have to look very far. There was an old Edwardian sideboard in the sitting room. On top of it sat a tray which held a glass decanter of whisky and a single whisky tumbler. Roxy opened one of the sideboard cupboards to reveal a cardboard storage box which held Captain's life – and death. Its contents included his birth certificate, details of bank and building society accounts, a brown envelope holding Captain's last will and testament, a few photographs – and a Royal National Lifeboat Institute medal for gallantry.

Roxy held the medal up to show Niall. 'Do you think this was Captain's?' she asked.

'Well, if it was, it'll be easy enough to find out,' Niall replied. 'He must have done something pretty special for it to have been awarded and there's bound to be a record of it.'

Having found all the documentation they needed, Niall went into the kitchen to deal with any perishable food that needed disposing of and to gather anything that was obviously Sailor's to take back to Roxy's with them. In the meantime, Roxy went upstairs, searching for she knew not what, but feeling the need to look, nonetheless. The spare bedroom was completely unfurnished and there were no curtains at the window. Captain had clearly never anticipated nor intended inviting any guests.

His own bedroom contained a neatly made double bed, a chest of drawers, a wardrobe and a single chair. On a bedside cabinet stood a reading lamp, an alarm clock, a glass of water and a book. Roxy picked up the book and inspected it. It was a volume of poetry by Tennyson. There were no pictures or photographs on the walls and no ornaments of any kind. Only one thing in the room was neither practical nor useful, but simply there, Roxy assumed, because it was wanted and it had meant something. A very old and, by the look of it, very well-loved teddy bear dressed as a sailor sat at the head of the bed. His once-golden fur was patchy and worn, and one of his eyes was loose, giving him a slightly bewildered air. The sight of him sitting there all alone was unbearably poignant, and Roxy had to cover her mouth with her hand to silence the sob that threatened to escape. She couldn't stop her tears, however, as she picked up the bear and the book and turned to leave the room.

Later that afternoon, with Sailor at her feet, Roxy sat at her laptop searching for Captain's past life. She soon discovered that his history with the RNLI had been long and distinguished but had ended abruptly just over thirty-five years ago – at the same time that he had moved halfway across the country. Her search also yielded several newspaper reports detailing a particularly dangerous and harrowing rescue in which Captain had played a major role. How had such a courageous man, who clearly loved the sea, ended up miles from the coast living as a virtual recluse? Roxy's only hope of answering that question was to try to find someone who had known him. There was a phone number for the lifeboat station where Captain had served as a volunteer, so she picked up her mobile and punched it in. She didn't expect it to be easy – that she would get to speak to someone who knew him straightaway – but it seemed like a good place to start. The man who answered was far too young to have served with Captain, but once Roxy had explained why she was enquiring, he said he would ask some of the older volunteers if they remembered him.

'Most people stay involved with the station when they're too old to be active crew on the boat,' he told her. 'They end up giving tours or working a few hours in the shop or fundraising. Hardly anyone ever walks away completely.'

But Captain had, thought Roxy. She gave the man her contact details and thanked him for his help.

It was a warm evening and Roxy took Sailor for a stroll in the park. He seemed to have accepted his new circumstances and situation with remarkable equanimity. As he trotted along in front of her, stopping every now and then to sniff or greet another dog, Roxy pondered how considerately Captain had prepared him for this. She thought about the box in the sideboard and how easy Captain had made it for them to deal with affairs. His will, recently altered, had, much to her surprise, made Roxy his sole executor. Provision had been made for a basic funeral, and a generous sum had been left to Roxy in recognition of her friendship and ongoing care of Sailor. The remainder of his estate had been left to the Royal National Lifeboat Institution.

Roxy had just given Sailor his dinner when her mobile rang.

'Hello,' said a man's deep voice with an unmistakably melodious Welsh accent. 'Is that Roxy?'

'Yes. Who's this?'

'My name's Gethin Williams. I understand you've been asking about Dylan Jones. Well, I served on the same crew as Dylan for twenty years.'

Roxy explained briefly why she had been searching for anyone who had known Captain. 'We became friends,' she told Gethin. 'He left his dog with me. But it seems he had no one else.'

There was a brief silence on the line before Gethin continued.

'Dylan was a very popular man. He had loads of friends here. True, he never married, but he had plenty of girlfriends.' Gethin chuckled. 'There was many a girl who tried to get him down the aisle, but Dylan liked the single life. When he left, he told no one. We had no idea where he had gone. I was worried sick about him. I even went to the police, but they said there was nothing they could do. It was clear that he had moved of his own accord and obviously didn't want to be traced. And that was true enough. He left no trail. I've tried to find him several times over the years, but I've had no luck. I even got my grandson to look on the internet – I'm not good with computers myself. But in the end, I had to accept that he was gone and that was what he wanted.'

There was another silence.

'But I suppose I always hoped that one day, he might turn up,' Gethin continued. 'I didn't really accept that I'd never see him again – until now.'

'I'm so sorry,' said Roxy. 'From what I knew of him, he was a lovely man. I'm going to miss him very much. But what made him leave? Do you have any idea?'

'There was a bad shout. Two little girls went missing. Sisters they were – Bethan and Erin. They were local kids, lived in the same village as Dylan. They got caught out by the tide and ended up stranded on some rocks.'

'I found the newspaper report,' Roxy told him. 'Wasn't Captain – sorry, Dylan – awarded a gallantry medal for his part in the rescue?'

'All three of us on the crew were. But Dylan was the one who put himself in the most danger that night. He risked his life to save those girls and nearly died himself. He got Bethan back to the boat, but when he went back for Erin – well, I suppose you know what happened next. He almost had her when a giant wave washed them both into the sea. Erin was smashed against the rocks and hit her head. And that was that. Dylan managed to get to her in the water, but by the time he got her back to the boat she was already dead. He never got over it. Never forgave himself.'

Roxy couldn't think of a single thing to say.

'It didn't help that he lived in the same village as the family. There was a possibility every day that he might run into one of them. I think he felt that he had let them down. Not just the family, but the whole community.'

'But that's crazy. Without your crew, both girls would have died.'

'I know. It was tough for me and Robert, the other crew member, too – he passed away a few years ago, God rest his soul. But then, we didn't live in Solva. Dylan was a very proud man, and he took it very hard.'

'Perhaps that's why he moved here,' Roxy mused. 'He couldn't have chosen anywhere further from the sea.'

'You could be right,' Gethin agreed. 'The sea was his life. He loved it – perhaps more than anything else. Leaving it so far behind would have been the greatest punishment he could have inflicted upon himself. As I said, he felt he'd let Erin's parents and his whole community down. But in truth, it was the other way around. It was us who let him down. We saw his pain and we didn't do enough to ease it. Everyone knew he was a hero that night. Everyone – except Dylan.'

Chapter 53

Captain's funeral was a fitting tribute to the man he never knew he was. A man who was courageous, loyal, trustworthy, hardworking and, above all, very much loved. There had been a good deal of debate between George, Roxy, Niall and Gethin about whether it should be held in Pembrokeshire or at the crematorium. They had finally decided that the service should be held in the town where Captain had chosen to live for so many years, but that his ashes would be returned to Wales and scattered across the sea that he had loved so fiercely. Briony had told Captain's story on The Light a Candle Society's website and the response had been overwhelming. Several florists had provided floral tributes for the chapel, and numerous people had volunteered to attend. There had also been many requests to donate money to the RNLI in Captain's memory, so Briony had set up a JustGiving page, which had already raised almost one thousand pounds.

A benevolent September sun bathed the day in golden light as George, Niall, Roxy and Sailor met up outside the chapel to say goodbye to their friend. They watched as a coach that had travelled all the way from Wales pulled into the car park, full of people who had come to pay their final respects to one of their own. As the coach doors hissed open, Gethin was the first to alight – a short, broad figure with white hair and a neat beard. Despite his age, he moved briskly, and his posture was ramrod straight. He was followed by a man whom he introduced to them as the Reverend Rhys Davies, the current priest at the church Captain had attended in Solva.

'I think it's wonderful what you're doing here,' the priest said to George as he shook his hand. 'Gethin told me all about your society and I felt I had to come today and do whatever I can to help. I never met Dylan – he was long before my time – but many of the people who came with us today remember him well, and very fondly, as I'm sure you'll find out before too long.'

Sailor was looking very dapper in a black neckerchief tied over his collar. He was the recipient of many compliments and admiring glances as people filed past him into the chapel. Elena arrived with Sid, closely followed by Mrs Biscuit and her Norman.

'I've done some Welsh themed biscuits for the wake,' she told Roxy, 'with a nod to the nautical!'

Overhearing her remark, Gethin raised his eyebrows questioningly to Roxy, who shook her head.

'Don't ask,' she told him. 'You'll find out soon enough.'

The last of The Light a Candle Society members to arrive was Briony, accompanied by Zach and a very elegant elderly lady whom Briony introduced as Allegra.

'I want to make sure that these funerals are up to scratch if I'm trusting you and your cronies to organise mine,' she had joked to Briony. But in truth, like many other people who had already taken their pews, she had been deeply moved by Captain's story and felt the need to acknowledge his bravery and sacrifice in some way.

Edwin had insisted on driving the hearse himself today, and by the time it came into view, making its stately progress up the winding gravel drive, the chapel was completely full. Captain's coffin was draped in an RNLI flag and crowned with his felt cap with the skull and crossbones badge, the teddy bear that Roxy had found in his bedroom and a huge anchor of yellow and white flowers lovingly created by Elena. The Reverend Davies led the coffin into the chapel to the accompaniment of 'Guide Me, O Thou Great Redeemer' sung by the male voice choir that had been amongst the coach passengers from Pembrokeshire. Once Edwin and his fellow pallbearers had gently settled the coffin on the catafalque, George got up and lit the candle that stood next to the coffin.

'We are here today to celebrate and give thanks for the life of an extraordinary man called Dylan Peter Jones – known to some of us as Captain,' he told the congregation. 'And today's service will be led by the Reverend Rhys Davies from Dylan's hometown of Solva.'

Reverend Davies began the service with a short prayer and then thanked everyone for coming. 'I am the current priest at the church where Dylan used to worship, and it's an absolute privilege to be here today to lead this celebration of his life. I travelled here from Solva with volunteers – past and present – from the St David's lifeboat station, Dylan's friends and former colleagues, folk who knew him and some who didn't but know *of* him and wanted to be here to acknowledge his huge contribution to the people and place where he once belonged. And I'd now like to invite Gethin, Dylan's oldest friend and fellow RNLI crew member, to tell us something about the man we are here to remember.'

Gethin walked to the front of the chapel and laid his hand on Captain's coffin, where it remained for the duration of his speech.

'Firstly, I'd like to thank The Light a Candle Society,' he began, 'because without them, the chances are that none of us would be here today, and we wouldn't have had the opportunity to say goodbye to a man who was once a dearly loved member of our community.'

Gethin's voice broke a little with emotion and he swallowed hard before continuing. 'Dylan was a huge character with a big heart. He always grabbed life by the balls – excuse me, Reverend, but there really is no other word for it – and went at everything full throttle. Don't get me wrong – he wasn't perfect.' Gethin patted the coffin in a placatory fashion. 'He certainly didn't suffer fools gladly and he was a bugger for practical jokes. He once hid a couple of spoonfuls of his vindaloo in my korma while I was in the toilet at the curry house and then choked with laughter almost as much as I did with pain when I ate it!'

Some of the Welsh contingent in the congregation laughed affectionately, clearly recalling Dylan's sense of humour.

'But as a friend,' Gethin went on, 'he was the best of the best, and he always had your back no matter what. And Dylan was one of the bravest men I've ever come across. He volunteered for the RNLI as soon as he was old enough and served as an active crew member for twenty-five years. Dylan loved the sea – but more than that he understood it. It was truly in his blood, and he could read it better than anyone I've ever known. That's why whenever I was on a shout, I always wanted him to be beside me in the boat. And I know that all the other members of our crew felt the same way.'

Gethin paused for a moment, as if gathering himself for what came next.

'As most of you probably know by now, after a particularly tragic rescue, Dylan left the RNLI and Wales behind and came to live here. We can never really know what went through his mind to make him leave behind everything and everyone he loved. But one thing I do know is that I wish I'd made more of an effort to understand what he was going through at the time. We Welshmen think we're so tough. We keep quiet and carry on, but sometimes we need to talk, even when we say we don't want to. I wish I'd ignored Dylan when he told me he was fine even though I knew he wasn't. I wish I'd tried harder to make him talk to me. Maybe it wouldn't have made any difference – but at least I would be standing here now knowing that I did my best. As it is, I know I didn't. I also wish I'd tried harder to find him – even if I had succeeded and he'd told me to bugger off!

'If I *had* found him, I would have discovered that he had made a new life for himself just about as far from the sea as he could get. He began working as an HGV driver and bought a little house on the outskirts of town here. And eventually, he made some new friends – Roxy and George from the library that he belonged to, and that handsome boy over there who was by his side when he died,' Gethin said, gesturing towards Sailor, who was sitting at the end of the front pew next to Roxy.

'Thank you, Dylan, for all your years of service in the RNLI. Thank you for all the lives you saved, and for all the times you risked your own life without a second thought. And thank you for being such a brilliant friend to me and to so many people back in Wales. Dylan, you deserved better from me. But I promise you that, from now on, I'll never let someone I care about disappear from my life without a fight – and neither should any of you,' Gethin said, looking out at the congregation. 'Because, in the end, all we really have is each other. Let that be Dylan's legacy.'

Gethin bowed his head slowly to the coffin and then returned to his seat.

'And now we're going to stand for our next hymn,' Reverend Davies announced, 'Known to most of us as "For Those in Peril on the Sea".'

When the hymn was over, Roxy got to her feet, and accompanied by Sailor, she made her way to the front of the chapel and read from the volume of poetry she had found in Captain's bedroom.

'Crossing the Bar' by Alfred Lord Tennyson
Sunset and the evening star,
And one clear call for me!
And may there be no moaning of the bar,
When I put out to sea,

But such a tide as moving seems asleep,
Too full for sound and foam,
When that which drew from out the boundless deep
Turns again home.
Twilight and the evening bell,
And after that the dark!
And may there be no sadness of farewell
When I embark;
For tho' from out our bourne of Time and Place
The flood may bear me far,
I hope to see my Pilot face to face
When I have cross'd the bar.

Roxy kissed her fingertips and pressed them to the side of the coffin before returning to her seat.

'And now Bethan Williams is going to say a few words,' Reverend Davies announced.

A small fair-haired woman in her mid-forties with round cheeks and blue eyes walked up the aisle and turned to face the congregation. She gave a sad half-smile and took a deep breath.

'My name is Bethan Williams and when I was ten years old Dylan Jones saved my life. My sister and me had been playing on the beach and decided to go climbing on the rocks. We were Solva girls born and bred, and we should have known better, but we were just kids and we lost track of time and ended up being cut off by the tide. The weather turned nasty and the pair of us were terrified. But my big sister, Erin, never gave up hope. She kept telling me that the lifeboat would come and rescue us and that we'd be okay.'

Bethan was clearly struggling to keep her tears in check and wiped beneath her eyes with her index finger. Gethin got up and went and stood by her side. He handed her a pristine handkerchief from his pocket, took hold of her hand and gave it a squeeze. She smiled at him gratefully and continued.

'It was dark, and we were so cold and wet, and I was sure we were going to die. I remember thinking that I'd never see my guinea pig, Puffball, again and hoping that mam would look after him and not give him away to Shelby next door. But Erin was right. All at once we saw a light coming towards us, and we heard shouting. Without Gethin and Robert and Dylan I'd never have grown up, got married, had children, been to Disneyland' – she said this with a smile – 'or made my lovely mam and dad grandparents.' Bethan looked towards a pew where an older couple were sitting, and they smiled at her encouragingly.

'It was Dylan Jones who jumped in the water that terrible night and came over to get us. The waves were so big that he kept disappearing, but he never gave up and just kept coming. I'll always remember the feeling when he climbed onto the rocks and hugged us in his big, strong arms.'

Bethan paused for a moment and then drew herself up, pulling back her shoulders and lifting her chin. 'He took me back to the boat first – because I was the youngest and smallest – and then he went back for Erin. Dylan did everything he could and more than most would ever dare to – he nearly died himself – but he couldn't save Erin when the sea took her. Dylan was never to blame for that in any way. If not for Dylan, my mam and dad would have lost both their girls on a single night, and I wouldn't be here now. And I know there are others sitting amongst us who also owe their lives to the brave men and women of the RNLI – some to Dylan in particular – and I know we are all grateful to them every single day. I only wish that we could have made Dylan believe he was the hero that we all knew him to be, and how much we loved him for it.'

There was a moment's silence and then spontaneous and thunderous applause.

'I hope you're listening to this, mate,' Gethin said quietly, looking towards the coffin, before releasing Bethan's hand and returning to the front pew.

The final hymn had, according to Gethin, been Dylan's favourite. The male voice choir sang the first verse of 'How Great Thou Art' before being joined by the rest of the congregation in a surprisingly rousing and tuneful rendition.

As the last notes died away, Reverand Davies once again addressed the congregation. 'The Light a Candle Society are holding a wake to raise a glass – or two – to Dylan at The Duck and Donkey pub, and you are all welcome to join them there.' Then he turned towards Dylan's coffin and spoke a farewell blessing. 'Go with a fair wind and a following tide.'

The music that played them out of the chapel had been chosen by Roxy and was – inevitably – 'Heroes' by David Bowie.

Chapter 54

The following morning, George awoke with a thick head to the sound of his doorbell. He checked his alarm clock and was surprised to discover that it was 8.30 am already. Captain's wake at The Duck and Donkey had gone on until late the previous evening. It had been a heartwarming party, and Lachie had done them proud with a delicious and generous buffet. Mrs Biscuit had surpassed herself with several batches of cheese and leek boat-shaped savoury crackers, which had been by far the most palatable of her offerings so far. George and the others had chatted with Bethan and her parents and many of the others who had travelled from Solva and were eager to share stories and memories of the man they had known as Dylan. Briony had introduced Allegra to the other members of The Light a Candle Society, and she and Sid had somewhat unexpectedly hit it off straightaway. George had also been delighted to see Keisha's friend, Shanice, at both the funeral and the wake. The coachload of people that had come with Gethin from Wales had booked into a local hotel overnight, and George had promised to go and see them off that morning.

He scrambled out of bed, pulled on his dressing gown and hurried down the stairs.

'Blimey, you look rough!' Roxy said with a grin when he opened the front door. 'What time did you get home last night?'

George shrugged. 'I'm not sure. That Gethin can certainly hold his ale. He was a bad influence on me and Edwin.'

Roxy laughed. 'Thank goodness Niall came home with me, then, otherwise you three would have led him astray too.'

George groaned and rubbed at his temples. 'I really need a cup of tea. I said I'd go and see Gethin and the others off, so I'd better get a move on.'

'And I need to get to work. Be good for Uncle George,' she instructed Sailor as she handed George the dog's leash and headed back down the garden path.

Since Captain had died, they had come up with a rota for looking after Sailor. He lived with Roxy, but when she worked full days, she would leave Sailor with George and pick him up on her way home. When George was at work with Roxy, Sailor sometimes came too and relaxed in the staff room. He was also a regular visitor with Roxy to her mum in the care home – much to all the residents' delight.

'Come on, handsome. Let's go and get some breakfast,' said George, 'and maybe a side order of paracetamols.'

A couple of hours later, man and dog were in George's car on the way to the hotel where they were to meet Gethin. It was another fine day, and when they arrived, Gethin was sitting at a table outside drinking coffee.

'Would you like one?' Gethin enquired cheerily, raising his cup to George.

'I would, thank you. I'm feeling a trifle delicate this morning,' George replied with a rueful smile.

Gethin laughed. 'You youngsters, you've got no stamina!' He called over a waiter who was clearing one of the other tables and ordered George a coffee which arrived moments later – hot, frothy and accompanied by a croissant.

'I just wanted to thank you again, before we left.' Gethin's face was serious now. 'I understand from Roxy that it was you who started The Light a Candle Society. It's funny, because when I told my wife, Betty, about it, she started calling you the TLC Society because of your initials. She was so sorry not to be here, but her arthritis is playing her up something shocking at the moment, and she couldn't face the journey. Anyway, Betty's right about you and your friends. It is tender loving care that you're providing – not just for the dead, but for the living as well. I can't tell you how grateful I am to have had this chance to pay tribute to Dylan and to say my goodbyes. Without you, God only knows when I would have found out where he was and what happened to him. Maybe I never would have. And I know how much it meant to Bethan too, and her mam and dad.'

George sipped his coffee thoughtfully whilst feeding the croissant to a delighted Sailor. 'It's strange,' he said, 'because in the beginning I only thought about the people who had died. I just wanted to make sure that, no matter how or why they had ended up on their own, they were given a decent funeral and their lives were recognised and remembered in some way. It never occurred to me that there might be friends or family out there who still cared about them but didn't know how or where to find them.'

'People like me,' Gethin replied, 'who tried, but maybe not hard enough.'

George shook his head. 'We can't rescue everyone,' he said. 'Captain couldn't rescue Erin, and you couldn't rescue Captain. Sometimes that's just how it is. All we can do is keep trying.'

'You're a good man, George McGlory. And I hope you'll keep doing what you're doing – because it really matters.'

George smiled. 'I don't think I'd dare stop now. Briony, our resident reporter, has set up interviews with local radio and TV stations on the back of Captain's story. You never know, we might see Light a Candle Societies popping up all over the country at this rate!'

George and Sailor stood in the car park and watched as the coach pulled away and began its long journey back to Wales. Their next stop was the cemetery, where George changed the wilting roses on Audrey's grave for some pink and white dahlias.

'I've been a bit of a fool, haven't I, love?' he said as he adjusted the flowers in the vase. He pictured Audrey smiling at him in the way she always had when she was pleased with him and nodding. 'I'm going to sort it out. I promise.'

Sailor sat on the other side of Audrey's grave listening intently to George. He tipped his head to one side as though waiting for him to continue.

'I was thinking,' George began hesitantly, 'would you mind if I asked Elena out for a drink or maybe for a meal? Just as a friend,' he added quickly.

Audrey had told him before she died that she didn't want him to be alone and that he would need to find someone else to keep him in line. But somehow it seemed only right to run it by her first.

George and Sailor made their way over to the memorial cabinet by the pond and George took a key from his trouser pocket and unlocked the doors. Today's additions to the display were Captain's cap and RNLI medal for gallantry. But there was something else too. George placed a battered silver penknife onto one of the shelves. Its label read 'In memory of my father, Douglas McGlory'.

On their way back to the car George spotted a familiar figure over by the bins. Edwin waved and Sailor dragged George over to say hello.

'That was a cracking funeral yesterday, George – and the wake was pretty special too!'

George nodded. 'And I've still got a sore head to prove it.'

Edwin grinned. 'You should be proud of yourself, George McGlory. Look how much you've achieved since we first met in this very spot. As I said before, the way we treat our dead is a measure of our own humanity.'

'I've had a lot of help from some very kind people – yourself included.'

'Yes, but it was your idea. You set the whole thing off. Without you The Light a Candle Society wouldn't exist.'

'To be honest, Edwin – if it doesn't sound too weird – I've enjoyed it. And I've made some good friends.'

Edwin took a final drag on his cigarette and stubbed it out. 'There's nothing weird about enjoying helping people, alive or dead. I love my job – always have. Anyway, I'm glad we've bumped into each other because there's something

I've been meaning to ask you, but I wanted to catch you by yourself.'

'I'm intrigued. Fire away.'

'I was wondering if you'd like to come round for dinner sometime with me and Esmee. And I was thinking of inviting Elena as well.'

George felt his face redden.

'Of course, if you'd rather not, or you'd rather come alone, that's fine,' Edwin added hastily, seeing George's embarrassment.

George shook his head. 'It's a funny thing you should ask because I've just been chatting to Audrey about Elena.'

Edwin smiled and flung his arm around George's shoulder. 'Do you think she'd mind?'

George's eyes filled with tears and he rubbed them away. 'Audrey told me that she didn't want me to be alone.'

'Well, I never met Audrey, but from what you've told me, you'll be in a lot of trouble if you don't do what she asked.'

'But do you think Elena would want to go out with me?'

Edwin laughed out loud. 'George – for a clever man, you can be as daft as a brush. She's just waiting for you to ask!'

That evening, after his tea, George sat nursing a shot glass of vodka. He very rarely drank spirits, especially vodka, which had been his dad's downfall. But tonight, it felt somehow appropriate. Since that first phone call to the Alcoholics Anonymous helpline back in late summer, George had spoken to one of their counsellors several times and had been gradually recalibrating his relationship with his dead father. He had learned to allow himself the happy childhood memories of his dad as well as the traumatic ones. The alignment of these jigsaw pieces of his past was difficult and painful, but necessary, he realised now, to paint a truthful picture. George had begun to distinguish the person from the addiction and to see his dad as two separate men – one sober and one drunk. And he was learning to accept that perhaps he could love one of them, without condoning or excusing the other, and that he could do this without betraying his beloved mum. He had also forgiven the little boy he had been for feeling scared and doing nothing. He was finally free to move on.

The penknife was the only thing he had left of his dad's. He had kept it in a box in his garage, along with a few family photographs that he couldn't bear to look at but couldn't quite bring himself to throw away. Last night, when he had got back from The Duck and Donkey, slightly befuddled by drink, he had retrieved it and emptied its contents onto the kitchen table. Perhaps it had been Gethin's words at the funeral that had prompted him –*'Because in the end, all we really have is each other'* – or perhaps it was just the beer. But whatever it had been last night, this morning George had made a decision. He had written the label and taken the penknife to the cemetery. And now he picked up one of the photographs and propped it up against a wooden candlestick that he had brought through to the kitchen from the sitting room sideboard. The photo had been taken on a family holiday at Ramsgate when George had been about eight years old. His dad stood grinning between his two sons, with his arms around their shoulders, beside an enormous sandcastle covered in paper flags. George knocked back the vodka with a grimace and set down his glass. He took a match from the box on the table, struck it and lit the candle. He watched for a moment as it flickered precariously before settling into a steady yellow flame, and then he pulled his phone from his pocket and selected a number from his contacts. It rang three times before a familiar voice answered. George took a deep breath and then exhaled.

'Roger – it's George. I think it's time we talked.'

Chapter 55

Lines clinked against the masts of the little boats in the harbour and squawking gulls pitched and wheeled in an impressive display of aerial acrobatics. Niall, Roxy and Sailor were sitting with Gethin outside the pub that faced the harbour, finishing their drinks. It was growing chilly, and Roxy was glad of her warm coat. They had come to Solva to bring Captain's ashes home and were staying for the weekend in a cottage in the village. Earlier that day Gethin had taken them to the St David's lifeboat station at St Justinian, where they had been given a private tour and were introduced to some of the crew members.

'I hope you're ready for the pub quiz tonight,' Gethin told them. He had heard about their Duck and Donkey exploits and had persuaded them to take part in the local quiz as guest members on his team. 'We take it very seriously here, you know.'

'So do we,' replied Niall with a grin.

Gethin checked his watch. 'It's time we got going,' he told them. 'It'll take us ten minutes or so to walk there.'

Roxy fed Sailor the last of the crisps that he had been allowed as a special treat and they all stood up. They descended the steps onto the sandy shore of the harbour and began to make their way towards its entrance and the open sea. Sailor ran ahead, rootling through clumps of pungent seaweed with his nose and splashing in and out of the water's edge. They passed the circular lime kilns that protruded from the hillside like stony knuckles and walked on and around the headland until they came to the beach. Ragged ribbons of cloud streaked the pale pomegranate sky as the sun slipped down towards the sea, its glowing sphere already sliced by the horizon. The water was calm and the whisper and fizz of the waves as they broke onto the shore was, Roxy thought, one of the most soothing sounds she had ever heard, as she stood with Niall and Gethin scanning the horizon. She reached her hand inside her pocket and pulled out Captain's teddy bear. The sound of the engine came only seconds before the sight of the orange lifeboat roaring through the water. It turned towards them but stopped once they could make out the figures of the men on board and bobbed gently on the waves as the crew raised their hands and saluted them. Gethin gave the thumbs-up signal they were waiting for, and a plume of grey ashes was released into the air and fluttered down onto the water.

'What was that poem you read at the funeral?' Gethin asked softly as they watched. 'Could you say it again now?'

Roxy couldn't remember it all. But what she could remember was enough.

Twilight and evening bell,
And after that the dark!
And may there be no sadness of farewell
When I embark ...

Author's Note

The Light a Candle Society was initially inspired by an article I read about a man in Scotland who had started writing poems and reading them at the funerals of those who had died alone with no one to mourn them. I also recalled my parents' funerals. Dad died on 13th March 2020 and Mum died just six weeks later. Their funerals, held during the first Covid lockdown, were brief, sparsely attended and pretty much pared down to the bare essentials due to the newly imposed Covid restrictions. I had to provide and arrange the flowers myself as florists were closed. But at least my parents had some family members to see them on their way. How much worse would it be to have no one I wondered?

I also drew on my own experience working in Bedford town library as a Saturday girl many years ago. I still remember some of the eccentric regulars who came not only (and sometimes not even!) to borrow books, but to sit and pass the time somewhere warm and comfortable, to people-watch or simply for some human companionship.

Whilst researching the book I worked closely with Kylie Dillon, Bedford's Funeral Co-ordination Officer, who is responsible for public health funerals in Bedford. I spent time behind the scenes at our local crematorium and witnessed several cremations first-hand, following the process through from beginning to end. I spoke with the Chapel Attendant, Steve Gaunt, who helps to arrange public health funerals, and I also had the privilege of meeting Jim Gaffey, the man who was responsible for cremating my parents. To see him at work and witness his unfailing respect and compassion for those people he looks after was a huge comfort to me, knowing that he had treated my parents in the same way. I also attended several public health funerals and continue to do so. I like to think that I have become George McGlory's representative in the real world.

Acknowledgements

I often wonder how many people actually read the acknowledgements at the back of a book, but if you've got to this point, you are one of the ones that do and I'm grateful. I was brought up always to send thank you notes, and these acknowledgments are exactly that – one enormous thank you note.

Thank you so much to my wonderful readers for buying, borrowing, reading, reviewing and recommending my books. Thank you too for brightening my days with your messages, support and pictures of your dogs. And thank you for paying my wages!

I am truly grateful to all the book bloggers, reviewers, booksellers and, of course, George McGlory's fellow librarians who help readers to find my stories. I really appreciate the brilliant work you do.

As usual, I am indebted to a huge team of awesome people who have helped to transform *The Light a Candle Society* into an actual book. Lisa Highton – super-agent and friend – you are a one-woman phenomenon (and yes, I did have to use spell-check!) Thank you for your steady and guiding hand, your wisdom, humour and unfailing patience. Every adventure with you is a joy! Huge thanks to all the team at Jenny Brown Associates for all your hard work on my behalf.

Once again, it has been an absolute pleasure working with the lovely people at Corvus and Atlantic Books. I'm hugely grateful to Sarah Hodgson for her faith in my stories, and for her sensitive and perceptive editing, and to the rest of the team, especially Dave Woodhouse, Felice McKeown, Kirsty Doole and Aimee Oliver-Powell for all their hard work, support and enthusiasm. And to Walter, the corgi, for graciously accepting my gravy bones. Thank you also to Emma Dunne for her meticulous copyediting.

Writers are curious animals, and it sometimes helps to know that there are others out there whose brains are wired in a similarly idiosyncratic way. So, I'd like to thank my fellow authors, Matt Cain, Celia Anderson, Annie Lyons and Kit Fielding and Peter Budek for their much-appreciated friendship and support.

There are a small group of very special people without whom I could not have written this book, and I am truly grateful to them not only for all their help with my research, but also for welcoming me into their world with such warmth and magnanimity. Based at Bedford's Norse Road Crematorium and Cemetery, Kylie Dillon is Bedford's Funeral Co-ordination Officer, Jim Gaffey is a Cremator Operative and Steve Gaunt is the Chapel Attendant. They carry out their roles with such diligence, dignity and compassion, but although they work with death, they are full of life, wit and humour. I am completely in awe of each of them. Kylie has been so supportive of this book from the very beginning, and all three of them have been amazingly generous with their time, knowledge and experience. Jim cremated my parents and spending time with him while he worked was an absolute privilege. Jim – if I die before you, please will you be the one to send me on my final journey?!

Thank you as always to Mum and Dad for teaching me the joy of reading – and the importance of thank you notes!

And finally, we get to the cornerstones of my world. Thank you, Squadron Leader Timothy Bear, Mr Zachariah Popov and Paul, for being my safe harbour.

Join the RUTH HOGAN mailing list

Members are the first to hear seasonal news, enter giveaways, receive exclusive chapter extracts and information on upcoming books directly to their inbox a few times a year

To join, simply scan the QR code or visit
www.ruthhogan.co.uk

Books with heart

CORVUS

Also from RUTH HOGAN

Books with heart

IT'S NEVER TOO LATE TO SPREAD YOUR WINGS

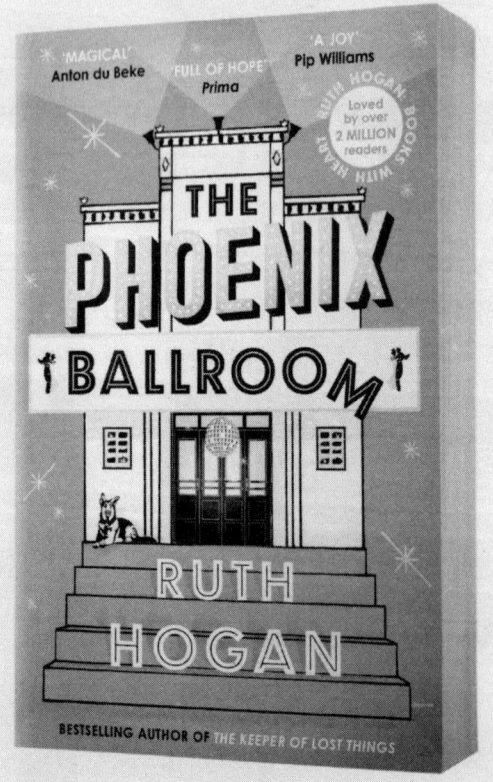